D1225994

Toe-to-Toe
A Nonie Broussard Novel

Deborah LeBlanc

Published by LeBlanc Laboratories
Copyright 2018 Deborah LeBlanc All
rights reserved.
ISBN# 978-1-937209-04-9

ALSO BY DEBORAH LEBLANC

Family Inheritance
Grave Intent
A House Divided
Morbid Curiosity
Water Witch
White Hot
The Wolven
Bottom Feeder
Voices
Witch's Hunger
Witch's Thirst
Witch's Fury

DEDICATION

This book is for Roe, Sarah, and Pookie.

CHAPTER ONE

Panting, Nonie Broussard struggled to pull off Dover Fontenot's underwear. The man weighed well over three hundred and fifty pounds and carried most of that lard in his barrel-chest, gut and butt. Fortunately, Nonie's father had been gracious enough to cover Dover's face with a sheet of black plastic so she didn't have to look at it.

In life, Dover had been no Brad Pitt. He'd looked more like a pit bull. A sixty-three-year-old, cigar-smoking, bourbon-drinking, foul-mouth pit bull and the mayor of Clay Point, LA. Now his face anyway, was little more than a mangle of blood, bone, and hair. From what Nonie had been told, Dover had reached over to grab a pack of cigarettes that had slid from the passenger seat of his car to the floor. When he looked up again, his sedan was burying itself beneath an eighteen-wheeler's flatbed.

It was bad enough that Nonie had to take off his underwear, but doing it in an embalming room made it ten times worse. The smell of formaldehyde made her stomach do flip-flops, and the stark sterility of the room, with its steel appliances and white tile floors, walls and ceiling made her dizzy. Had Dover's bloody goo of a face been exposed, she'd have bolted in a heartbeat.

"So come on and get those damn things off already," Guy Skinard said, leaning against the counter near one of the embalming machines.

Nonie shot him a look. "The elastic keeps catching on the hitch in his butt. It sticks out so far you could sit a dinner plate on the damn thing. And why are you so anxious for me to get his underwear off anyway? You're not even supposed to be in here. Don't you have somewhere else you need to be?"

Guy scowled. "No," he snapped. "And I just wanna see, that's all."

"See what?"

"How big his wiener is."

"Guy Philip Skinard!"

"Aw, come on. You can't tell me you're not a little bit curious."

"Not even," Nonie said emphatically.

"We can call it research," Guy said. "You know, like disproving an urban legend."

Nonie pulled a bit harder on Dover's shorts and felt them give a little. Sweat beaded up on her forehead from the effort. "What the hell are you talking about?"

"You know, he's a big guy and all, but he's got small feet and hands, which usually means a small wiener. I just wanna see if it's true. See? Research."

Nonie glared at him. "You're sick, you know that, right? Go on and get the hell out of here. You know this room is off-limits to the public."

"I'm not the public."

Nonie huffed. "Right. You're a pain in the butt. Now go."

"And what're you gonna do if I don't? Kick me out?"

None let out an exasperated sigh. Life used to be far less complicated.

Only fourteen days ago she'd been working at Garmin's T-shirt factory, located on the north end of town. Sewing labels on T-shirts had been a tedious, boring job, but it paid the rent on her half of a duplex, kept fuel in her '98 gas-guzzling Acura, and food in her pantry.

Nonie had started working at Garmin's fresh out of college—all three semesters of it. It hadn't taken long for her to figure out that extended academia was not for her. She'd applied at Garmin's two days after dropping out. That had been nearly three years ago.

She'd been content with her mindless tasks at the factory. Then one morning, out of the blue, all three hundred and forty-five employees came into work to find the kiss of death smacked on small pink slips in their time sheet box. Evidently the head honchos who owned the factory figured it would be more cost effective to manufacture their

T-shirts in Indonesia, Mexico, or somewhere in bum-pluck China. Anywhere but Clay Point, LA. or any other city in the vast U S of A for that matter.

The Garmin gorillas had doled out small compensation checks, but nothing close enough to cover Nonie's monthly expenses. She'd needed another job and quick, but so did three hundred and forty-four other ex-Garmin employees. That left finding another job in Clay Point all but impossible.

She'd had one job offer from Red Barn Feed & Seed, which she turned down. They'd wanted her to lug fifty-pound sacks of seed from trucks to storage bins for minimum wage. Another option had been for her to drive to Lafayette and look for work. But that meant she'd have two, forty-five-minute drives to make per day. With her resumé being so limited, Nonie figured that even if she did find a job in

Lafayette, half of her salary would go to gas and repairs on her already abused car.

That had left her with only one other choice. One she dreaded. One she'd avoided her entire adult life—working for her family's funeral home. She'd grown up around the business and never could understand how her parents tolerated so much sadness every day without mentally cracking. Although, where mentally cracked was concerned, her mother, Rita Broussard, could be considered slightly questionable.

So, stuck like a rock in hardening concrete, Nonie had sucked it up and talked to her father about hiring her, emphasizing her employment would be temporary, only until she'd found another job.

Evidently Elmo Broussard—who most people in Clay Point called T-boy—suddenly experienced selective hearing when she'd mentioned the temporary part because the man damn near went into seizures from excitement. Finally, his prodigal daughter had come to him, wanting to work at the funeral home. To him, that meant that the Broussard Funeral Home legacy would live on once he passed away. It had already been handed down from father to son from two previous generations, so, for all intents and purposes, it should be going to her brother, Matthew, who was five years old than Nonie. More than likely that discussion of passing from father to son had already taken place, though, because last year Matthew conveniently moved to El Paso with his wife, Jeannie, and their two kids.

That left Nonie to deal with her father's hopes and struggling with Dover's underwear.

"You almost got it," Guy said. "Look, I see a little bit of hair. Just a little more—"

"Shut the hell up," Nonie snapped, then heard the snick of the lock on the embalming room door.

Her Uncle Fezzo stepped inside and smiled when he saw her struggling with the stubborn underwear. "Looks like I got here jus' in de nick of time," he said.

Fezzo was her father's older brother and one of Nonie's favorite relatives. He stood at least six foot three, had a stocky build, walked with a limp, spoke with a heavy Cajun accent, and, even at seventy-years-old, had a head of thick, gray hair. For years, Fezzo had made a living hunting alligators and running trout lines in the swamp. That came to an end when he lost a struggle with a five-hundred-pound gator. The beast's jaws had clamped onto Fezzo's right calf. Had it not been for Buzzard, Fezzo's hunting buddy, he'd have lost that leg for sure.

Fortunately, after three surgeries and a lot of physical therapy, Fezzo managed to walk again, but his alligator hunting days were over. That was when her dad had asked Fezzo to help at the funeral home. He knew Fezzo had too much pride to ask for a job, so Nonie's dad had made it sound like the family desperately needed him. Evidently smelling a rat, Fezzo had taken some time before he consented. Now he helped with removals, kept the hearse and flower car in top running condition, and stood sentinel at viewings. He also lent a hand in the embalming room, undressing the deceased.

Then he'd gussy them up after Butchy Thibodeaux, a short, blond, chubby man in his early thirties, and the funeral home's apprentice, embalmed them.

Earlier, Fezzo had been sent to retrieve Mrs. Inez Trahan, a ninety-four-year-old resident of Our Lady of the Oaks Nursing Home. She'd passed away quietly in her chair while watching a soap opera on television. With Fezzo gone, Nonie's dad had asked her to help with Dover. They needed the mayor undressed stat in order to embalm him. This would then free up the embalming table for Mrs. Trahan. Grudgingly, Nonie had agreed. So far, she'd managed to strip off Dover's button-down shirt, slacks, shoes and socks, then got snagged on his tighty-whities.

"The mayor's got a big hitch in his giddy-up," Nonie said to Fezzo, "and I can't lift him high enough to get his underwear off."

"Mah, don't worry 'bout dat," Fezzo said. "You don't need to see that old saggy sack anyways. I'll take care of it. By de way, you friend, Buggy, is in de coffee room, and she's hoppin' around like she got a few bees up her butt. Said she needs to talk to you right away. So you go and see what she wants, and I'll finish here. Don't forget though. Dey want to do de viewing tomorrow, and you know what dat means."

Nonie rolled her eyes. "Yep, mega busy. Dad's probably already taking Rolaids and Mom's worried about everything being perfect and what she's going to wear for the viewing."

Fezzo chuckled while donning a surgical gown. "You got it. So try to make it fast wit' you friend. Den go see what else you daddy wants you to set up for tomorrow. Don't want you mama to know you not workin'. She'd pass a stroke."

Nonie kissed her uncle on the cheek, then stripped off her surgical gown, hair cap and shoe covers. "Thanks for covering for me."

"Not a problem, mon petite fille. I'm supposed to be doing dis anyways."

Nonie smiled, left the embalming room and was about to head for the coffee room when she spotted Guy flanking her on the right.

"You need to stay put," she said. "For Buggy to come here, it must be important. That means private convo. You're not invited."

"Aw, come on," Guy protested. "You wouldn't let me see Dover's wiener, the least you can do is let me in on this."

"I said no," Nonie said, and marched down the carpeted hallway to the coffee room. She chanced a glance over her shoulder and saw Guy standing at the end of the hallway, pouting. She couldn't help but think how sexy he looked with that pouty mouth, shoulder-length, blond hair, and those deep smoky gray eyes and dimpled chin. He wore scruffy jeans and a white T-shirt with the word Budweiser emblazoned in red across the front. It was so him.

Nonie and Guy had been childhood sweethearts since high school. They'd been inseparable. Swore they'd marry, live in Clay Point and raise a brood of kids. Spend the rest of their lives simply loving and growing old together. Their dreams had roots in reality, save for one small problem.

Guy Skinard had died in a freak boating accident nine years ago.

CHAPTER TWO

Nonie's sneakers whispered across the maroon, olive, and gold swirled carpet that lined the hallway to the coffee room. The funeral home was shaped like a T, with a sitting area and two viewing rooms taking up the base. Just inside the oak double-doors of the entrance sat a receptionist's desk and a viewing room marquee. Beyond it were two brown leather sofas and four wing-back chairs, upholstered in tan and maroon striped fabric. The sitting area then led to the two viewing rooms, which sat on opposing sides of the funeral home. Viewing room A had been enlarged over the years so it held pews for chapel services for anyone choosing to veer off the traditional Catholic mass route. Room B was standard size and used most often.

At the intersection that formed the top of the T of the funeral home sat her father's office to the far left. Beside it was a women's bathroom, followed by the coffee area then a men's bathroom. The embalming room capped off the far right of the T.

The coffee area held three, round, wooden tables with four matching chairs assigned to each, a snack bar and a small kitchenette. Since 98 percent of Clay Point's forty-one hundred residents were Catholic, it wasn't unusual to have family members bring gumbo, étouffée, or some other meal for family and friends gathered to mourn. Unlike other places around the U.S., funerals held in Cajun country were a process due its course. It called for a full day's viewing with an occasional request for overnight stays, then two to four hours of viewing the following morning, and ended with a funeral mass, usually held at St. Anthony's, located four blocks from the funeral home on Main Street. Burials most often took place in the cemetery that sat behind the church.

Buggy hated funerals and funeral homes as much as Nonie did, so her friend coming here gave Nonie pause. Something had to be wrong.

The moment Nonie swung into the lounge she spotted Buggy pacing impatiently around the tables. When she saw Nonie she started jumping up and down and clapping her hands like an eight-year-old, her face bright with excitement.

Nonie had met Buggy Mouton in second grade and they'd been steadfast, best friends ever since. Buggy stood about five feet tall and weighed maybe ninety-eight pounds if she had ten dollars worth of quarters in her jean pockets. She wore her jet-black hair in a pixie cut with bangs, had huge caramel-colored eyes and a tiny nose that sat above full lips. Her choice of clothing very seldom swayed away from jeans, tees, and sneakers. Both Nonie and Buggy were quickly climbing the hill to thirty, so she couldn't imagine what had set her friend off, causing her to act like an adolescent on speed.

Before Nonie had a chance to ask, Buggy ran up to her, grabbed her by both arms, stared at her with wide, sparkling eyes and said, "Girl, you're not going to believe the news I have. You've gotta sit 'cause it's gonna knock you on your ass!"

When someone asked you to sit before they gave you news, that news was usually horrid. But Buggy looked too damn near orgasmic for this to be the case, so Nonie pulled a chair out from the nearest table and sat.

"What's up with you?" Nonie asked.

Buggy flapped her hands at her sides like a young bird ready to take flight. "Okay, okay . . . Wait let me get a Coke first."

Before Nonie could protest, Buggy ran into the kitchenette, grabbed two Cokes from the fridge, then hurried back to Nonie and sat beside her. She handed Nonie a soda and pulled her chair up close.

"All right, I'll give you the scoop, but you have to promise not to say a word until I'm finished, okay?"

"Um . . . okay," Nonie said.

"Promise?"

"Yeah, sure."

"No, I'm serious," Buggy insisted. "Like cross your heart, pinky-swear."

"Geez, we're not in kindergarten, Bug. I promise I won't say a word 'til you're done," Nonie said, starting to get annoyed and anxious at the same time. "Jesus, you look like you're about to jump out of your skin. What's the deal?"

Buggy opened her Coke, took a long gulp.

"Tell me already," Nonie said, waiting for Buggy to finish guzzling her soda.

Buggy placed the soda can on the table, let out a little burp then said, "Okay, here's the skinny. You know how Lyle works for that cable company in New Orleans, WXRT, right?"

"And?"

"He drives the van. You know, the one with the satellite domathingies on it? The one they use when they have to film something live? Well, yesterday he's driving the van to this big shindig they had to cover on Bourbon Street and guess who's riding in the van with him?" Buggy looked at Nonie expectantly.

Nonie sighed. "No clue."

"The producer of two of their highest-rated weekly shows and the owner of WXRT!"

Having no idea where this was going, Nonie tried to look impressed for her friend's sake. Buggy and Lyle had dated since high school just like her and Guy. "Driving the bigwigs. Pretty cool."

"Are you kidding? Like that *never* happens. Even better, Lyle's not just driving the van, he hears them talking about a new show they want to put together called *Something's Out There*. It's like a ghost hunting thing, but only in the South. And get this—they want to start in Louisiana 'cause we've always got some weird shit going on down here. If it works out as good as they hope, it might air

farther than Louisiana. Like Texas or Arkansas."

Nonie eyed her suspiciously. "What's that got

to do with you flapping around here like a

madwoman?"

Buggy drummed her fingers on the table.

"Well, see, the producer wants to put a scouting

team together." She suddenly held up a finger."Wait

a sec." She glanced around the room. "Is he here?"

"Who?"

"Lover boy."

Understanding Buggy meant Guy she shook

her head. "No."

"Whew, got so excited I forgot for a moment.

Anyway, like I was saying, they're looking for a

team of people who'll go to different locations that

are supposedly haunted. Once there, they have to try

and get some kind of concrete evidence on audio or video that the place is really haunted, then bring the evidence back to the production team. If the producer thinks it has merit, enough to send a film crew to do a real investigation, he'll pay the scouting team five hundred dollars a head for the find. You got that, girl, five hundred dollars. That's a five with two zeros after it!"

Nonie rolled her eyes. "I know what five hundred dollars is. But what does that have to do with us? Specifically me?"

Buggy shot up from her chair. "Are you kidding?" She put her hands on her hips. When Lyle told me about this at lunch yesterday I almost had a shit fit. I started thinking like we could really be rolling in cash with this deal. With what you know . . . you know what I'm talking about—"

"Buggy . . ." Nonie warned.

"Swear to God, I didn't tell a soul," Buggy promised. "I didn't tell anyone anything about that thing you can do."

Nonie swiped a hand over her face.

Still standing, Buggy started to fidget from one foot to the other. "You promised to wait until I was finished before you said anything, so let me finish already. If we put a crew together . . . which I kinda sorta already did—I'm calling us the Boo Krewe, only I spelled Krewe like in Mardi Gras? Is that cool or what? Anyway, this idea hit me so hard, I told Lyle to go right back to the producer and tell him he had a crew already lined up and ready to start work whenever they were ready. 'Cause with you on the team, Nonie, the money's in the bag. They're going to supply the scouting team with all kinds of cameras and woo-woo equipment to find ghosts, but with you there, who in the hell needs equipment? We'll know right up front if we're working with a dud or have something legit. Then we can go about recording or taping evidence on whatever thingamajigs they give us. "

Nonie slouched in her chair. "What the hell do we know about scouting for ghosts? We've never done anything like that before. And who else is in this crew you supposedly put together?"

"What's there to know about scouting?" Buggy said, a note of indignation in her voice. "We've all seen those ghost hunting shows on TV a million times. Half that shit's made up anyway. But with you on this gig, now we're talking about the real deal. *And,* I bet if we do a stupendous job, we might actually be part of the real team that's on the television show. Then we'd get paid major bucks. Major!" Buggy's hands started to flap again. "Look, I know this sounds over-the-top, and I'm a little excited about it. Screw it. I'm a lot excited about it. I mean, for real, how often do people get opportunities like this?"

Nonie sat up, about to tell Buggy to go home and have a beer and chill out, when Buggy started up again.

"I know you hate working here, girl, and I'd sure like to do something better than waiting tables at Meemaw's Café. With the kind of money we'd be bringing in from this scouting gig, we could go into some kind of business for ourselves."

Nonie's head began to swim, trying to absorb everything Buggy had said.

"So whadda ya say?" Buggy said, in her face again. "Come on. Tell me you're in."

Nonie raised a hand and stood. "I can't, Bug. I just can't."

Buggy's eyes widened with shock. "Why the hell not? You have to Nonie. We can't let this gig slip through our fingers."

Nonie picked up her soda, popped the top on the can and took a sip. "You know why. If I do something like that then everybody's going to find out."

"No, they won't. I swear. We'll make sure that doesn't happen," Buggy insisted.

"And just how in the hell are we going to do that? Use sign language? Learn Italian so nobody understands what we're talking about? And you didn't answer my question. What do you mean you've already put together a team? What team? Who's in this Boo Krewe?"

Hope lit up Buggy's eyes. "Shaundelle Washington is one of them and—"

"Hold up," Nonie said, and cocked her head. "Are you talking about that big woman that runs the Tint and Tips on Sixteenth Street?"

"Yeah, but she doesn't only do nails and hair. She's awesome with a camera. I've seen some of the pictures she's taken. They're fabulous. Most of them were of naked guys, but the quality was awesome."

Nonie opened her mouth to tell Bug she'd not only fallen off the deep end, she'd completely missed the pool. Before she had a chance to voice it, though, Buggy grabbed the second of silence to jump back into her litany.

"And we've got Tatman."

"What's a Tatman?"

"You know, that big guy that works over at Guidry's Hardware."

Nonie thought for a moment. She'd been in Guidry's a few times for her dad, but the only big man she remembered working there had been covered in tattoos and had long, thinning, scraggly hair that he pulled back into a messy ponytail "Are you talking about that biker looking dude? Heavyset? The one that looks like he hasn't showered since . . . birth?"

"Yeah, yeah," Buggy said with a clap. "That's him. His real name is George but everybody calls him Tat because he's all inked up."

"And you picked him why?"

"Muscle mostly. We're gonna have a lot of equipment to lug in and around different locations. I figured he'd come in handy. And just 'cause he's inked doesn't mean he's stupid. He knows a lot about fixing stuff. He'll kinda be like our insurance guy. If we run into problems with something, he can beat the shit out of it or fix it."

"How's he going to beat up a ghost?"

"Well . . . just in case. And anyway if equipment breaks or the van breaks down—"

"What van?"

Buggy bounced in place. "Wait, didn't I tell you? We get to use one of the WXRT vans! Not the ones with the satellite stuff on it. A supply van. So there's another bonus. They're supplying the techie equipment, a van, and moolah if we find ghoulies."

"But—"

Buggy didn't allow Nonie to get another word in edgewise. She was more than wired for sound. "Oh, and we get a real deal investigator to add to our Krewe, too. I think he's one of the producers' nephew or something like that. He's done investigations before and knows how to use all that techie stuff. His name's Jack Nagan. Real smart guy from what I hear."

"You haven't met him?"

"Uh . . . not exactly yet."

Nonie felt sweat drip from her armpits. She didn't know why she'd allowed Buggy to get her so worked up. All her friend had done was put together a gaggle of misfits plus a producer's son, nephew, whomever. No way that production company was going to give them the gig.

"So," Buggy continued, "the plan is we'll all meet up, and Jack will show us how to use the equipment. We'll be pros before you know it. I can handle a digital recorder, Shaundelle a camera, Jack all the other tech stuff, and Jesus H Christmas you're smarter than all of us put together. I know if Jack shows you how to use some gizmo you'll catch on," Buggy snapped her fingers, "just like that."

Nonie stood and rubbed her temple with a finger. "Look, Bug, I've gotta get back to work. We've got the mayor's viewing tomorrow. We'll talk more about this later, okay? I'm sure there'll be a lot of people trying out for this job. Not to knock your blocks down, but the chances of any of us getting on this bandwagon I'd say were slim to no way." She gave Buggy a quick hug. "Give me a call later.

Maybe we can catch a late feature at the Round Up
—"

"Uh . . . We've already got the gig," Buggy said,
then flinched like a puppy waiting to get its snout
popped with a rolled-up newspaper.

Nonie took a step back. "W-what? How? Who . .
.?"

"I told you as soon as Lyle told me about the gig,
I jumped on it like white on cotton. He went to the
producers, told them there was a crew ready to go
and bing, bang, boom, the big man okayed it. Even
called his nephew to let him know."

Nonie scowled. "You did all that thinking I was
your ace in the hole and didn't even talk to me
about it first?"

Buggy grabbed both of Nonie's hands and
squeezed. "Look, I'm sorry about that, but I know

you, kiddo. You'd have kicked like a mule against this. So I made a couple calls to Shaundelle and Tatman, told Lyle what to tell the producers, then said a quick novena to St. Jude that you wouldn't kill me when I told you."

Nonie pulled her hands out of Buggy's grasp and threw them up in the air. "Hell, Bug, I really don't want to do this."

"Think of the money, girl. I mean we're talking pretty big bucks. Where else you gonna find a deal like that around this podunk town?"

Regretfully, Nonie had to admit that if she pushed her own fears aside Buggy was right. But that didn't mean she had to like it.

When she was about six years old, Nonie had seen her grandfather standing at the foot of her bed, smiling. That had been the night after his funeral.

She'd told her parents about seeing him, but they hadn't believed her and told her not to talk to anybody else about it because people would think she was crazy. Rita and Elmo, T-boy, Broussard were not the sort of parents or people who believed easily. They had to see everything for themselves for it to truly have stock. Her mother had even talked about possibly taking Nonie to a psychiatrist to make sure something wasn't wrong with her daughter's brain. That had scared Nonie more than seeing her grandfather.

For the most part, the dead left her alone after that. Then, after Guy died, everything changed. The moment she'd found out about his death she'd wanted to die herself. She'd always known he'd be her husband one day, and Guy's demise had sent her world spinning off its axis. She'd cried for days, barely able to get out of bed. Couldn't eat, couldn't sleep. Then one night, after a huge tear-fest, Guy had simply appeared beside her bed. She'd gasped as if waking from a nightmare and quickly reached out for him. All she'd felt was a cool breeze whisper through her fingers as her hand passed right through him.

"My Nonie, one and only," Guy had said. "Don't cry, baby. I'll always be with you. I promise."

And he'd been true to his word. Seeing him had been a constant over the past nine years. After a while, she'd grown desperate to tell someone about her experiences with Guy. Her parents were out of the question, and the only other person she trusted wholeheartedly was Buggy Mouton. As she'd expected, Buggy had been slightly taken aback by the news but in short order her attitude changed to enthusiasm and total belief. And as far as Nonie knew, to date, Buggy had yet to tell another soul, as promised.

It wasn't as if Nonie saw and heard the dead wherever she went. She sensed more than she saw. Except for physically seeing Guy, seeing others who'd passed on seemed to come and go at their own discretion. Like the time Mrs. Gail Roy, the wife of a local grocery store owner in Clay Point, died after a long illness. Nonie had attended the funeral, as did most of the town, to pay her respects. While everybody whispered and gossiped, moved in and out from the viewing room to the coffee lounge, Nonie saw and heard Mrs. Roy standing at the foot of her casket, bitching the entire time that her daughter had put her in a purple suit when she knew she'd wanted to be buried in pink.

"Mah dat's a shame, yeah," Mrs. Roy had said. "Look how bad I look in dat dress. Why she put me in dat purple thing? I tol' her and tol' her, when de time comes to bary me, I want you to dress me in pink. I look good in pink. But does she listen to her mama? No. She put me in purple. Lawd, look how I look bad."

Mrs. Roy had all but yelled her complaints, and Nonie looked around, figuring others had to have heard her, as well. But everyone was either talking amongst themselves or sniveling into a tissue. Nonie had been the only one to witness the tantrum, and she certainly didn't share the news about color preferences with Irene, Mrs. Roy's offending daughter.

Although this scouting gig sounded like a financial hit, it made Nonie extremely nervous. She feared someone might slip—that someone being Buggy—and others would find out Nonie's secret. And if the wrong person caught wind that she could see and speak to the dead, word would spread through Clay Point like ants at a picnic. She imagined the entire populace chasing her down Main Street, carrying torches and straitjackets. Okay, so maybe her imagination had a bit of a cayenne in it, but still, small towns—small minds.

Nonie sighed, and tried to be open-minded. Maybe, just maybe they could pull this off. The fact that the money was the enticer made her feel a little guilty, but being able to breathe easier financially and doing so away from the funeral home softened the guilt somewhat. As for the other members of the Boo Krewe finding out about her so-called gift, she and Buggy would have to find a work-around for that issue. Nonie knew enough about Shaundelle Washington to know the woman was totally self-absorbed. So if Nonie gave Buggy some kind of signal that a place had a spirit attached to it, more than likely Shaundelle wouldn't notice. Same with George—aka Tatman. The few times she'd met him, he'd seemed a little slow on the uptake. But the Nagan guy made her fidgety. She knew absolutely nothing about him.

Puffing out her cheeks then slowly releasing the air, Nonie finally said, "If. . . and I'm saying *IF* I go along with this, I'd need more info on this Jack Nagan guy. When are you supposed to meet him?"

Buggy clapped and twirled in place, her round face red with excitement. "Tonight! We'll meet him tonight."

"What do you mean *we*?"

"Well, I left it sorta open-ended with everyone until I had a chance to talk to you, but I told them we'd maybe meet at your house around eight tonight."

Nonie let her jaw drop, flabbergasted. She glared at Buggy. "You mean to tell me you invited strangers to *my* house! Why not your apartment?"

"It's too small."

"Why not the Hole in the Wall bar or Tatman's house?"

Buggy shrugged. "The bar's too loud and there're too many people. Somebody might overhear our conversation and start asking questions. I don't want to have to explain anything to anybody. We don't want the competition. As for Tatman, he lives with his mother. Your place seemed like the most logical location."

"I live in a duplex, you know that. It's maybe a third larger than your apartment. And what about Dora Arsemont, the woman who lives in the other half of the duplex? She's nosier than a Labrador with its nose up a duck's butt."

"So? Is there a law against you having a few friends over? It's not like she'll be inside your place to see or hear what we're doing."

"Dora's got ears like a bat, and the walls are thin."

Buggy let out an exasperated sigh. "So we'll talk softly, work quickly. She'll never know what we're up to. She—"

Nonie held up a hand, stopping Buggy's tirade. "I need some time to think about this."

"Well, you better get to thinking 'cause we're going to be at your house at eight."

"What were you thinking, inviting all of those strangers to my house without talking to me first?" Nonie said, flustered. "Suppose I had a date?"

"You, on a date?" Buggy clicked her tongue against her palate. "Like with who? Lyle and me aren't going anywhere and the last person I know you went out with was Kyle."

Kyle was Lyle's identical twin brother who worked offshore. Occasionally, when he was in town, Nonie tagged along with Buggy, Lyle and Kyle to the movies or a concert. But it was far from what Nonie would call a double date.

"For your information, Miss Know-It-All, that new deputy, Nate Lopez, who just started working for Sheriff Buchanan? He's asked me out a couple of times."

Buggy's head snapped back in surprise and her eyebrows shot up. "Really? Wow, he's quite the hunk."

"And what am I? A dog?"

"No, no," Buggy said. "With him being new in town, I just thought . . . well, figured it kinda weird that he'd start asking anyone on a date. At least get to know folks in town first."

"He's been here a little over a month, and Clay Point is a small town. Even being brand new here, I can't see it taking that long to get a lay of the land or the people in it."

Buggy waggled her eyebrows. "So give me some scoop. Where did you meet him? What did he say? And how come you didn't tell me—"

In the middle of Buggy's barrage of questions, Margaret Simms, the funeral home's receptionist for the living and hairdresser and cosmetician for the deceased, walked into the coffee room. She marched up to Nonie, hunchbacked and scowling. She wore a dark blue dress with a wide white belt cinched around her narrow waist. As usual, her eyeglasses, which were half the size of her narrow, pinched face, sat on the end of her nose. She'd worked for the Broussards for over twenty years, since Nonie's grandfather ran the place. Although Margaret would never reveal her age to a soul, Nonie guessed her to be nearing seventy if not slightly over.

"Where have you been, missy?" Margaret asked Nonie. She glanced at Buggy but didn't acknowledge her. "Your mama's been looking everywhere for you. There's a lot of work to be done. You know we've got a big viewing tomorrow and look at you. Hanging out with a soda, chitchatting without a care in this big ol' world."

Margaret had come from Georgia and was somehow related to some second cousin's cousin on which side of the family Nonie couldn't remember. Even after all these years, Margaret still carried her Georgian accent, a nasally twang that thickened when she got agitated. To make matters worse, Margaret chain-smoked, although she'd swear on all that was holy that she didn't, so her twang came out deep and raspy.

"I was helping," Nonie said defensively. "Uncle Fezzo came in and relieved me. Buggy hasn't been here long. We're talking."

"Well, chat time's over. I think you need to march your little butt over to the reception area, where your mama is. She's beside herself, being there's so much to do and all. Flower deliveries are already coming in, and they're piling up near the front door. The viewing room needs to be set up, prayer cards need printin'—you know the drill. Your daddy's going into the embalming room right now to do his business with Mayor Dover, Lord bless him, then I've got to go in right after to see if I can do anything with hair and makeup. Given the mayor's condition, though, I doubt it."

"Where's Butchy? Why isn't he doing the embalming?" Nonie asked, referring to the resident apprentice.

"Polishin' the hearse with Fezzo," Margaret said. "Your daddy decided to take care of Dover with him being the mayor and all. Plus the poor man's face needs some reconstruction 'cause his wife's demanding an open casket viewing. Anyway, it's none of your beeswax who's where and doing what. All you need to be worrin' about is where you need to be. Now get!"

Nonie turned to Buggy and rolled her eyes. "Gotta get back to work."

"Okay, but call me," Buggy said. "Like soon. Or, well, just be ready. We'll be there at eight. We'll talk more about it then. It'll give you time to come up with more questions."

Nonie gave her a warning scowl.

"It'll be fine. Great. Don't worry."

"Nonie Marie Broussard, don't make me tell you again," Margaret warned, as if Nonie were a petulant child. She stood stock-still, determination deepening the wrinkles in her face, obviously set on not leaving until Nonie followed her out.

"I'm coming," Nonie said, wondering how many years it had been since Margaret drew up the nerve to talk to her as if she were her mother. Then she remembered . . . ever since Nonie could remember.

CHAPTER THREE

Death sucked.

Especially when it was your own.

Guy Skinard watched Nonie veer off into the coffee room and itched to follow her inside. He wanted to eavesdrop, find out what Buggy had to say, know why she'd come here. Must have been important or some real juicy gossip for her to come to the funeral home. Even from where he stood, he could hear Buggy talking loudly, excitedly. Something about ghosts . . . and money. He wasn't sure.

As anxious as he was to find out the scoop, he knew better than to try and sneak into the coffee area. Nonie would spot him in a heartbeat and that would be the end of that.

Sulking, Guy turned around and walked through the back wall of the funeral home, closest to the embalming room. He paid little attention to the drywall fibers, insulation and two-by-four studs as he walked through them. There'd been a time, not long after the boating accident, when he'd thought walking through walls, people, basically anything and everything had been really cool. Now it was simply something he was able to do. Like fishing, hunting and playing blackjack had been the talents he possessed when alive.

Living, breathing, seeing to be seen, hearing to be heard, felt like it had been his reality only hours ago. So did his memory of the accident that had taken his life. Guy remembered it all too vividly. He and his best friend, Too Tall Touchet, had been fishing for catfish in the Atchafalaya late one afternoon. They'd just pulled out of a slough to find a more productive fishing hole, when a speedboat came of out nowhere and plowed into the back of Guy's skiff—right where he'd been manning the outboard motor.

The next thing Guy knew he felt like someone had perched him on the top of a cypress tree for a bird's-eye view of everything happening below. Too Tall flapping around in the water with one arm, yelling and gulping for air. There'd been very little left of the skiff, and the speedboat with its shiny red and white striped body looked like a crumpled Coke can. Guy had spotted its driver lying in a heap at the bottom of his boat, covered in blood. The weirdest part, though, was when Guy saw himself floating face down in the bayou about sixty feet away from the wreckage.

Dead.

He'd died. Plain and simple. And it pissed him off. Left him frustrated and disappointed. Where had all the guardian angel crap they'd fed him in catechism gone to? He'd seen no angels, seraphim, archangels or pearly gates. No one to show him the ropes now that he was dead. What the hell was he supposed to do?

The notion of being dead refused to fit in Guy's brain. He couldn't be dead. He knew that the speedboat had hit them, but he'd felt no pain, didn't remember landing in the water.

Then, while trying to absorb all he surveyed, Guy's mind suddenly took a hard, involuntary detour. He no longer saw the basin, the boats, or Too Tall. He found himself standing at the edge of some field he didn't recognize and staring at a strange purple light that appeared to grow brighter with each passing second.

Guy felt the light beckon to him, warm and welcoming. He felt love coming from that light, a sensation so powerful, it had been difficult for him to comprehend. Its call had been so enticing he'd taken a couple of steps closer to it. Then he'd thought of her.

Nonie.

He'd made promises to her. Loved her. Needed her. Wanted to protect her always. The love he'd felt coming from that light was powerful, but not as strong as his love for Nonie. And besides, he'd never heard of any dead person seeing a purple light. It was supposed to be white. Something had to be off here.

So he'd turned away from the light—from the warmth and welcome and made a conscious decision to stay earthbound for as long as Nonie needed him.

As Guy popped out from the outer wall of the funeral home, he faced a sunny afternoon, which gave him no sense of pleasure. He shuffled around the building, hands in his pants' pockets, waiting for Nonie.

Once Guy came to terms with death and the fact that he'd tossed away whatever might have been waiting for him on the other side of that bright purple light, he'd struck out on his own.

Dead man walking. Literally.

No matter. He tackled it like he did most things when he was alive. Figure it out on his own as he moved about.

It was odd to walk around Clay Point, recognize people you'd known your entire life, yet not be able to communicate with them. He listened to their conversations, could follow them anywhere and there wasn't a damn thing any of them could do about it. Although the gossip he'd picked up had been exciting, it left him feeling like the odd man out. What good was great gossip and secrets if you had no one to share them with?

Although alone where conversation was concerned, it didn't take Guy long to realize that he was far from being alone. He'd been surprised to discover just how many spirits occupied Clay Point and the surrounding small towns. So far, the spirits he encountered appeared to fit in one of four categories.

The first simply refused to move on due to fear. What remained on this earth was familiar to them, felt safe. The light, no matter the color or how inviting it appeared, was still strange territory and caused them great anxiety.

The second group seemed to remain earthbound due to unfinished business. Things they didn't know how to wrap up now that they were dead. It left them angry at everything and everyone they came into contact with. The third group refused to move into the light because they inherently knew the light would cause them to lose control over their environment and they were used to maintaining control. They had managed and manipulated everything and everyone in life and expected to do the same in death. A bunch of sad saps if you asked him.

The fourth group was one Guy avoided to the best of his ability. They were evil spirits, people who created chaos and havoc in life and saw death as a kick-ass tool to produce mayhem at every turn simply because they could.

Guy figured he sat between groups one and two. He ached for the familiarity of Nonie. They'd been inseparable in life, and he didn't want his death to terminate that. He regretted that they'd not been able to marry before he died, but that didn't mean he couldn't watch over her as a husband would his wife.

For some reason Guy still couldn't explain, it had taken him some time to find Nonie. Every street and alley in Clay Point looked the same as it did when he was alive. He knew the directions to Nonie's house as well as he did his own. The problem was every time he'd get within two blocks of her house, in a snap, he'd suddenly find himself sucked back into a gray vacuum of sorts that inevitably took him back to the scene of the boat accident. He felt like a hunk of metal and the bayou a giant magnet that refused to let him go very far.

Each time that occurred, he'd trek from the swamp to Nicholson Street, which sat two blocks from Nonie's, and the trip seemed to take forever. A thousand endless miles. Maybe it was some macabre punishment for turning away from the light in the first place.

Punishment or not, the one quality he'd maintained in death that he'd carried strongly in life was stubbornness. So no matter how many times he got sucked back to the swamp, he'd storm back toward Nonie's.

Then one night, seemingly out of nowhere and for no apparent reason, Guy found himself crossing Nicholson Street, then walking through Mrs. Banks' petunia garden on Guidry Street. The next thing he knew, he'd not only made it to Nonie's house, he'd marched right through it and into her bedroom, where he'd found her asleep. He was glad she slept for had she seen him at that moment she'd have seen a bug-eyed fool. He still couldn't believe he'd managed to break the barrier that had kept him away from her for so long. He never understood why the barrier had been there in the first place. Nonie must have had something to do with it. He could only speculate that he was finally able to break through the barrier because she was mentally ready to see him. He hoped.

A deep ache filled him when he spotted the tear stains on her pillow. He wanted so much to touch her, reassure her. But when he placed a hand on her cheek, he might as well have swiped through thin air. He felt nothing. She, however, stirred, eyes fluttering open, brow furrowing, as if waking from some undesirable dream.

Within seconds, she'd turned in his direction and her eyes widened. That's when Guy knew she saw him. Neither of them spoke. She raised a hand to his chest. He felt the heat and energy of her skin go through his being.

He'd been so shocked when he realized that Nonie could actually see him that if the dead were able to piss their pants, he would have right then and there.

His death and her life had never been the same since.

Suddenly feeling a little spring in his step, Guy bounced his way over to the funeral home garage, where he saw Buggy's Taurus backing out of the driveway. In front of the Taurus, parked inside the garage was the hearse, all shiny and black and protected from the elements. Between the hearse and a garage workbench, Guy spotted Margaret squatting and sneaking a quick smoke.

Grinning and unable to help himself, Guy went over to Margaret, stood right in front of her and put his right hand on the hood of the hearse, where the battery was located. One thing he'd learned since dying was that in order to manifest anything in the physical world, he needed to borrow energy from other sources, like batteries, lamps, anything that produced an electrical current.

Guy felt a tingling sensation ride up from the palm of his right hand, flow into his chest, then over to his left arm and hand. It was enough energy for him to pound on the hearse's hood once, which sent Margaret jumping upright and squashing out her cigarette in one stomp. Wide-eyed, she kept watch on the hearse as she squeezed herself past the vehicle and back into the funeral home.

Being dead did suck.

But sometimes it had its advantages.

CHAPTER FOUR

After Buggy left, Nonie halfheartedly followed Margaret to the reception area, where her mother, Rita, sat behind a large oval mahogany desk. As usual, her auburn hair was coiffed to perfection, her long nails painted the same tint as her rust-colored suit and matching pumps.

"Nonie, for heaven's sake, we have so much to do," her mother said, then let out a theatrical sigh. "I'm so glad you're here. I need you to start placing all these flowers in the chapel." She waggled manicured fingers towards the thirty-plus arrangements clogging up the front entrance. "The Fontenot family has already chosen the prayer cards, and Margaret has them set to print. I need you to handle the obit, too. Here's the info they gave me about Dover." She handed Nonie a slip of paper.

"Aw, Ma, not the obit," Nonie protested. "Can't you do that?"

"I just had my nails done. What would tomorrow's visitors think if I ran around with chipped nails? I need you to type the obit and send it off to the *Gazette* before two so it makes the paper run for this evening."

Nonie blew out a breath. Rita Broussard's maiden name was Menard, which was a surname as Cajun as the rest of the town, save for a handful like Margaret. And the funeral home was a small business that worked maybe fifty funerals a year. Why then, did her mother have to act so uppity, like she'd come from some fancy city out West or East? It puzzled Nonie. It was almost as if Rita was ashamed of her inherent culture. She loved her mom, of course, but sometimes she had to swallow the things Rita said or did a little at a time, so she wouldn't choke.

Margaret stepped in and waved a hand with two-inch red-painted fingernails. "I'll finish the prayer cards because it's gonna take a little while I'm suspectin' before I can get to the Mayor's hair and makeup anyway. That's if T-boy was able to do something with his face." She turned to Nonie, "You do the obit and flowers, then vacuum up a little. You know how the baby's breath in those arrangements leaves those little white diddies all over the floor when you move them."

Nonie held back a groan. Why her father had chosen to stay in this business boggled her to this day. He was a talented man in so many ways. He could've easily told his father no when he'd been offered the funeral home baton. But Cajun was Cajun, which meant traditions and responsibilities were seldom taken for granted or shaken off.

Without a word, she gathered the funeral sprays closest to the front entrance and started to haul them away. She stopped and turned to her mother. "Which parlor?"

Rita tsked. "Nonie Marie, we're talking about the mayor of Clay Point for heaven's sake. Which parlor do you think?"

"It's a chapel service? No mass?" Nonie asked, surprised. The Fontenots were devout Catholics, at least every Easter and Christmas devout, and it surprised her that they weren't going to run Dover through St. Anthony's.

"Mrs. Fontenot hasn't decided yet. They're talking cremation. I should hear either way relatively soon." She dismissed Nonie with a wave. "Go on now. Get this front area cleared out so we can clean it."

"Who's we?" Nonie asked with a dig.

Rita sighed heavily. "You, Nonie Marie Broussard, so *you* can clean it. Now stop with the nonsense and do your job." She slapped a hand on top of the huge box of unprinted prayer cards sitting on the reception desk. Can't you see we're busy here? Now where in God's name did Margaret run off to?"

Nonie shrugged, knowing full well that the seventy-year-old woman had probably sneaked off to the garage for a smoke. As obnoxious and bossy as Margaret was, Nonie liked her. She had a no-

nonsense, do-as-I-please attitude, which Nonie couldn't help but admire. Margaret's voice, with its raspy twang, reminded her of magnolias and whiskey. There was a significant difference between a Southern woman and a Cajun woman. A Southern woman carried herself with grace and charm, the way Margaret did, even though she was hunchbacked. Nonie could picture her as a young woman, wearing a hooped skirt, perched on a porch swing, and drinking mint juleps. A Cajun woman, on the other hand, you'd more than likely find wearing cutoff jeans and sitting on a riding lawn mower, steering wheel in one hand, Budweiser in the other.

"I swear, do I have to do all the work around here?" Rita whined.

Turning away with an eye roll, Nonie took the sprays into the largest viewing room. She hated the smell of multiple flowers compacted into one room, regardless of its size. It was like going to a perfume counter and sampling every brand at once, the scent overwhelmingly sweet, spicy and confusing to the brain.

After placing the flowers in hand against the wall closest to the casket bier, Nonie turned on her heels, ready to head back for more, when she ran into—or more to the point—through Guy. She gasped as a rush of cold air whooshed through her body. Usually that cold air was a precursor to his presence. He'd never sneaked up on her like that before. He appeared solid in form, yet she'd walked through him as if he was mist.

"Don't do that!" Nonie hissed in a loud whisper.

Guy grinned. "'Just having a little fun, babe."

"Well, that wasn't fun or funny. You scared the hell out of me!"

"Aw, baby, you know I'd never hurt you."

Nonie threw a quick glance over her shoulder towards the viewing room door to make sure Margaret or her mom hadn't decided to follow her and give floral placement tips. So far, the coast appeared clear.

"You need to leave," Nonie whispered. "What if my mom comes in here? Or worse, Margaret?"

Still grinning, Guy shrugged. "It's not like they can see me, hotcakes."

"I know but having you around when other people are talking to me screws with my head, and you know it. Now, go. Shoo. Be gone." Nonie turned and took a step towards the door. In a blink, Guy was in front of her again.

"Jesus!" she cried. "Why are you doing this?"

"'Cause you're leaving too fast, and I've got a present for you." Guy waggled his eyebrows, a habit Nonie had always hated.

"Don't do that," she said, and waved a dismissive hand. "I've got to get back to work."

"Nonie?" Rita's voice rang throughout the funeral home. "You okay in there?"

Nonie winced, then growled at Guy. "Fine, Mom. Just touching up the sprays."

"Did you say something earlier?" Rita called to her. "I thought I heard you talking."

"Nope," Nonie lied, and glared at Guy. He held a hand over his mouth as if to stifle a laugh.

"Well, hurry up, dear," Rita said loudly. "More flowers just arrived."

"Coming."

Nonie heard Margaret cough then start talking to Rita.

"Go," Nonie demanded, and scowled at Guy. "You're going to get me in trouble."

He held his arms out at his sides. "Nothing stopping you, babe. You can walk right through me anytime."

"Move," she whispered. "I don't want to do that walking through you thing again. It makes me feel . . weird."

"Feels pretty good to me. A rush actually. In fact. . ." Guy looked down at the fly on his slacks. "I don't know if ghosts can have woodys or not but—"

"Oh, don't even," Nonie warned, holding up a hand. She quickly slipped around Guy and hurried towards the door.

This time, instead of popping back up in her face, he called out, "Don't you want to know about your present?"

She batted a hand behind her, dismissing him, and crossed the threshold into the sitting area. That's when Nonie heard Guy whisper in her right ear. "You're going to love what I've got for you. Tonight, baby. I'll show you tonight."

Nonie winced. Where Guy Skinard was concerned, alive or dead, surprises could easily become troublesome.

CHAPTER FIVE

Nonie arrived at her duplex around seven-thirty already exhausted. There'd been thirty-five floral arrangements to set up in the viewing room, vacuuming the stray baby's breath, and writing the obituary, which had been painstakingly hard to do. It's one thing when a family pays tribute to a loved one at the time of their death and you didn't know that family. It was another when you did.

The entire town of Clay Point knew Dover cheated on his wife, stuck his hands in the city's till, and was a loudmouth, arrogant old fart. He made certain that for every favor he granted the recipient stayed forever in his debt. Taking the flowery hero write-up the family had faxed over to the funeral home and what she knew about Dover, and melding the two together in her mind was like trying to turn a cow's tongue into filet mignon. It had taken Nonie over three hours to write, but she'd gotten the job done. And Margaret, true to her word and smelling like she'd inhaled an entire pack of Camel cigarettes, had completed printing the prayer cards.

Much more work lay ahead in the morning. Dover would have to be casketed and set up in the viewing room before the family arrived at nine a.m., with the general public viewing starting at ten.

As Nonie stepped towards the porch of the duplex she spotted Dora Arsemont, her neighbor, sitting in a rocker on the duplex's porch. The old woman's face held more wrinkles than a shar pei and her white, scraggly hair had been curled haphazardly around plastic rollers, each held in place with a plastic pick that stuck out like small

Martian antennas. She wore a purple and pink flowered housedress and bright red lipstick that wavered up and under the line of her lips. A red dot floated when she moved, the ever-present cigarette Dora had hanging from the left side of her mouth.

Nonie groaned softly. She wasn't in the mood to chat with Dora and wasn't looking forward to the houseful of visitors Buggy planned to bring over. Nonie wasn't the most fastidious housekeeper in the world, which meant she had dirty clothes, dishes and empty pizza boxes to stash before they arrived.

Dora nodded from the rocker as Nonie clomped onto the porch and started to head for her side of the duplex. At full height, Dora stood no taller than five feet, weighed barely a hundred pounds and thought she was the remake of Gloria Swanson. She was puffing on a cigarette with one side of her mouth and blowing smoke out of the other, all the while applying mascara sans a mirror.

"Evenin' Ms. Dora," Nonie said politely, while she scrambled for her house key in her purse.

Dora lowered her mascara wand and cigarette ashes plopped onto her housedress. She quickly brushed them off, then pinched the cigarette out of her mouth with a thumb and forefinger. "Mah you late tonight, huh?" Dora said, her Cajun accent so far from the fluid sensual tone of Swanson she might as well have been a duck. "I heard about de poor mayor. It's a wonder he didn't drop dead sooner. Big man like dat. All de booze he drank. He was nuttin' but a heart attack waitin' to happen. I knew dat, me."

Nonie wasn't about to correct the woman on the details of Dover's death so she kept the small talk small. "How've you been?"

"Not too bad, not too good. My art'ritis you know. My son Brian came over dis morning and brought me my new med'cine but it don't seem to be workin' too good."

"Sorry to hear that."

"Want to come eat a little bit before you go in you house?" Dora asked. "Got some shrimp sauce picante on de stove."

"No, thanks, Ms. Dora. I've got some friends coming over."

One of Dora's painted eyebrows shot up. "Yeah? Who's comin'? Dat's not usual for you to have comp'ny like dat."

"Just some friends."

"Hmm," Dora mused. "You don't wanna say who dey are? You embarrassed?"

"No, Ms. Dora. Buggy's coming, and she's bringing over a few people."

"Who's dem few people?"

"A couple of people from town, and one I haven't met yet."

"Oh, you bes' be careful wit' dat," Dora warned. "We two good-lookin' ladies livin' alone out here. Dat person you didn't meet yet, it's a man?"

"Yes, ma'am."

Dora stuck her cigarette back into the corner of her mouth and puffed. "Bes' be careful, dat's all I'm gonna say. Dat strange man could wait 'til I'm sleepin' in my bed, den bus' through the window and have his way wit' me right dere in my sleep." A look crossed the old woman's face that looked a little like wishful thinking. "Jus' be careful, and y'all don't make too much noise, okay? Don't let 'em play dat rat music and drink too much. If y'all do, I'm gonna have to call Sheriff Buchanan. Not to be mean, you know, but I gotta get my beauty res'."

"Yes, ma'am, I understand," Nonie said, relief flooding over her when she finally latched onto her house key.

"And none of dem sex orgies, no," Dora added.

"No, ma'am, they're just coming over to visit," Nonie said, quickly unlocking her door.

"Mah, okay. We'll see," Dora said, and went back to her cigarette and mascara.

Nonie hurried into her apartment, closed the door and leaned against it for a moment and said a quick prayer to anyone listening that Dora would turn in for the night before Buggy showed up with the rest of her gang. If not, each would be drilled with more questions than a police interrogation.

After her ten-second reprieve, Nonie dropped her purse on the couch and started scurrying around the apartment, tossing dirty clothes into a hamper, dirty dishes into the sink, which she covered with a dish towel, and newspapers and pizza boxes into a large trash bag, which she stashed in her bedroom. Her place wasn't big, thankfully. Living room, one bathroom, one bedroom, small kitchen with a dining table that sat four.

She tossed a dirty pair of jeans under the couch. Then grabbed a coffee-stained newspaper and whirled about to head to the kitchen trash bin when she found herself almost nose to nose with Guy.

"Crap! Would you stop jumping out at me like that?"

"Aw, Nonie, my little bologna." He smiled, and she was suddenly awash with the scent of him, the way she remembered way back when. Soap, wintergreen mouthwash, and the air after a spring shower. It made her heart ache every time she smelled it or saw him for that matter. She could no longer hold him the way she used to.

"I don't have time to wrangle with you right now," Nonie said. "You're gonna have to go wherever you go when you're not around me. I've got company coming."

"I know," he said.

"What do you mean?" she asked, glancing over her shoulder as she tossed the newspaper into the trash then hurried over to a pile of old mail and hid it under the couch. Nonie suddenly stood and propped a fist on her hip. "Wait . . . Were you eavesdropping on Buggy and me at the funeral home?"

"Just a little actually," Guy said. "I stayed in the embalming room and got to take a look at Dover's wiener, by the way. Just as I figured. Nothing to write home about."

"You're a pervert."

"Am not. Just curious. After I saw it I got bored and just kinda hung around for a little while. Not long. That's when I heard Buggy. She was talking so loud, people from the next parish probably heard her. All I picked up on before leaving like you asked me to was Buggy saying something about ghost hunting and money. Then something about people coming to your house." Guy frowned, giving her a serious look. "Look I don't know what the whole ghost thing is about, but Nonie you have to listen to me. Don't get involved with stuff you don't understand. You don't know what you're getting yourself into where ghosts are concerned."

"Since when've you become my father, my priest, or my big brother for that matter?"

"I'm only saying you know it's different here on the other side, but you don't know the whole of it. Some spirits are good, some bad."

"But living people are like that. Do you think I'm stupid enough not to know the difference, dead or alive?"

"Yeah, it's like in life, only when the bad ones die and stick around instead of crossing over they can do things to you when you least expect it."

Nonie huffed. "Like when you appear in front of me out of the blue and scare the crap out of me?"

"Worse," Guy said, a hint of exasperation in his voice. "Hell, even some of the good ones are so desperate to be seen and heard again they'll latch onto you."

"What is it with you guys anyway? Isn't there some kind of bright light you're supposed to go to once you die? I know you already told me about your purple light, but what about everybody else who's hanging around? Why don't they just go to the doggone light and get it over with?"

Guy shrugged. "Fear. Unfinished business. Unable to let go of the past. I don't really know. I can only answer for myself."

Nonie shook her head, hoping to clear it. "Never mind. I don't have time to get into all this hoohah. Buggy and the rest of the crew will be here any minute, and I have to get the apartment looking half decent."

"Just hear what I'm saying, please. Don't do it."

"Look, we're talking five hundred dollars a pop. Do you realize what that means? No more dressing up to go to work at the funeral home every day. Having to show up early, work late. I can go back to doing exactly what I want and wearing what I want. Besides, the work will be a hell of a lot more interesting than sewing labels on T-shirts."

"I know about the dressing up part. I heard you arguing with your mother during the last visitation about the dress she wanted you to wear." Guy laughed, a sound that made her heart thud. It brought back memories of the times they'd laughed so hard together over the stupidest things that they'd cried.

"Anyway, I really want to give the scouting gig a shot," Nonie said.

Guy sighed. "Whatever. You'll find out about the different type of ghosts soon enough. I guess all of the spirits who haven't moved on have their own reasons. The bad ones may see the light as a scam, the same way they saw most things in life. Maybe they're afraid that although the light is warm and exudes love and welcoming, they're afraid that beyond it is really a fiery pit, just waiting for them because of the terrible things they did when they were alive."

"Is there a fiery pit?" Nonie asked quietly.

"If there is, I haven't seen it."

Nonie suddenly made a shooing motion at Guy with her hands. "Enough. I can't go there right now.

Like it or not, you're gonna have to bleep yourself out of here and go somewhere else. I can't have you hanging around when everyone gets here. It'll be too distracting for me. I'm supposed to be paying attention to whatever equipment some man's bringing over so we can learn how to use them."

"Nonie, don't—"

"I've already made up my mind. I'm going to do it. I've gotta get out from underneath my dad and mom some time. I'll only work at the funeral home until this new project gets off its feet then it's bye-bye dead people. If I never walked into that place again it would be too soon. Now go, shoo. Take yourself and any of your ghost friends you might have hanging around nearby with you."

"But—"

"No buts. Go," Nonie said, while brushing Frito crumbs off the kitchen counter.

In that moment, she heard a knock at the door, then Buggy's voice shout out, "You've got company!"

"Damn," Guy said, then quickly faded out of sight.

"Be right there," Nonie called back. She quickly threw a second dishtowel over the sink full of dirty dishes and hurried around the kitchen corner into the living room and unlocked the front door.

Buggy led the pack into Nonie's apartment, followed by Lyle, her boyfriend. The rest of the crew trooped in behind him. One Nonie could only assume was Tatman since he had inked sleeves that rode all the way up to his neck. He wore a T-shirt with the sleeves cut off and a pair of jeans with grease stains.

Following Tatman was Shaundelle Washington, a large black woman with beautiful long dreadlocks. She wore black spandex leggings and a yellow and red blouse that reached just below her ass and sparkled every time she moved. She immediately settled herself into the only overstuffed chair Nonie owned. Tatman, Lyle and Buggy took over the couch.

With her living room full to overflowing, Nonie went to her small dining table, grabbed two chairs and carried them into the living room. She placed one near the couch, half listening to Buggy blabber to Lyle about some movie he'd promised to take her to. About that time, a man walked through Nonie's open front door. The sight of him made her breath catch. He gave a whole new definition to fine-as-hell. Black, collar-length hair, a strong chiseled face with high cheekbones, bright green eyes, and a slim, muscular body. She assumed him to be Jack Nagan. He wore khaki pants with a maroon polo shirt that had the television call letters, WXRT, stitched over his left breast. He carried in two metal cases, both larger than briefcases but smaller than trunks.

"Mind if I place these here?" he asked, aiming his cleft chin at her coffee table.

"N-No problem," Nonie said. Then to herself, *You can put those cases any damn where you want as long as you always come along with them!*

"Nonie," Buggy said, nodding to the tattooed man. "This is Tatman, and you remember Shaundelle, of course."

"What's shakin', girl," Shaundelle said in greeting. She wiggled herself deeper into the overstuffed chair. "Decent digs you've got here."

"And the man bringing in the luggage," Buggy continued, "is Jack Nagan."

Jack was the kind of man women fantasized about when they wanted sex, Nonie was sure of it. He laid his two cases down on the coffee table then stood upright. His movements were fluid, and she couldn't help but watch his large biceps flex when they were in motion.

"Nice to meet you," Nonie said, then walked up to shake his hand, forgetting that she was still holding onto a kitchen chair. "Sorry," she said, and placed the chair on the floor. One of the legs slammed down on her left big toe.

"Shit" she cried, then slapped a hand over her mouth and looked up at Jack. "Sorry. Chair got my toe."

"I hate when shit like that happens," Shaundelle said, crossing her legs as best she could considering the size of her thighs.

"Me too," Tatman said. "Hurts like hell. I'm always dropping piping and stuff like that on my feet at the shop. Hurt one of my toes so bad a few months ago, I thought they'd have to cut it off."

"I'm assuming all of you already know each other?" Nonie asked.

"Yeah," Lyle said. "I drove everyone over in the company van. The one you guys will be using on your scouting gigs."

"You should have seen my neighbors," Shaundelle said, beaming. "They was staring out their windows and whistling. I felt like I was a movie star or something. Hey, you got any snacks up in here? Coke? Beer?"

"I've got a couple of Buds in the fridge but that's about it," Nonie said. "Didn't have time to stop at Roy's." Roy's was the local grocery store that kept residents from having to drive twenty miles to a larger supermarket.

"I'll take a Bud," Tatman said, getting up from the couch and making his way into the kitchen.

"Me, too," Shaundelle said, struggling to get up from her chair. After a few tries she gave up and sat back. "Bring me the second one, hon, since you're already up."

"Will do," Tatman said, and seconds later he showed up with two Bud Lights, one in each hand.

"I'd be happy to run over to Roy's if anybody else would like one," Nonie offered. "Tonight's meeting sort of took me by surprise." She glowered at Buggy. "Otherwise I'd have been better prepared."

"I'm good," Buggy said.

"Yeah, guess I am, too," Lyle said, watching Tatman down his beer, a hint of envy on his face.

"Jack?" Nonie prompted as she watched him open his cases and start laying out equipment on the coffee table.

He looked up at her with a surprised, slightly confused expression on his face. "Huh?"

"I was saying I can run over to the grocery store if you'd like a beer."

"Oh, sorry, I didn't catch that. No thanks."

"You ain't a coonass are ya?" Tatman asked.

"I'm originally from New Orleans. Live in Lafayette now," Jack explained. "Not sure what that makes me."

"A bit off your rocker if you don't drink," Tatman said with a hardy laugh.

Jack joined in the laughter good-heartedly and went back to unpacking his cases.

"Aw, man, is that a Canon 5D Mark III," Shaundelle asked when he pulled out a camera.

Jack looked at Shaundelle, amused. "You seem to know your cameras."

"Hell, yeah, I know them. I've got a Mark III, a Wista 4 x 5 Field Camera, a Nikon D3S, and a Sony Alpha a99.

"Impressive," Jack said. "So you're a professional photographer?"

"Damn straight. I do weddings, funerals, and beauty shots. Most of those are half-naked men, but you know how it is. If you're going to shoot something, you need to have the right ammo to get the beat down. Know what I'm sayin'?"

"Sure do," Jack said. "Since you're so familiar with cameras, I'll put you in charge of the Mark III and our night vision camera. Same style as a D3S, only you don't need a flash to take a picture. It's made to detect low light spectrum objects."

"Now that's what I'm talkin' about." Shaundelle scooted to the edge of her seat so she could reach for the Mark III and check it out. Jack handed it to her.

"What am I going to be using?" Buggy asked, her large, dark eyes wide with wonder.

"Audio," Jack said. I've got two digital recorders so take your pick. We use them to do EVPs."

"What's a VPE?" Tatman asked.

"It's EVP, short for electronic voice phenomena. Whenever we do a hunt, we turn on the recorder and ask questions, like, 'Is there someone in this room who'd like to talk to us? What's your name? Are you male or female? Does it bother you that we're here?' Then we analyze the recordings later to see if we received any responses."

"Oh, I can so do that," Buggy said. "I'll question their butt off. If there are any ghosts where we're going, I'll get them talking. Don't you worry."

Jack smiled, seemingly impressed with her enthusiasm.

"What about me?" Tatman asked. "What're you going to have me doin'?

"I'll need your help setting up infrared cameras in the rooms we're going to investigate and wire them to a fifty-five-inch TV with splitters. We'll put the TV in an area we'll call our command center. From there, we'll be able to see what's going on in five rooms at one time."

"I've done that shit at the shop. Set up an entire security camera system by myself. So I'll be a tech guy sorta?"

"Yep, you'll be my tech guy."

Nonie grimaced. Jack hadn't assigned any equipment to her. Aside from seeing or hearing the dead, both of which she couldn't let anyone know about, Nonie didn't have any special talents that might impress Jack. There were still so many gadgets spread out on the coffee table, she feared he'd pick the most complicated one and hand it over to her, expecting her to make it work.

"Are you going to be on this crew?" Nonie asked Lyle, who'd been sitting quietly on the couch taking in all Jack had to say.

Lyle shook his head and grinned. "Just here to make sure the intros went okay and that everyone played nice."

Nonie gave him a small smile. There went her hopes for handing off some of the more complicated equipment.

"And you," Jack said to Nonie, his green eyes sparkling like dewy clover, "will handle a Rem Pod."

Nonie worked hard to swallow her saliva. "What's a Rem Pod?" She'd heard about them on ghost hunting shows but had never paid attention to how they worked.

"All you have to do is turn the switch on underneath the gadget." He showed her where it was located. "Then place it somewhere in any room that may be a hot spot. A hot spot is usually where the owner of the location has either seen an apparition or shadow figure. Occasionally a spirit may show up but not in a way that can be seen by the naked eye. But the minute they get close to this antenna on the Rem Pod, it'll start beeping loudly and these bulbs on top of the Pod will start flashing multicolored lights."

"Then what?" Nonie asked.

"We'll be watching from the command center. If we see the lights go off, I'll radio Shaundelle to go in there with the I.R. camera and take pictures.

Nonie nodded. Easy enough to understand. The problem she had was if the Rem Pod went off, more times than not she'd be facing the spirit that set it off. What if she showed up in every shot Shaundelle took? She feared it would be too obvious. Someone as smart as Jack would put two and two together quickly and blow the whistle on her to the others. And heaven only knew what chaos that would create.

CHAPTER SIX

By the time Jack finished explaining all of the equipment he'd brought with him, Nonie's head was spinning. Aside from what he'd already explained to them, he'd brought an OvilusV, a PX, an IR thermometer, a P-SB11, a Trifield meter, an EMF Field tester, a Flir TG165, sage, extra batteries, flashlights, cameras, digital recorders, and external speakers. Along with the Rem Pod Jack had already assigned to Nonie, he put her in charge of a second digital recorder, like Buggy. The rest of the crew and he would manage the remaining equipment.

As if reading her thoughts, Jack said to Nonie, "I know this all looks intimidating, but you don't have to worry about using all of it. Most investigations don't require the use of all this equipment. But the instruments are great to have around if you hit a hot spot. Then you can use them to verify that you've picked up on something."

"Oh, I ain't 'timidated with none of this stuff," Shaundelle said. "All you've gotta to do is show me once, and that's gonna be locked in my head forever. I know I'm supposed to be workin' the cameras and all, but I can take more if you need me to."

"I'll keep that in mind," Jack said. Then he looked around the room. "So does everybody know what they'll be responsible for on our first scouting trip?"

Heads nodded.

"I think you've made it pretty easy for them to understand, Jack," Lyle said. "At least the equipment they'll be operating."

Silent, Nonie looked down at the Rem Pod in her hand and frowned, fearing more than the bells and lights that might go off on it.

"Nonie, you look a bit disturbed," Jack said. "Want me to go over the way the Rem Pod works again?"

She looked up at him, pursed her lips, then said, "No, sounds easy to use." Her eyes flickered about the room and the people filling it. "I do have a question, though."

"Ask away," Jack said.

"Why would the producers at WXRT choose us to do the scouting for the program, "*Something's Out There*?"

"Girl, stop with your stupid questions," Shaundelle said with a scowl.

"It's not stupid," Jack said. "If I was in your shoes, I'd be asking the same thing."

Nonie tilted her head, looking at him quizzically. "There are quite a few legit paranormal investigation teams in the state, some as close as Lafayette. Why would they pick us when we don't have any experience with investigations?"

"You tryin' to blow the deal?" Tatman asked, then downed the last of his beer.

"Of course not."

"Sounds like it to me."

"No one's blowing any deal," Jack said. "Nonie's question is legit, and I can answer it. You may not like the answer, but it's the truth."

Tatman belched. "Give it to us, big guy. What won't we like?"

Jack looked at Nonie. "You're right. There are active paranormal groups around the state who would give their left arm for this chance, but they come with problems. First is cost. There wasn't one group out there who would do a scout for less than fifteen hundred. A thousand if it was a dud. We were concerned that with prices that high, people might have a tendency to, let's say . . . make up spooks and ghouls when there really wasn't anything there. Second, every one of them wanted to be the stars of the show, and we already have the lead people chosen. They wanted cameo spots, which we disagreed with. The last thing we needed was them claiming on camera that they were the ones responsible for finding the ghouls. And finally, they might call themselves professional paranormal investigators, but a lot of their members think they're demonologists. A cat could move from one room to the other, and, sure as hell, one of them would declare it's demon possessed. That's simply not the direction we want to head."

"So it's easier and cheaper for you to use people who have no clue as to what they're supposed to be doing?" Nonie asked.

"Cheaper, yes," Jack said and looked about the room. "But if the money doesn't work for any of you, you're welcome to back out now."

"Hell, no on the backing out," Shaundelle said. "That money works for me."

Everyone else in the room nodded in agreement.

"Good," Jack said, then turned to Nonie. "As far as inexperience is concerned, every investigator started as a newbie. Unless you've got a few marbles missing up here," he tapped a finger against his right temple, "it's far easier than it looks, and all of this intimidating equipment will soon become second nature as far as use."

"So when do we get started with this ghoul patrol?" Tatman asked. "I'm itchin' to get going. Oh, hey, is our scouting these boogers a secret or can we tell our friends and family? I mean, most of them see me as a loser who can't do more than stock shelves at the hardware store. It'd be nice to let them know I'm part of something that had some gonads to it."

"Now that we have our team in place, you're welcome to throw all the gonads you want at them," Jack said and grinned. "As for when we get started, that'll be tomorrow. We'll be heading for a place about forty minutes from here. Opelousas. Supposed to be an old haunted house out there."

Nonie felt panic ride up her spine. "What time tomorrow? I mean, we all have jobs. I work at Broussard's Funeral Home with my family, Buggy at Meemaw's Café, and Tatman at the hardware store."

"No worries," Jack said. "It'll be at night. We'll meet here, if that's okay with you, around seven-thirty. I'll have the van so we can all ride together."

Buggy clapped her hands like a school girl. "This is so exciting. I can't believe we're really going to be scouting for ghosts!"

Lyle patted one of her thighs as if signaling for her to calm down.

"Now what happens if we find us one?" Shaundelle asked. "Besides run like hell. I can take all the pictures you want, but if I sees me a ghost, like up close and personal, I'm outta there faster than poop down a toilet."

"Shaundelle," Nonie said, eyeing her. "Think we can keep the language decent?"

"What? I didn't say nothin' dirty. Ain't nothin' bad about poop going down a toilet. We all seen it happen."

Jack chuckled. "Look, y'all, I'm about the easiest guy you'll ever work with. Hell, I've been known to throw an expletive around myself from time to time."

"See?" Shaundelle said. "He throws exploits around, too. So there. Ain't nobody gotta act Miss Prissy Prissy around the man. That's what he's sayin', right?"

"Right," Jack said. "All you have to do is watch what you say when you're near one of the cameras we'll be setting up or one of the digital recorders. Don't need the big boss to hear all the shits and damns."

"Not a problem," Buggy said. "I promise not to say shit or damn or worse when we're recording something."

Lyle, who was sitting beside her, gave Buggy a quick hug. "That's my girl."

"But you didn't answer the more important question," Shaundelle said. "What we supposed to do if we find some ghoulie or ghost somewhere? Offer them a drink? Dinner? I'm for running like hell out the place myself."

"Just grit your teeth and work that camera, girl," Jack said. "I know you've got the grit to do it. You wouldn't be on this team if I didn't think you had it in you."

"Grit," Shaundelle said, rolling the word over and over in her mouth. "Yeah, I gots grits out the ass. I'll get them pictures. You'll see!"

"How long does a scouting event take?" Nonie asked.

"Depends," Jack said.

"On what?" Tatman asked.

"We might luck out and get something right away. Or we may have to hang around for hours waiting for something to make itself known."

"What if there's nothing there to be known?" Buggy asked. "We can't stay until eight in the morning. I've got to work the breakfast shift at Meemaw's."

Jack shook his head. "Nothing like that. If we don't pick up something, anything within a couple of hours, three at the most, we call it a bust and head home."

"To hell with a bust," Shaundelle said. "You best have a lot of them haunted places lined up 'cause the cash we get is goin' right in my bra. Savin' for my own Tint and Tip shop. That way I ain't gotta work for Ricky Rich no more. He can find hisself another gopher to do his work. Hell, that man don't even know how to do a decent shampoo much less tint a woman's hair."

Nonie couldn't help but grin. Judging from the size of Shaundelle's breasts, she could've held a bank load of cash in her bra, and no one would notice.

"Not to worry," Jack said. "There are so many places that claim to be haunted in this state that it would take us two years to cover them all."

"Now we're talking," Buggy said. "Let's get this thing rolling."

"When do we start?" Tatman asked. "Oh, yeah, yeah, tomorrow. We start tomorrow. Meet here at seven-thirty. Gonna do a place in Opelousas. I got it now."

Jack nodded. "Hopefully we'll pick up something there."

Tatman stood up and headed for Nonie's kitchen. "You sure you don't have another Bud hiding in the fridge?" he asked Nonie.

"If I do, it's hiding from me, too," she said. "You're welcome to look, though."

Tatman was already in the fridge before she made the offer. While he rummaged through the few condiments and milk she kept inside, Jack came over and sat on the arm of the couch, close to where she was sitting in her kitchenette chair.

"You up for this?" Jack asked her. "You've been pretty quiet tonight. Not that I know you to be a talker since we just met. But, well, I don't know. Maybe quiet isn't the right word. Worried maybe?"

"I'm good," Nonie said, lying through her teeth and offering him a small smile. "A little nervous since I've never done this before, but this Rem Pod thing you have me working with seems easy to operate. I'm not worried about that at all."

"Then what are you worried about?" Buggy asked. She leaned forward on the couch so she was able to look past Jack and eye her friend. "You worried about . . .him?"

"Who's him?" Jack asked.

"Oh, I meant them," Buggy said. "You know small towns. A lot of blabbermouths. I'm sure as soon as word gets out that we're doing this, rumors will be flying from the Exxon to Sonic."

Jack gave Buggy a long, wary look as if knowing in the pit of his gut that she was lying. He obviously, and thankfully, decided to drop the subject when Tatman came back into the living room.

Behind him, as clear as the tattoos on Tatman's arms, Nonie saw Guy walk into the room, fury on his face. Evidently it had been fine with him for Tatman, with his long scraggly hair and tats to sit beside her, but a hunk like Jack, no way.

Guy plopped himself down on the arm of the couch, right behind Jack. Nonie glared at him, tried to signal for him to leave, but he ignored her. He glared at Jack, then looked over at Nonie and waggled his eyebrows, a gesture he knew she hated. She claimed it made him look like a letch.

Suddenly, Guy turned ever so slightly and flicked a finger hard against Jack's cheek.

"Whoa," Jack said, putting a hand to his face.

"What's the matter?" Lyle asked, leaning forward to look over at Jack.

"Something just flew against my cheek. Stings. Must have been one hell of a bug."

"Nonie doesn't have bugs in her house," Buggy said defensively. "You sure you didn't accidently hit it on the edge of the couch? You know, on that wooden piece near the headrest?"

Jack rubbed his cheek and evidently chose not to make a big deal out of it. "You're probably right."

In that moment, Guy with the biggest grin Nonie had ever seen on his face, turned and slapped Jack hard on the top of his head.

Jack's hand went from cheek to head. "What the hell?"

"What now?" Shaundelle asked. "Another bug? I ain't seen one since we got here."

"Not a bug. Felt like somebody just whacked me on top of the head with a hand or a book. . . something."

Jack glanced over at Nonie. "Are you sure your place isn't haunted?"

Nonie did her best to laugh off his question. "You think I'd be living here if it was?"

Buggy, evidently catching on that Guy had made his way into the room and planned on making Jack's life miserable because he sat too close to Nonie got up from the couch. "Okay, guys. What say we call it a night. I know Nonie's got a big funeral to work tomorrow, and we all have jobs to tend to before the hunt."

Everyone stood at once, except for Shaundelle, who had to scoot her butt to the end of the chair until she was able to get traction with her feet to stand. As she worked herself upright, Jack stood and began repacking his cases. A look of confusion and something else Nonie couldn't quite identify clouded his eyes. His expression had gone from open, friendly, and helpful, to get me the hell out of here.

Embarrassed, but trying to act cordial, like nothing happened, Nonie walked everyone to the front door. Fortunately, Ms. Dora wasn't sitting on her porch, chain smoking and swiping mascara on her lashes. She must have gone inside shortly after Nonie because Buggy would have mentioned being interrogated by Ms. Dora if she'd still been outside.

"See you tomorrow," Nonie said. "Seven-thirty."

"You got it, girl," Shaundelle said. Before getting into the van, she suddenly stopped and put her hands on her wide hips. "Wait up a second. We didn't talk about the most important thing for tomorrow."

"What's that?" Nonie asked, anxious for them to leave before Guy pulled another stunt.

"What we supposed to wear?" Shaundelle asked. She stuck her head into the van and asked the question again. Probably this time to Jack.

When Shaundelle turned and looked back at Nonie she had her lips pursed. "The man say wear whatever you want. Wear black, girl. It's slimmin', not that you need any slimmin' with your skinny self, but it makes me look like I've been dietin' for a week. I don't want to be the only one wearin' black, so wear black, okay?"

Working in funeral service, the one color Nonie had plenty of was black. "No problem. Black it is. See y'all tomorrow."

Nonie waited on her porch until the van pulled out of view, then she turned and stormed back into the duplex. Guy Skinard had better have gone to meet the Lord because if he hadn't after what he pulled tonight, she planned on showing him how to

get there—the hard way.

CHAPTER SEVEN

Suspecting what was coming from Nonie, Guy made himself scarce. For him, scarce meant leaving the house because no matter where he'd try to hide in Nonie's duplex, she'd see him and give him what for.

It wasn't like he could've helped it. That bastard, Nagan, had been sitting too close to his girl. Was getting too friendly. He couldn't just stand there and watch that happen without doing something about it.

Nonie might be going ghost scouting with that good-looking pain in the ass, but that didn't mean he couldn't follow along to make sure Mr. Jack, whatever his name was, kept his hands to himself.

Dead or alive, Nonie belonged to him, and Guy planned to make sure it stayed that way.

There'd been an occasion or two when Nonie had gone out on a date with Kyle, Lyle's twin brother, but that hadn't bothered him. On the first double date with Buggy and Lyle, Guy saw immediately that Nonie really had no interest in Kyle. Not sexually anyway. She enjoyed the company and the chance to get out and have a little fun, but he knew her well enough to know that sex wasn't ever going to happen between the two of them. The only time Guy's hackles rose was after their first double date when Kyle kissed her goodnight. Fortunately, and confirming what he figured Nonie thought about the guy, there'd been no tongue or groping involved. She'd given Kyle more of a peck on the lips, like she'd have been kissing her brother good night.

Two men concerned him. First was Nate Lopez, the new deputy in town, who definitely had the hots for Nonie. The guy stood about six feet tall, was muscular and had blue eyes and collar-length black hair. He seemed to be a nice guy, as far as Guy had witnessed, and more Nonie's type, which made him a hazard Guy knew he'd have to keep an eye on.

The second man that concerned him was this new guy Jack. Not that Jack or Nate had done anything inappropriate. . . yet. And tonight, when he found Jack sitting way too close to Nonie, he'd done something about it. Chances were Mr. Ghost Hunter wouldn't return to Nonie's duplex anytime soon.

The only other man who'd shown serious interest in Nonie was Edward Roy, the grocery store owner's son. The man was about thirty-five with short brown hair and lips that held a perpetual pout. Definitely not Nonie's type.

To keep himself out of Nonie's wrath path, Guy walked around Clay Point, checking out what was going on that evening. So many times, when he'd see old friends hanging out at places he used to frequent, it made him feel homesick. Worse than homesick because being dead meant he'd never be able to enjoy those friends or hangouts again. All he had to hang onto while stuck in Clay Point was Nonie, and she was worth sticking around for.

Now, because he'd made her so angry after he messed with Jack, Guy would have to wait until she fell asleep before going back into her apartment.

That made him feel the loneliest of all. He hated being away from Nonie even for a moment. Of course, there were times when she'd all but tell him to get lost, like when she went into the bathroom, was at work and had to concentrate, or had important company.

And, for the most part, when she asked him to leave, he complied. Except for this whole Boo Krewe gig. It made him nervous. Nonie, much less Tatman, Buggy, and Shaundelle didn't know what the hell they were getting themselves into. Big man Jack might have done paranormal investigations for years, but they never included Guy's Nonie. He feared for her. He knew what spirits were out there. Some benign, kind of like himself, stuck here because they refused to leave a loved one, some mischievous, causing just enough chaos to scare the hell out of anyone who entered their space. Then there were the evil ones. The ones who'd never been human in the first place. He'd heard some investigators call them demons. Guy called them assholes. They hurt people. Made them fall down ladders, flights of stairs, made them sick until they'd become little more than a blubbering, drooling mess. Since his death, Guy had run into one or two of them, and it hadn't taken him long to see the evilness that drove their game. Each time he came across one, he veered off in a different direction. He wasn't about to confront something he couldn't fight.

Guy had already made up his mind to follow Nonie on every scouting trip. He knew she often saw and heard the dead, but to his knowledge, she'd never run into a demonic asshole. He might not be able to defeat it, but he could deflect its attention to something other than his girl.

The biggest challenge Guy thought of was how he'd get to the scouting site without Nonie knowing he was around. It wasn't like he could hitch a ride in the van. She'd see him in a nanosecond and pitch one of her notorious fits. The vehicle was a van, which meant it had no trunk. The only way Guy figured he'd be able to hop a ride was to place himself on top of the van. Nonie was too short to see him up there from ground level. If she stood on the bumper, however, he'd be busted. Logic insisted that she'd have no reason to stand on the bumper. If anything was placed up there for safekeeping until they reached the location, they had Tatman the muscle man to handle the job. And Tatman couldn't see him.

Although Guy knew why Nonie had decided to take this gig, and his warning to her about it seemed to fall on deaf ears, he thought up a plan. He knew she needed the money to make ends meet and to scrap working at the funeral home. So, if he worked hard enough at it, Guy was certain he could make that happen.

He wondered . . .What if, no matter the location they went to, he showed up and start moving things around? Rang doorbells, threw pots around, made will-o'-the-wisp smoke appear out of nowhere?

He bet he could even make those gadgets Jack had brought to show everyone tonight light up and ding or do whatever they were supposed to do to validate a "ghostly presence."

He'd have to do it in such a way that Nonie wouldn't get freaked out, of course, but if he worked that plan at each location, Nonie would get five hundred bucks per scout, and the numbers would start adding up fast.

And if they found a location that held a legitimate spirit in it, all the better. Guy would make sure to rile that spirit up until the walls shook.

He chuckled, seeing it in his mind's eye. Mr. Jack, the investigator, getting so freaked out he'd run out of the place, leaving his crew behind. That would show Nonie the man he really was. Hopefully. For all Guy knew, Jack might actually be good at this investigation thing. Instead of scaring him, it might excite him to the point that he'd be shooting film until dawn.

After strolling around Clay Point for what seemed like hours, Guy decided to sneak back into

Nonie's, hoping she'd gone to bed and was asleep by now.

Instead of walking straight into her bedroom, he just poked his head inside the wooden door. She was lying in bed on her stomach as usual with an arm curled under her pillow. Her breathing sounded slow and easy, like she'd already drifted off to dreamland.

Feeling safe enough to give it a try, Guy pulled his head out of the door and did a full body walk in. He kept his footsteps light to make sure no air caused the floor boards to creak, and he didn't stir any additional breeze around her.

Guy stood at the foot of her bed, loving the sight before him. Nonie's long, curly brown hair with bangs that reached the top of her eyebrows, her smooth complexion, her small nose and perfect lips.

He could have stared at her all night and probably would have if she hadn't suddenly sat up in bed.

"What the hell's wrong with you?" Nonie asked.

Guy frowned. Nonie had been faking sleep to lure him inside. He hated being tricked.

"What are you talking about?" Guy asked.

"Give me a frigging break, Casper," Nonie said. "I'm talking about you poking Jack in the cheek then slapping the top of his head. What the hell were you trying to prove?"

Guy felt anger roil in his gut. "He was sitting too close to you, and I didn't like it. Just showing him who was boss."

"Boss over who? Me? Since when? The guy couldn't even see you for heaven's sake." She lay back down and pulled her pillow closer to her face. "And for the dumb move you made tonight, I don't want to see you right now either. Go poke somebody else. Go ride the moon. Just go."

"But I always stay with you during the night."

Nonie turned her head slightly and glared at him. "Until you learn how to behave yourself, you can sleep in a barn filled with cow shit for all I care. You're not staying here tonight, and that's a frigging order!"

With that, Nonie turned her face back into her pillow. Guy stood there for a moment, regretting what he'd done to Jack, even though he'd felt justified doing it at the time. He hated making Nonie mad, but sometimes he found himself pissing her off without even trying.

Taking her at her word, Guy exited Nonie's bedroom the same way he'd entered. He left the house, and for the first time he walked for two miles to visit a place he'd avoided since his death. The cemetery. And the grave with his name and dates etched in marble.

CHAPTER EIGHT

By seven the next morning, having only one cup of coffee under her belt, Nonie dragged herself into the funeral home, wearing a black blouse and blazer, along with a knee-length black skirt and pumps. She'd been warned by her mother, Rita, more than once to dress appropriately for the funeral and to get there early in case they needed help prepping before the mayor's family arrived at nine. The only prepping she did when arriving, though, was head for the coffee room and add sugar and cream to a large mug of coffee. Her sleep last night had been sporadic. She'd dreamed of Jack. Intimate dreams. Sex dreams. And each time a dream came close to driving her over the edge of panting, Guy appeared in her dreams, screwing it up.

"Good morning, mon petite," Fezzo said to Nonie, when he limped into the room and went straight for the coffee urn. Evidently he needed the same caffeine buzz she did.

Nonie gave him a kiss on the cheek. "Morning. Where is everybody? I didn't see Margaret or Mom at the reception desk."

Fezzo groaned and pulled out one of the chairs near a table and sat.

"Your leg hurting you this morning?" Nonie asked, worried.

"Aw, the leg, the back, the head. When you get to be my age, even you butt hurts sometimes just 'cause it's part of you body."

Nonie grinned. "You're not old. You'll wind up outliving us all."

Fezzo swallowed a sip of coffee and said, "Poo yi, bébé don't say dat. Outlivin' you means I'd be over a hund'erd years old. Who wants to live dat long when parts are already starting to sag, fall off, or disappear when you in you seventies?"

Nonie laughed. "Just make sure you stick around for the important stuff in my life, you hear? Like if I ever get married and have babies. I want you around when that happens."

"Mah den you bes' get somethin' movin',", Fezzo said. "I don't see no boys hangin around 'cept the twin of that boy Buggy dates all de time."

"Kyle's not so bad," Nonie said.

"No, not bad. But if I was fishin' and caught dat on my line, I'd throw it back to the water. Find me a bigger, better fish."

Nonie sat beside her uncle. Being alone with him was very rare. She wanted so much to tell him about Guy. To ask his opinion about what she should do with him. Fezzo had been right, she rarely dated but it was all because of Guy. Not that she felt she'd be cheating on him, but because she knew he'd pull some kind of stupid stunt like he had with Jack and chase the guy away. She knew in her heart that her Uncle Fezzo wouldn't think she was crazy or make fun of her. His advice would be as real as he could make it.

"Uncle Fezzo?"

"What mon petite?"

"Remember when Buggy came over yesterday?"

"Yeah."

"Well, she came over to tell me that I could be part of a paranormal investigation scouting group. I'd get paid decent money if we got any evidence. It's for a show called *Something's Out There.*"

"What's dat a paranormal what you called it?"

"It means we'd go to different places and look for ghosts." '

Fezzo studied her face carefully. "What you think about dat?" he finally asked.

Nonie shrugged. "I'm thinking about doing it. I mean, the money's good."

"You know why dey want you to be part of dat group?"

Nonie looked down at the table, unable to keep her eyes on her uncle. "I . . . yeah," she said simply.

"'Cause you can see de dead, huh?"

She looked up at him, startled. "How did you know?"

Fezzo reached over and patted her arm. "I know from way back when you tried to tell you mama and daddy dat you saw you grandpa the night after his funeral."

"And you believed what I said was true?"

"Mah, you said it, so I had no other reason to believe it wasn't de trut'"

"Why didn't you say something to me then? It would have been nice to know that someone believed me."

"I know, mon bébé. I didn't want to cause no fight wit' you mama and daddy. So nonc just left well enough alone. I figured sooner or later we'd have de chance to talk about it. Now is not dat time though. We gonna have a full house today. We'll talk about it later, okay?"

All Nonie could do was nod. She still couldn't believe that after all these years Fezzo had known she saw the dead. Well, her grandfather anyway. She wanted to talk to him about Guy, about her concerns with doing the scouting gig. But he was right, now wasn't the time for that talk. Soon the funeral home would be packed with people, and with a subject that serious, she wanted, needed more time with her uncle.

"Where're Dad and Butchy?" Nonie asked, getting her mind off of Guy and the real discussion she wanted to have with Fezzo.

"Well, let's see—Margaret, her, is in the embalming room with Butchy seeing about Mrs.

Trahan. Remember the one we had to pick up last night from the nursing home?"

"Sure, but aren't we showing her today?"

"No, you daddy talked the family into waiting until tomorrow because he was afraid there'd be too many people with the mayor being here. The Trahans didn't mind. Dey a small family anyway, so it made them no never mind. Dey gonna have de viewing for Mrs. Trahan in the morning, early 'cause they wanted to get her through the church by eleven. That only gives 'em a two-hour viewing, but hey," Fezzo shrugged. "each person got their own way to send off de dead."

"And what about Dad? Where's he?"

"Back at his house wit' you mama. He wanted to wear his black pinstriped suit for the funeral, but you mama say no. De suit would crash wit' what she wanted to wear."

"Crash?" Nonie squinted for a second. "Oh, you mean clash."

"Yeah, dat's what I said, crash." And you know how hardheaded you mama can be. If she don't want him to wear de suit he wants to wear, he's gonna put on de one she wants him to wear."

Nonie sighed, wondering if there were other families in Clay Point this dysfunctional.

"Did the Fontenots decide if they were going to run the mayor through church or go for cremation?" Nonie asked.

"Dey gonna do de visiting hours until four dis afternoon, den he's goin' to the crematorium. I already called Claude over dere to warn him. You know how de mayor's wife and kids can be a little coo-coo in the head sometimes. I wanted to warn Claude in case they all decided to show up to watch de burnin.'"

Nonie shivered. "Who on earth would want to watch that?"

"You'd be surprised, mon petite. Some people gotta see so dey know it's real. Some gotta see just to say dey saw. And others go and just take a peek, like when you pass a wreck on the road. You look and see how bad de cars is messed up but you don't wanna see no dead bodies."

"Nonie Marie!" There was no mistaking that heavy-smokers southern drawl. Margaret must have finished in the embalming room. Nonie heard her footsteps hard and heavy on the carpeted floor of the hallway.

"Mah, it looks like our coffee breaks over," Fezzo said. "De bulldog from Atlanta's lookin' for you, and I don't need her to find me."

Nonie grinned. "I know you're not scared of Ms. Margaret."

"Scared, no. But dat mout' on her can drive a man to de bottle until it's empty." He chuckled. "I'm gonna go check the hearse, make sure it's all shiny. No fingerprints. Don't need your mama having another hissy fit over fingerprints on the car."

As Fezzo left and before Margaret made it into the coffee room, Nonie heard her confront him. "What were you doing in there? It's not time for coffee or breaks of any kind. The mayor's family is going to be here in about an hour and a half. Everything needs to look top-notch, shipshape."

"I'm goin' shape de ship right now," Fezzo answered, and it took all Nonie had not to burst out in laughter.

In that moment, Margaret stuck her head in the lounge. "I should have figured you'd be sipping on coffee like you were company. You need to get busy, young lady, before people start arriving."

"But everything's done," Nonie said. "The mayor is casketed, all those flowers are set up perfectly in the chapel, and I even set a stack of prayer cards at the end of each pew."

"Yes, but you know what happens with some of those flowers when left overnight. Some wilt or lose a leaf or two. The baby's breath leaves all those white diddies all over the floor. I need you to go in there and make sure everything's perfect. No wilting flowers. No white diddies. Now go, girl, before your mama and daddy get back here and start inspecting."

That's when Nonie realized that it wasn't so much that Margaret meant to be bossy or ride Nonie's ass just to ride it. She didn't want Rita, Nonie's mother, to ride *her* ass. T-boy, Nonie's dad, could've walked into a room filled with wilted flowers and walked right back out and sworn everything looked fine. Rita, on the other hand, would've had a stroke if one leaf had fallen and had been left on the floor unattended.

Instead of giving Margaret grief, which she would have loved to do if for no other reason than to break the monotony of the place, Nonie got up from her chair, excused herself as she bypassed Margaret and headed for the chapel.

Margaret had been right. The baby's breath on the floral arrangements had left little white diddies, as the Georgian gueen said, on the floor, and two to three plants that had been sent as condolence acknowledgments had a drooping leaf or two.

Knowing the protocol, Nonie vacuumed up the loose baby's breath and removed the drooping leaves from the plant arrangements so they looked freshly delivered.

Once that was done, Nonie checked the clock in the lobby and saw that it was eight-thirty. Private family viewing wasn't supposed to start until nine, but inevitably, most personal family members came early. If you noted in the paper that public viewing started at ten, you could bet dollars to screwdrivers that friends and distant family members would start showing up around nine-thirty to nine-forty-five.

Nonie wondered if most funeral homes had that issue. People just showed up any damn time they pleased. They had no idea the prep time it took to get the funeral home ready for a viewing, especially a large one like they anticipated for the mayor. They expected such a large crowd that Nonie had caught wind that the local television station would be filming in the funeral home. The only things they weren't allowed to film were the body and the procession to the crematorium, much less the cremation itself.

Nonie didn't think that would be a problem for any small-town television crew. Just the thought of seeing someone's body crispy fried in a retort turned her stomach. In with flesh, out with ash. No thank you. When it was her time to go, they could put her in the ground wrapped in newspaper, she didn't care, but cremation was out of the question.

Just as she suspected, five minutes later, two men walked through the front doors of the funeral home. Although they looked to be in their mid to late forties, both were potbellied and balding badly. They were dressed in black suits, had bulbous noses and each wore a gaudy LSU class ring and eyeglasses that appeared too small for their chubby faces. Save for the acne scars on one of the men's cheeks, they could have passed for twins. Nonie had little doubt that they were Mayor Fontenot's sons.

Unsure of what to do since seating or directing guests had never been her job, she welcomed them, and asked them to have a seat in the lobby. She promised to get someone to help them right away.

"Don't make the wait long," acne face said. "Our mother will be here shortly, and we'd prefer that she doesn't have to suffer the indignity of sitting in a lobby while her husband, and our father, lies dead in another room."

Nonie wanted to tell him to get his highfalutin nose out of his two-ton ass but said instead, "Absolutely. I certainly understand. Now, if you'll excuse me, I'll get someone right away."

After speed walking through the lobby and turning the corner to the lounge, Nonie didn't see Margaret anywhere. Instinct sent her running to the garage, where she caught the woman puffing on a Marlboro as fast as her lungs would allow.

When Margaret spotted Nonie, she threw the cigarette out of the open garage door and eyed her. "You saw nothing, right?"

"Right. But there are already people here for the viewing. Isn't it your job to greet them and tell them where to go?"

"Don't think just because you caught me taking a puff or two on a cigarette that you can talk to me that way, young lady. I've been doing this job before you were born."

"Then go do it," Nonie insisted, almost frantic. "Right now there are two guys in the lobby, and by the way they're acting, I think they're Dover's sons."

"Why? How're they acting?"

"Like their shit doesn't stink."

"Yeah, that's them all right. Clarence and Stefren Fontenot. Both born with a silver spoon up their backside."

"How can you tell who's who? They look almost identical."

"Stefren's the one with the bad acne scars, like his mama. Got her attitude, too. Uppity."

"They claimed their mother was only five minutes behind them, and they didn't want her to suffer the indignity of having to wait in a lobby." Nonie rolled her eyes and started chewing her fingernails. "These folks are going to be a handful."

"Lawd, yes," Margaret said, brushing ashes off her mauve dress with its wide white belt. "Just stick close. If something turns bad, get Fezzo. If he's not around, get your daddy. All you've gotta do is keep your eyes open, child. Them folks are definitely going to be a handful, but for Pete's sake, it ain't rocket science, so quite chewing your nails. We'll manage just fine."

About an hour later, Nonie would have given anything to hear Margaret say those words again, "We'll manage just fine." Because that was the last thing they were doing.

As Nonie suspected by nine-forty-five, the funeral home was packed. Just when they managed to get one wave of people settled, another, bigger wave showed up, this one complaining because there was nowhere left to park. Most had opted to park in St. Anthony's parking lot near the funeral home, but that meant they had to walk across a ditch that separated the two properties. That didn't serve well for highly polished shoes or egos for that matter.

When the funeral home had neared capacity, Rita—dressed in a new navy blue suit with shoes to match, along with pearl earrings and necklace—

gave Margaret the job of hostess. She claimed her new shoes were giving her feet blisters, and she could barely walk.

"There're Band-Aids in the bathroom," Nonie told her mother. "I bet if you put one on the back of each heel, those new shoes won't be rubbing against the blisters so bad."

Rita looked incensed. "Don't you think if I thought Band-Aids would help I would've already seen to that?"

"Then change your shoes," Nonie insisted. "The white ones you wear with your coral suit would look wonderful with navy blue. They're already broken in so you wouldn't have to worry about your feet. Want me to run home and get them?"

"Most certainly not," Rita said. "I'll simply sit right here and direct people as they come in." She turned to Margaret. "Margaret, darlin', if you don't mind, keep an eye on the lounge. Make sure the coffee urn stays full and that the sandwich trays sent here from MeeMaw's Café are set out so everyone knows they're welcome to them."

"And what are you going to do, Miss High and Mighty?" Margaret asked, plopping a hand on her hip. "Sit here on your throne like you're too good to help the help?"

Nonie took a step back, not wanting to get hit with the stapler or printer or whatever her mother decided to throw at Margaret.

"How rude of you to say such a thing," Rita said in a stage whisper.

"It's not rude, it's the truth," Margaret insisted. "Now if your heels are hurtin' go do the Band-Aid thing. You're the wife of the funeral home owner. You need to step up and mingle, you know that."

Rita pouted. "But my feet really hurt."

Nonie turned on her heels and headed for the viewing room. She couldn't take her mother's pouting and ten million excuses why she couldn't mingle. The truth was she didn't want to take the chance that someone might spill coffee on her suit, or bump into her and mess up her hair, and Lord help anyone if they played any part in chipping one of Rita's fingernails. For small funerals, you couldn't ask for a better hostess than Rita. She dodged the viewers with drink cups, extended a person's personal space by ten feet, and smiled like the corners of her mouth had been set in place with superglue.

With all Rita's faults, and who didn't have any, Nonie loved her mom. But sometimes Rita Broussard was a bit much to handle, and it didn't take an Einstein to figure out it was time to make a quick exit when she was in one of her moods.

Nonie inched her way through the crowd, searching for her dad and Fezzo. She noticed that a few of the funeral sprays had been knocked over, so she straightened them out and thought, *To hell with the white diddies from the baby's breath.* They were everywhere. Maybe it was a good thing Rita stayed at the registration desk.

As Nonie made her way to the casket, which was closed, she saw many familiar faces along the way. It seemed like the entire town had shown up for the viewing. Although she didn't see her dad or Fezzo, she spotted Butchy, their apprentice, Sheriff

Buchanan, Jan and Sarah Mitchell from Cajun Eatery, Gerard Guidry, Tatman's boss, from Guidry's Hardware, Jerry Manville from SuperTators, Stuart Burleigh from the Feed and Seed, Pench Richard the postmaster, and Scott Leger, Clay Point's fire chief. In the far corner of the room she spotted Buggy, Tatman, Lyle, and Shaundelle the four of them huddled quietly together. She also saw Ms. Dora Arsemont, her duplex mate, and Ed Roy, the grocer's son, who bugged her weekly for a date. He sat near the back of the room, as did Nate Lopez, the new deputy.

Out of all those people, the one drawing the most attention, of course, was Hazel Fontenot, Dover's wife. She sat in the front pew, crying like a four-year-old who'd stubbed her toe. On either side of her sat chubby and chubbier, her two sons. Nonie sucked it up and went over to Mrs. Fontenot to offer her condolences. She was surprised to find that from all the boo-hooing the woman had been doing since they'd opened the funeral home, not a tear stained her cheeks. Her hair was teased high, and the ends curled under. Not a strand out of place, and her makeup sat perfectly on her face, not a smudge to be seen. Her sons, Clarence and Stefren looked even less worse for the wear. If anything, they looked utterly bored.

"My condolences for your loss," Nonie said, offering Mrs. Fontenot her hand. The woman didn't take it. Instead she dabbed the bottom of one eyelid with a tissue.

"Thank you," she said, then turned to her sons. "I wish we could have had an open casket, don't you?

I wanted it to be open. I specifically asked for it to be open."

Both sons shrugged as if it made no difference to them whatsoever.

Getting the message loud and clear that it was best she leave them to family business, Nonie, meandered her way through the throngs of people, intending to meet up with Shaundelle and Tatman.

Before she made it to the back of the viewing room, where her fellow investigators stood, Nonie spotted Pastor Morton from First Assembly of the Holy Trinity being escorted to the front of the viewing room by her dad and Fezzo. They chatted quietly as they walked.

When her dad finally made it to the casket with Pastor Morton by his side, he said loudly, "Friends and family, if you would, please take a seat so we can begin the service."

As though caught in a game of musical chairs, people rushed to find seats, knowing there were more butts than chairs. The ones left standing were directed by Fezzo to stand along the east and west walls of the chapel room, so the aisle remained clear.

There was a lot of whispering and shuffling of feet and chairs. Ten minutes later, when the silence became pin-drop quiet, Pastor Morton finally walked toward the center of the casket and held his hands together. "Brothers and sisters, today we celebrate the life of our beloved Mayor Dover Fontenot. Let's join together—"

"What the hell?" someone said from the back of the room, and the entire congregation began to mumble. A few people gasped. Everyone turned their heads to see who'd interrupted the service. For all they knew, Satan himself had just walked into the room.

In truth, Satan, had nothing to do with the interruption. But to Nonie and the rest of her family, it might as well have been.

CHAPTER NINE

"How did it go?" Warren Chinsaw, one of the producers for WXRT asked. He sat at a large mahogany conference table with Peter Segan, head editor, Michael Versille, an investor in WXRT and Jack Nagan. Michael had been the one who came up with the idea for the television program, *Something's Out There,* and he was anxious to hear a progress report.

"It went fine," Jack said, "but you do realize we didn't have a scouting trip last night. It was all about the group meeting each other and going over the equipment we'll be using."

"Of course," Peter said. "You told us that was your plan, but when are we going to see some action?" He glanced nervously over at Michael who was drumming his fingertips on the table.

"What is this group like?" Michael asked, leaning back and crossing his arms over his chest. "Do they have what it'll take to scout fast and well?"

Unsure of how to answer that question honestly, Jack simply laid it out on the table. "I have no idea as I just met them last night. All seem to have great potential, so I think if we go to a place that's supposedly haunted, and it winds up being so, we'll get the evidence you need."

"Did you have to go into a lot of detail about the equipment or were they sharp enough to catch on quickly?" Warren asked.

"Well, you couldn't tell by looking at them," Jack said, "but I think they're going to work out better than some of the professional investigators you were originally considering."

"And let's not forget," Michael said. "We're getting them at a great price."

Jack gave him a sour look. Michael might be an investor, but Jack Nagan was not a man who kissed anyone's ass.

"They asked me why they'd been chosen," Jack said. "And I told them it was because they were cheaper than hiring a professional group who had been doing investigations for a number of years."

"Why would you tell them that?" Michael asked. "Sounds a bit demeaning if you ask me. I'd have turned it down after hearing that."

"I told them about the money because it's the truth," Jack said. "Look, if the three of you want me to run this scouting group, you're going to have to trust my judgment."

"What did they say when you told them?" Peter asked.

"They didn't make a big deal about the money. They'll be grateful to get it." Jack leaned against the table and eyed the three men. "You've got to remember or at least know that most paranormal investigators in the business started with zero from the get-go. They weren't paid and shouldn't be paid in my opinion, to help others out when it comes to paranormal activity. Especially if the investigators are good at what they do." At the mention of money, the three top heads looked at Jack like he had corn growing out of his nose. "Most investigators started with nothing more than a disposable camera, a compass, and a set of brass balls. That was all they needed just to walk into a creepy building. Most do it just to answer their own internal questions about what exists after death."

"We didn't ask for a lecture." Warren sighed. "We're interested in the people who'll be involved in this scouting group."

"I'm getting there," Jack said, "but it's important that you get the back story about paranormal investigations first. This new scouting crew is no different than all the groups who are out there now. Every one of them had to start at ground zero. The only difference with our group is they'll start off with much more sophisticated equipment."

"Fine, yes," Peter said. "We get it. Now you've got to get it. We can't afford to waste time training people over and over again, that's why we're asking about them. We have a pilot and six episodes to shoot for a first season run. That's the only way we'll be able to tell if the show will fly or drop like a turd from a flying pigeon."

"How many people do you have on this scouting team?" Warren asked.

"Five, including myself." Before they could complain about the number being too large, Jack asked. "How many do you plan on having on the real investigation team?"

"Five," Peter said.

"And let me guess, two women and three men?" Jack said.

"Yeah, so?

"And the guys are buff, young? The women in their mid to late twenties with plenty of ass and tits?"

"What are you getting at, Jack?" Peter asked.

"Did you think we were going to hire eighty-year-olds or people who've never seen a beauty salon or had a manicure in their life? Do you think an audience would stay tuned to some Jethro with two missing front teeth and a jumbo broad who wears a triple D bra and muumuu because she can't fit into anything else?"

"That's sexist and just downright wrong in so many ways," Jack said.

"Look," Peter said, "Just because the crew we hired happens to be good-looking it definitely won't hurt the show. If anything it'll help. Aside from the ghost stuff, women will tune in to see the muscles on those guys and men will tune-in to check out tits in low cut T-shirts."

"You mean to tell me that you're actually going to dress that crew to show off their bodies?" Jack asked.

"Hell, yeah," Michael said. "Before I put all the money I did into this speculative venture, it was one thing I thought was unique and might add flavor to the show and keep people watching. Think of it like wrestling. Fake or not, women love to watch those wrestling hunks running around in spandex tighties, and the men love the women wrestlers for the same damn reason." He turned to Warren. "Why are we having to explain all of this crap to him? I thought you said he was on board and knew the ropes. He's making me nervous, Warren. Sorta sounds like a preacher warning a congregation about the sins of their ways."

"I'm far from a preacher, and your sins are your own. I have enough shit on my plate to keep track of," Jack said.

Michael seemed to relax after Jack let out the

expletive.

"So who are you working with?" Peter asked.

Jack hesitated, already knowing the three amigos were going to throw slur bombs his way.

"Their names are Shaundelle Washington, Tatman Guilbeaux, Buggy Mouton, Nonie Broussard, and me, of course."

"What do they do for a living and what do you plan on having them work with during an investigation?" Warren asked.

Jack drew in a deep, silent breath. "Shaundelle works for a beauty salon called Tint and Tips. She sidelines as a photographer for weddings and glamour shots. I've seen her work. She's got a good eye. I'm giving her the night vision camera and the Mark III to work with."

"You're going to let a beautician handle a

thousand dollars worth of camera equipment?" Michael asked.

Jack shot him a look. "She knows what she's doing. I wouldn't have assigned the task to her if she didn't."

"What does she look like?" Warren asked.

"What's it matter?" Jack shot back.

"Damn, don't get your jocks in a twist. Just wondering was all. If we need a backup on the real shoot, I'm just wondering if any of them can make the cut. You know, fit in with the rest of the investigators."

"If you're looking for tits and ass," Jack said angrily, "you'll need to find backup somewhere else. These people are serious about this scouting gig, not about showing off their bodies."

"So she's ugly," Michael said.

"Shut up," Warren told him. "We might be in a boardroom, but you never know who might be listening. You want to get sued?"

"Pfft." Michael eyed Jack again. "So what about the others?"

"I've got Buggy, who works in a café and has a good ear for people, handling the recorders for EVPS, and Nonie, who works at her family's funeral home, will be setting up the Rem Pods and keeping an eye on them."

Jack tucked his hands under the table so the men wouldn't see that he'd rolled his hands into fists. "Tatman is going to help me set up the cameras in each hotspot, then wire them to the monitor in the command center. He's worked for an electrician and a mechanic, so he knows wiring, and if some piece of mechanical equipment breaks down, I'd bet my balls on a block that Tatman can fix it."

"And you?" Michael asked.

"I'll be at the command center. From there I'll be able to keep an eye on everyone and the equipment they're responsible for."

"Smart move," Peter said. "We don't need anyone running off with any of that expensive equipment."

"They're not thieves," Jack snapped.

"How do you know?" Warren asked. "Like you said earlier, you only met the entire team last night."

"I just know," Jack said firmly. "They might be a little rough around the edges,"—Except for Nonie, he thought, and couldn't help but let a picture of her long dark brown hair and soft blue eyes fill his mind. She had a smile that could light up any room and perfect, kissable lips, although he'd not had a chance to confirm that yet.—"but I trust them. It's a gut feeling."

"A gut thing, huh?" Peter said.

"Yes," Jack said. He turned and scowled at Warren. "Look, the only thing the three of you have been doing since I've talked about this team is complain and question my decisions. If you'd prefer someone else take over the lead on this gig, fine. Go for it."

Warren glanced at Peter and Michael, then eyed Jack. "We're not looking to replace you. We want results. We have every right to ask questions so we'll have some idea of the percentage of and potential for success we're looking at here."

"By my account," Jack said, "if a place is haunted, we'll get the evidence you need."

"But what if they try to fake out a job?" Michael asked. "I mean, if they're not complaining about the money, five hundred for a positive location is a decent amount of money for those folks."

"No one will be faking anyone out," Jack said loudly.

"Jack . . ." Warren warned.

"You forget that I've been a paranormal investigator for ten years," Jack said to Michael. "I know fake from real and know all the tricks in the book. Nobody's going to pull the sly on this gig. No strings pulling doors shut so it looks like they've closed on their own, no fishing wire opening and closing kitchen cabinets or knocking over bric-a-brac. It'll be the real deal or nothing. And talking about nothing, the three of you need to realize something. Just because a location is supposed to be haunted doesn't mean we'll get evidence on the first night we go there. Sometimes a truly active location takes two to three visits before anything viable shows up. It's not like spirits just show up on command. The same can happen during the scouting and filming of an episode. We can bring you evidence out the ass, then the paranormal investigation crew you're using as your stars may go there and nothing happens at all."

"That's shitty," Michael said, frowning. "Does that happen often?"

"More times than not, but not because one group is a scouting crew and the other crew is the one you're filming. It just happens when it happens. It's frustrating as hell, but it is what it is. You just need to know up front that that might be the case at times."

"Easy enough problem to solve," Peter said. "If the real crew doesn't pick up anything, I'll simply edit in the real deal that the scouting crew came up with. Only it'll look like our crew found it."

"Now that's a shitty deal," Jack said. "Your crew finds nothing and gets paid thousands and the scouting crew who did find evidence that you plan to use to cover a bald spot gets paid a measly five hundred bucks."

"What the hell else do you expect me to do?" Peter said loudly. "We're already behind on schedule, and you throw that ball in my lap. Nobody's going to know but me and the crap lying on the editing room floor."

"I'll know," Jack said. He looked at Michael, the man fronting the money for the show. "If we use the scouts' findings, they get paid more and get credit on the end roll."

"Just how much more money are you talking about?" Michael asked.

"At least double. I don't think a grand a person's going to break you, right?"

Michael pursed his lips. He stared at Peter. "Are we that far behind schedule?"

Peter nodded solemnly.

Michael turned back to Jack. "Deal. But don't make it too damn often, understand?"

"I have no control over what spirits do," Jack said. "But I will tell you this. The scouting crew we have is sharp, anxious to do a good job, and are serious about the gig."

"I'll tell you what," Michael said, scratching his chin. "If they are as committed as you say they are, and we wind up having major issues with the real paranormal investigators I'll swap them out. I'll take the best of your crew and exchange them with the worst we've got in ours. I think that's a fair deal, don't you?"

"Sounds okay," Warren said. "But what if you do this exchange and the other members of the scouting group get jealous and quit? Then we're back to square one."

"They're not like that," Jack insisted. "The others would be happy for the ones chosen."

"When it comes to money and kudos, kid, I know my stuff. If that scenario happens and the rest of them don't quit, I'll eat my left shoe."

"Uncle Warren," Jack said. "With all due respect, you can be a big pain in the butt. Your last name should be Chainsaw not Chinsaw because you sure as hell know how to cut off a good thing, even if it's in theory."

CHAPTER TEN

The chapel had fallen into such a deep silence it might as well have been deserted. Nonie didn't know if it was because someone had said the word hell in front of the pastor or if it had anything to do with the two women suddenly making their way down the center aisle. One of the women looked to be in her late fifties. She had platinum blond hair cut short with wispy bangs across her forehead, and her makeup, especially around her eyes, was exquisitely done, showing off blue-green eyes. She had a smile that would have caught anyone's attention, such bright, perfect teeth. She wore dangling sapphire earrings with small crosses that hung beneath the blue baubles. She wasn't dressed in traditional funeral black but wore a white linen pants suit with a cruise jacket that zipped up the front and was decorated with starburst rhinestones along the shoulder and collar.

Following Ms. Rhinestone was a more homely woman, someone you wouldn't have been surprised to see living in Clay Point, and when Nonie took a second glance at her, she realized she *did* live in Clay point. It was Clara Grubbs, a grocery clerk from Roy's. Clara also had short platinum blonde hair, but it was cut in a bob. She wore a white, shift-style dress with floral print and had eyeglasses hanging from a silver chain around her neck. Her small eyes were brown and wide as she trailed after Ms. Rhinestone to the front of the chapel.

"Who's that?" Nonie whispered to Fezzo when he sidestepped the women, who were now three pews up from the casket.

"Trouble," he said. "Nuttin' but trouble."

As the two women made their way closer to the casket, Fezzo caught up to Ms. Rhinestone and took her by the arm and tried to get her to turn around and walk to the back of the chapel. A wave of whispers suddenly filled the room, and many people were frowning, pointing and shaking their heads.

About that time, Hazel had become so curious regarding the commotion that had broken the reverent silence, she stood up from her pew. She turned around at the same time Ms. Rhinestone struggled against Fezzo's grasp, claiming that she had every right to see her Dover. That she *needed* to see him.

"It's not right that I don't get a chance to see him," she proclaimed.

"You can't," Fezzo insisted. "De casket is

closed."

"But I have to—"

Hazel suddenly clasped her hands over her chest, like she was about to have a heart attack, and said to the woman in Fezzo's grasp. "You bitch! I can't believe you came to this chapel on this most horrible day. You have some nerve coming here and making such a commotion!"

"I'm not making the commotion, deary. You're the one who seems to be getting a bit loud."

About this time, Margaret Simms hurried into the chapel. "Is there a problem, Mrs. Hazel, Ms. Anna Mae?"

"Yeah," Hazel said, "But it's none of your business. So, if I were you, I'd go back to your little desk up front."

With a scowl and a harrumph, Margaret turned

on her heels and marched out of the room.

Hazel shot Ms. Rhinestone, Anna Mae, a look that could've killed. "Don't you dare call me deary, Anna Mae Turner. You have no business being here, and neither does your cousin, Clara." She glanced over at the woman who'd been shadowing Anna Mae. "Clara, I'm sorry. You're always nice to me in church on Sundays, but your cousin here needs to burn in the pit of hell for showing up in front of all of these people. Dover was my husband," Hazel proclaimed, turning back to Anna Mae. "Till death do us part."

"Well, he may have been your husband by law, but he claimed that he was mine for many years before he died," Anna Mae said. "This whole town knew it. Even you knew it, Hazel. You just chose to ignore it. Kept him out of your way. So now you've got what you wanted. He's dead, out of your way. So there's no reason why I can't come and see my Dover in his coffin."

"The coffin's closed," T-boy said, having joined Fezzo in his attempt to calm the women down.

"Can't you open it just a little?" Anna Mae whined. "So I can see him one last time?"

"That casket will not be opened," Hazel declared. "He . . . his face . . . It will not be opened." She put the corner of a tissue to her right eye where a real tear appeared.

"But I haven't seen Dover in at least two weeks. I need to see his face just one more time."

"If you don't quit your goddamn whining and get out of here, you hussy," Hazel snarled. "I'm going to make sure you don't see anything out of either of your eyes for a hell of a long time."

"Ladies, please," the pastor said. "We're in the house of God. This may be a funeral home, but it's a chapel nonetheless."

"I don't give a damn whose house is it," Hazel said. "That hag is going to get outta here."

T-boy leaned over, said something to the pastor, and the pastor nodded and sidestepped away from the casket then around the room towards the exit. With a simple hand gesture, T-boy signaled Fezzo to make sure the pastor got out without any issues.

Clarence and Stefren, as if just waking from a deep sleep, finally stood up near their mother.

"What's the problem?" Clarence asked.

Hazel pointed to Anna Mae. "That . . . That thing came here to see your father."

"And that pisses you off, why?" Stefren asked.

"Yeah," Clarence said. "There are tons of

visitors here. Why does her being here have you so

angry?"

Hazel looked at her sons like they suddenly had brain fluid leaking out of their ears. "Where have you two been? Don't you know? That hussy has been sleeping with your father for probably eight years now."

"Nine," Anna Mae said. "We were close to our ninth anniversary."

Clarence plopped back down on the pew and Stefren said, "Well, I'll be a sonofabitch."

Suddenly, Hazel wheeled about and slapped Stefren in the face. "Every time you say that word, you're saying I'm a bitch. So shut up and sit down and be quiet like your brother. I don't need either of you in my business right now. This is between me and Anna Mae."

Loud mumbling came from the crowd standing against the walls and filling the pews. Nonie stood on tiptoe, spotted Sheriff Buchanan in the crowd then signaled to her dad. She mouthed, "Do you want him to get involved?"

T-boy shook his head, probably feeling confident in his ability to stop these women from making it a full-blown WWE event. Nonie cautiously made her way to the fifth row of pews and stood at the end, watching the women like she was watching a tennis match, looking from Hazel to Anna Mae.

The women inched closer to each other, and Nonie suddenly realized her mistake. If slaps and swings were going to start flying, she'd be right in the middle of the fight. She felt in the pit of her gut that if she didn't get out of the way and fast, she'd wind up with a wayward punch or slap across her own face.

"You could at least have shown some respect and stayed away from here, no matter what you'd been doing with my husband," Hazel said, nostrils flaring. "But, no, you've got to come out here and show your behind. What you've done is going to send you to the pits of hell, Anna Mae Turner. Not only for what you've done with my Dover, but for showing up here and disrespecting him and our family. Embarrassing me in front of the whole community. We didn't need or want your ugly face here! Nobody likes you, don't you get it? Nobody wants you here."

"How can you say nobody wants me here? Not everyone in town knows me. Only those who've seen me with Dover. Nobody *really* knows me."

Anna Mae suddenly turned to Butchy Thibodeaux, who just happened to be in the right place at the wrong time. "Do you know me?" she asked Butchy.

With his pudgy cheeks turning crimson, Butchy shrugged his shoulders and shook his head.

"See what I'm saying" Anna Mae said. "Not everyone knows me, but they know you. That big mouth of yours and the way you strut your stuff all over town. Just because you were married to the mayor you thought you were all that. But the truth is you're really nothing, Hazel, but a worn-out old woman with a horrid complexion. Dover stayed with you during the day and left you at night. He came to meet me so he could get what he needed. Not just sex, but compassion and understanding. I was the woman he really wanted. Being a mayor, he couldn't cause a stink by divorcing you, not with a new campaign for mayor about to begin. He didn't want to look bad in the eyes of his people, the hearts of his sons and the minds of his constituents. That wasn't his style, but you wouldn't know that. Just how many conversations did you have with Dover other than, 'Hello,' and 'How was your day?'"

Hazel suddenly let out one huge growl and took off in a flat-footed run straight for Anna Mae.

Anna Mae dropped the purse she'd been carrying in the crook of her arm, lowered her head and held out both hands now curled into fists, waiting for Hazel to get to her. Before T-boy or Fezzo or even Sheriff Buchanan could reach the women, they latched onto each other and started swinging with full fists to the gut, slaps to the face, hair pulled until strands were yanked out by the handful. So much pushing and shoving. All of the flowers Nonie had so neatly set around the casket bier and along the walls were tossed over, stomped on, leaves and petals showering the floor.

"You witch," Hazel said between slaps. "You leave my husband alone."

"You leave my Dover alone," Anna Mae yelled. "He didn't deserve to be married to somebody like you. He needed a *real* woman."

No sooner had Anna Mae uttered those words than Hazel got one good solid punch to Anna Mae's gut, knocking the wind out of her and dropping her to her knees.

About this time, Nonie spotted her mother near the entrance to the chapel. One second she was there, mouth agape, and the next second she was on the floor, having dropped into a dead faint. T-boy hurried over to his wife as quickly as he could to get her out of the way of a sudden stampede.

By this time, people began to shuffle out of the chapel, not wanting to get involved in the brawl. People were stumbling over chairs, knocking into other people, everyone scattering to get out of the way.

In the background, Nonie heard a loud, familiar laugh. She glanced in the direction it came from and saw Guy standing not far from Shaundelle. He'd obviously been eavesdropping on Shaundelle and Tatman's conversations. Now he was watching the show between Hazel and Anna Mae and evidently thought it to be the funniest thing he'd ever seen. As if by radar, Guy suddenly caught Nonie watching him. She scowled, held a finger to her lips, indicating for him to shut up even though she was the only one who could hear him. This was a somber catastrophe. Not a laughing matter.

While more than half the people in the chapel were scrambling to get out, others were starting to take sides. Some with Hazel, others with Anna Mae.

"Bust her ass, Hazel. With Dover gone, she's gonna go after somebody else's husband. You can—"

"Gut punch her Anna Mae before—"

" . . . best damn funeral I've ever been to."

Nonie tried to make it over to the folks egging them on, to ask them to be quiet, but in truth, there was nothing she could do with anyone right now.

Even Shaundelle was getting into the act. Hands on hips, she yelled over the din, "If you gonna do it, do it right. Put those two broads in another room where they can duke it out. Winner walks out the door. Then it's over. Otherwise we'll be here all damn day waiting to see who's got enough balls to beat the shit out of the other."

Nate Lopez, despite the no-go T-boy had given Sheriff Buchanan, started working his way to the women, dodging swings and people shoving up against him. As if to protect their viewing turf, the remaining onlookers stood side by side, refusing to let Nate past them.

By now, Anna Mae's hair was no longer short and perky. It stuck up in uneven spikes around her head like she'd stuck her finger into an electrical socket.

Hazel no longer looked freshly spewed out of a beauty parlor. Her coiffed hair was now just a tangled mess that made her look like she'd been on an alcoholic bender.

Suddenly, Anna Mae got some wind beneath her wings and started shoving Hazel hard until she pushed the woman right up against Dover's casket. The casket teetered on its bier and while the women were still punching and shoving, Dover's casket flipped off its stand and wound up behind it. Fortunately the lid didn't pop open so no one saw the mess that had been left of his face. From what Nonie'd heard, her father had done the best he could to reconstruct Dover's face, but too many bones were missing to make him viewable.

By now, Fezzo wasn't waiting for T-boy's direction. He had seemingly had enough of all the stupidity. Never being a man of many words, he was definitely one for action. He marched over to the women, took hold of Anna Mae by the waist, lifted her up and threw her over his shoulder. Amidst much cheering and a few boos, he carried her out of the chapel and the funeral home. Anna Mae kicked and screamed and beat Fezzo on the back with her fists.

"Let me go, you big bastard!" Anna Mae yelled. "I have as much right to be here as anyone. I'll call the police, call them and have you arrested for assault."

As Fezzo carried Anna Mae outside, Sheriff Buchanan showed up beside him. "Just take her to my squad car. Don't think she's in much shape to drive. I'll take her home."

"Put me down, you big ox," Anna Mae yelled. "I swear I'll call the cops and have you arrested."

"I *am* the police," Sheriff Buchanan said. "And if you don't stop running that mouth of yours and go peacefully I'll have you behind bars within the next fifteen minutes."

From the front door of the funeral home, Nonie watched them load Anna Mae into a squad car. Personally she thought it was pretty tacky for her to show up at Dover's viewing with his wife there, but who was she to judge?

Nonie went back into the funeral home to check on Hazel's condition and hoped she didn't have to be hauled off in Lopez's squad car.

When she walked back into the chapel, all seemed relatively and unusually calm.

Hazel stood near the bier where the casket once sat, looked at the coffin lying askew on the floor, then turned back to see that most of the chapel was now empty. She pulled a tissue out of her skirt pocket and blew her nose. Grabbed a second tissue and wiped away a true flood of tears.

Although Dover's funeral was scheduled for a four hour viewing then a trip to the crematorium, with all of the hoo-hah that took place, Dover wasn't shipped off until nearly five that afternoon. Once the funeral home had cleared out, Nonie helped her dad, Fezzo, and Margaret clean up the mess that had been left behind.

Flowers were strewn throughout the viewing room and all the way into the lobby, coffee cups and Coke cans left empty or half-full on the coffee lounge countertops.

"I never seen nothin' like dis in all my life, me," Fezzo said. "All dem fancy people here and not one of 'em knows how to use a trashcan."

Nonie took a trash bag from a bottom cabinet and started tossing everything worthless in sight.

When that was done, she soaped up a dishtowel and wiped down the countertops and coffee urn.

Margaret suddenly appeared in the lounge and plopped down in a chair and slouched. "Lawd, I'm more tired than when I was eighteen and helped Daddy pick cotton. Have you ever seen such a crazy bunch of people?"

"Not here, no," Fezzo said. "I mean everybody in dis town knew Dover was cheatin' on his wife. Why dat woman wanted to come here and start all that bull, I don't know. Me, I'm not going to have dat problem. When I pass on to de good Lord, ain't nobody's gonna have nothin' to fight about. I ain't married and ain't getting' married. Poo yi, dat's too much drama."

Nonie nodded. "Drama for sure." She looked over at Margaret, who looked ready to fall asleep in her chair. "Have you seen Mom or Dad?"

Margaret yawned, then did a little eye roll. "Your mama's resting since she had that faintin' spell. Claims she's too weak to help out. Has a headache. Your daddy, though, is outside picking up garbage. Cigarette butts, Styrofoam coffee cups, even beer cans. Guess a few folks decided to indulge before the service."

Nonie scowled. "My mother's headache is just to get out of cleaning up this place."

"No matter what be de reason, don't talk bad about you mama like dat," Fezzo said. "The good Lord don't like when we talk bad about our mamas and daddies."

"But it's the truth, Uncle Fezzo. You know that."

"Don't matter. If you can't say something good, just don't say nothin'."

Nonie pursed her lips for a moment, then asked, "Have you ever seen anything like what happened today with Hazel and Anna Mae before?"

Fezzo tried to hide a grin, but Nonie caught it. "Only one time since I been workin' wit' you daddy. Two men got mad over some woman and decked it out right in the viewing room. It wasn't like today, though. A man's going to punch for the knockout. I ain't never seen a catfight like I did wit' dem two women."

Nonie didn't hide her grin. "They looked like two old hens fighting over an egg neither one could hatch."

Fezzo let out a loud belly laugh. "Good way to say dat. It's true. It looked just like dat."

Something niggled Nonie in the gut and she looked up at the clock on the kitchen wall. It was

nearly five-forty-five. Jack and the rest of the crew
were supposed to pick her up at seven-thirty.

"I've got to go," Nonie said. "How're we
looking for tomorrow?"

"All we have is old Mrs. Inez Trahan," Margaret
said.

"Should be an easy one," Fezzo said. "Poor old
soul was ninety-four years old. Only one son and
grandson. By this time, unless people come from de
nursing home, dats all who's gonna show. I'm sure
most of her friends have already passed on."

"Why don't you take the day off tomorrow,"
Margaret said to Nonie. "We can easily handle Inez.
Get yourself some rest. You worked real hard
today."

"You sure did," T-boy said, walking into the
coffee lounge. "I'm proud of you."

"Thank you, Daddy," Nonie said. "I've got to run off, shower and dress. I've got some people coming over this evening, and we're going out for a while."

"Anywhere special?" T-boy asked. "Anyone special?"

Nonie shrugged nonchalantly. "Not really special. Just Buggy and three of her friends. One of the guys in the group wants to check out a few houses and wants our opinion on them I guess."
Liar, Liar, pants on fire.

"Well, be careful out there," T-boy said.

"Oh, I will," Nonie said, then left the lounge before her dad could ask any more questions.

Nonie was halfway down the hallway when she heard a low voice call to her.

"Mon petite."

She turned to face Fezzo. He had a serious, almost fearful expression on his face.

"I don't know what you plan to do wit' you friends,' Fezzo said. "But one thing Uncle Fezzo knows is that you know more than most."

Nonie looked at him quizzically.

"Your grandma and her mama had de same thing you got. Dey see things other people can't see and hear things other people can't hear."

Nonie's heart started pounding hard in her chest. Her uncle knew what she was capable of yet had never said a word about it. Why now?

Fezzo smoothed her hair with a hand. "If you gonna go chasin' after what other people can't see, you got to be really careful. I'm not going to say a word to nobody because that's all you business, and you a big girl now. I remember when you was a little girl how you try to tell you mama and daddy that you saw you grandpa in you room and both of 'em thought you was coo-coo. I couldn't say nothin' 'cause you know you mama and daddy. They gonna believe how they gonna believe. Me sayin' different would have just made 'em mad. But me, I believe in stuff like that. I never had the chance to see it, but I believe you do. Just be careful, mon petite. Say your prayers so that the good Lord takes care of you and watches over you and your friends. Okay? You'll do that for me?"

"I will, Uncle Fezzo, I promise," Nonie said, then kissed him on the cheek and hurried out of the funeral home more afraid about tonight than ever before.

CHAPTER ELEVEN

Guy was emotionally torn. He couldn't stop thinking about the chaos he'd witnessed earlier at the funeral home, which kept him laughing. To see those old ladies punching at each other, slapping, kicking, people rushing out of the door or sticking around and choosing sides. It was like watching a boxing match gone awry.

The highlight had been when Fezzo had to sling Anna Mae Turner over his shoulder to get her out of the funeral home. Guy had laughed so hard then he didn't know how anybody other than Nonie hadn't heard him.

The conflicting emotions he had now, however, did everything but make him laugh. The fact that at any moment Nonie would be leaving with that Jack

Nagan guy made him angry, sad, and jealous. He didn't care that Shaundelle, Buggy, and Tatman were going on this scouting expedition, too. He just didn't like the fact that Jack would be with Nonie.

Guy was also concerned for Nonie because she really had no idea what she might be sticking herself in the middle of. Nonie might be able to see the dead, but not all of them. It wasn't like she walked through a cemetery and saw the ghost of everyone buried there. Guy knew Nonie saw them only at certain times and certain people. He had no idea why she saw some and not all. The fact that she was able to see and communicate with him was all that really mattered.

Maybe she was able to see him because she still loved him. Guy knew she'd seen her grandfather, as well. But that seemed to be a no-brainer. He was family, and Nonie had been very close to him.

But love wasn't the only catalyst that caused her ghost sightings. Nonie had mentioned how she'd seen a couple of people standing near their caskets at the funeral home. Strangers, no family attachment at all, yet she'd seen them.

Knowing that, Guy didn't understand why she'd want to purposely go out and hunt for ghost, save for the money, of course.

Guy worried about what spirits she might run into, but what worried him more was the time she'd be spending with Jack. He'd seen the way the guy had looked at her as he explained how to operate the Rem Pod she'd be responsible for, and the other doodads he'd brought with him during their visit to Nonie's. When he'd handed her a piece of equipment to show her how it worked, Jack's hands lingered a little too long on Nonie's. Seeing this

infuriated Guy to the point that he'd come out of

hiding just to piss Nonie off and get her attention

off of Jack. The only reason he hadn't done more to

Nagan was he knew Nonie would have immediately

reacted to him, which would have embarrassed her

and given up her little secret—that she could

actually see the dead. Had that happened, she'd

have forced Guy to stay away from her for good.

And he couldn't imagine that ever happening.

Guy knew the real reason Nonie had agreed to do

these ghost hunting gigs was because she needed

the money so she wouldn't have to work at her

family's funeral home anymore. That he

understood. Nonie had such a lively personality,

such a zest for life, that being stuck in a place that

only had sorrow and pain attached to it would

eventually drain the life out of her.

Thinking of this, Guy suddenly had a brain bulb go off, just like before. Create the evidence.

There was the real film crew to consider, however. If he'd be the one creating the evidence and the film crew never picked up a thing, unless there truly was a spirit around, they'd start to question if the evidence the scouting crew gave them had been faked. He certainly didn't want that to happen to Nonie. The only way to keep that from occurring, that he could think of anyway, was for him to show up at the same location while the film crew was there and create the same havoc.

Although it sounded like a good plan, the thought of doing it made Guy feel a bit sleazy. He loved Nonie, just as much now as when he was alive. He didn't want to screw things up for her.

Although his idea would have been lucrative for Nonie, it had the potential of getting her tossed out of the gig altogether, along with the rest of the crew. He couldn't take that chance. All he knew to do was somehow figure out how to discreetly watch her back and hope she'd have enough sense to know when she was in over her head at a location and get out.

Later, when Nonie returned home, Guy purposely stayed out of her way, which was difficult to do since she showered. Oh, how he loved watching her shower from afar. Even when the shower glass steamed up, he could easily see the curves of her body. Tall, thin, exquisite. After her shower, she dressed in black jeans and a cobalt blue pullover, which set her eyes ablaze. He didn't know of any model that looked so beautiful, even in sneakers. After she dressed and busied herself cleaning the bathroom, Guy went into the living room.

From the front window, he saw a white van with the letters WXRT stamped on the side of it pull up in front of Nonie's. He spotted Jack Nagan behind the wheel of the van with Tatman riding shotgun. Behind them, in the large passenger bench seat sat Shaundelle and Buggy.

He let out a sigh of relief. Since Tatman was riding shotgun, that meant Nonie would be sitting with Shaundelle and Buggy, which was fine by him. He saw large cases of equipment in the storage area at the back of the van.

No sooner did Guy finish giving the van the once-over than Nonie ran outside toward it. Guy hadn't been expecting her to react that fast. He didn't know how she knew the van was waiting for her, but she flew right past him and through the front door without acknowledging he was there. A good thing since she'd have given him hell.

As he watched Shaundelle and Buggy move over so Nonie'd have room to sit, Guy thought over his plan. If he squeezed into the van, Nonie would surely see him and pitch a fit, thus blowing her cover to everyone except Buggy, who already knew Nonie saw the dead.

Running out of time, Guy racked his brain to figure out how he could sneak into the van when mother luck suddenly struck. As Nonie, Shaundelle, and Buggy were settling into their seat, Tatman got out of the van, went around it and opened the back, cargo doors. He tightened up a couple of bungie cords used to hold the equipment cases together, then pushed the cases closer to the front of the van to minimize any jostling on their drive to the scout site. The back of the cargo area was a perfect place for him to lay in hiding.

Knowing Tatman couldn't see him, Guy hurried to the back of the van so quickly that even if Nonie had been looking out of the window, he would have looked like an obscure shadow. By the time Tatman grabbed hold of the first door to swing it shut, Guy had already rolled himself onto his side in the back of the van's cargo area. Both doors slammed shut, and he heard Tatman scrambling back into the front passenger seat.

Guy felt relatively safe from Nonie's ever-prying eyes. The stack of equipment cases was high enough that even if she looked back, she wouldn't be able to see him. Getting out of the van without her noticing once they reached the location would prove to be a different challenge. But he'd figure that out once they got there. For now, all he could think of was making sure he stayed out of her way so she wouldn't see him.

"So where are we going again?" Shaundelle asked.

"Opelousas," Jack said, glancing at her from the rearview mirror.

"Aw, man, Opelousas ain't that far," Shaundelle said."I thought that we were going to do some real scouting."

"Opelousas is a pretty good drive," Buggy said. "At least forty minutes from here."

"Yeah, but I figured we'd be doing things like those big guys on television. You know, going to castles and caves and shit."

"At least we get to start somewhere," Nonie said. Even if it's only forty minutes away. That's more than we had yesterday."

"What's in Opelousas anyway?" Shaundelle said. "Besides Taco Bell and Walmart?"

"There's an old, historical house out there," Jack said. "I know the man whose mother owned it. She passed away a year ago, and he wants to renovate the house. He swears his mother claimed it was haunted, so I asked if we could scout it out before they started tearing walls down, and he agreed. Even better, down a graveled road just past that house is a deserted plantation I want us to check out. No one's been in it for at least ten years."

"And the owner of the plantation gave us the okay to scout it?" Nonie asked.

"Not exactly," Jack said. "As far as I could tell

by all the court records, no one owns the house. It's literally deserted."

"You mean we're going into that plantation without anyone's permission?" Nonie asked, seemingly appalled.

"Technically, yes," Jack said. "But it's not like I didn't try to find the owners. The state and feds don't have a lien on it, and the last owner of the house on record died seven years ago in a nursing home."

"Sounds like breaking and entering to me," Nonie said, then chewed on her bottom lip, which she always did when she was nervous.

"Look, I wanna do this gig just like everybody else," Buggy said. "But I don't want to go to jail over it."

"Nobody's going to jail," Jack assured them. "I

spoke to the St Landry Parish Sheriff's Department about us scouting it. They didn't even know the place existed. Said as long as we're careful and don't take anything from the house, they didn't have a problem with us going in."

"Now you've sprinkled some bullshit on that one," Shaundelle said. "Cops don't give anybody free reign to do stuff unless there's something in it for them. How much did you pay them?"

Jack grinned. "Not one red cent. Did tell them they might have a shot at being on one of the episodes, though."

"Were you serious, bro?" Tatman asked. "We can't even get on the real show. We're just the help. How are you going to get those cops involved?"

"Big difference between being the help and a cop," Jack said. "I think the producer will like the added seriousness of having cops there."

"I'm all for it then," Shaundelle said. 'That little house with all of us in it is one thing. A big-ass plantation is something else. Sounds like the place is just sitting there, waiting for us. Nobody else wants it, we can sure make use of it. I bet all the lights and dings from all them gizmos you got will go crazy in a big ol' deserted place like that. That's gonna be our first five hundred bucks."

"I hope you're right," Buggy said. "I don't understand how somebody can just leave a plantation house deserted, though. After ten years, you know it's gotta be dilapidated. And why would there be a house in front of it?"

"I don't know why it is the way it is," Jack said. "The actual film crew will do historical research on the place. But for now, we've got the perfect setting. Two houses for the travel price of one."

Guy harrumphed, not liking the "know-it-all" attitude that he thought he heard in Jack's voice. He put a hand over his mouth, remembering that Nonie was in the van and that she could hear him.

Sure enough, Nonie jumped in her seat and turned about, looking right then left. "Did y'all hear something?" she asked.

"What you talkin' about, girl?" Shaundelle asked.

"It sounded like a hiccup or a muffled hum."

Shaundelle blew out a loud breath. "Girl, we ain't even at any of the houses yet and you already wanna put the juju on us?"

"If you so scared of things like juju," Tatman said to Shaundelle, glancing at her over his shoulder, "then why did you sign up for this gig?"

"The money, my brother," Shaundelle said. "Same as you."

"Yeah, but if you're that scared, how are you going to work the cameras?"

Shaundelle snapped her head to one side, tossing some attitude. "Don't be worrin' about Shaundelle. I'm gonna work. I'm just going to set myself up and say Shaundelle Washington, you gots more nerve than any woman in the state of Louisiana, and you gonna take them pictures and be glad if something shows up. That don't mean I might not be shakin' inside, you know, and have to run to the little girls' room."

"So, what do we do, Jack," Buggy asked, "if the place is really haunted? I mean, like if we see stuff moving around, hear voices?"

"We take pictures and record," Jack said with a

shrug. "That's it. Then we leave. That's the name of this gig. Find it. The film crew will either see and hear the same things or they won't. And if they do, they'll either do something about it or they won't."

"What they gonna do if they see shit?" Shaundelle asked. "Take more pictures and haul ass like us?

Jack chuckled. "I have no idea, That's always a possibility. But that's the thing about paranormal investigating. You can go to a location one day and hear pounding on the walls, footsteps everywhere, hear people whispering over your shoulder and nobody's there. Then you go back the next day with a full film crew and you don't even have a June bug flying around anywhere."

"What happens if that happens with us?" Nonie asked. "We get evidence, hand it over to them and they send out a film crew who comes back empty-handed. Is the network going to want their money back from us?"

"No way," Jack said. "We got the evidence they wanted on film and audio. The film crew not being able to pick up the same is their problem. We did our job and will get paid for it."

"I like that plan," Shaundelle said. "We on our own, they on their own. Fair is fair. I just want my five hundred dollars."

Jack slowed the van to a near stop and looked at everyone in the van. "Now remember everybody, I know the money is important to all of us but no fooling around while we're there. No slamming the doors, no pulling drawers open. We get legitimate paranormal activity or nothing. If they find out one of us is trying to rig this gig, it's over for all of us."

"I ain't gonna be touchin' nothin' but my camera," Shaundelle assured him.

"And I'm just going to do the recording like you asked me to," Buggy said. "No funny business from my end."

"The Rem Pods are my priority," Nonie said. "You're not going to get any door or cabinet activity from me. If one of them goes off, I'll be yelling for somebody to come and take a picture of it, but that's all."

"We got this, bro," Tatman said to Jack reassuringly. "Nobody here wants to screw up a good thing. No worries."

They drove the rest of the way in silence with Guy lying in the back behind the equipment,

When they finally reached what Guy assumed was their destination, he had to think quick. How was he going to get out of the van without being seen by Nonie? The only thing he could think of was as soon as Tatman or Jack opened the cargo doors, Guy would roll out and hide under the van. Then he'd wait for them to go into the house before slipping out. After that, he had no clue. If Nonie was one of the first ones to go inside the small house, he'd be able to sneak in behind the last one who entered and dart off into a side room, any room where Nonie wasn't. He'd have to simply keep room hopping and closet dodging in order for him to keep an eye on her but keep her eyes off him.

The van doors opened and within minutes, Tatman had the cargo doors open. Guy rolled out of the van and slipped under it. He heard the twang of bungee cords being released and soon saw Tatman's feet and equipment cases being set gently on the ground.

"Shaundelle, why don't you take your camera, and Buggy you take a recorder, and Nonie you bring an EMF meter. Tatman and I will get the cameras and monitor set up," Jack said.

"Uh . . ." Nonie said. "You showed me a Rem Pod and how it works but what is an EMF meter? I forgot."

Jack pulled a Trifield meter out of one of the equipment cases and turned it on. It gave off a high-pitched whining sound, then settled into silence. "EMF stands for electromagnetic field. If it spikes," he showed her how the measurement apparatus fluctuated," then Shaundelle should take pictures around that area. It means that something has changed in the electromagnetic field around you, and we want to measure that. Take pictures in the area around it. Buggy, you can do an EVP session then. Do you remember what EVP stands for?

Buggy looked down at her digital recorder and back up at Jack, frustration on her face. "Yeah, electronic vomit and piss machine, 'cause that's what I'm going to do if Nonie's doomathingy goes off!"

Jack grinned. "Close. It means electronic voice phenomena. If there's a spirit around, you may not be able to hear it with your human ears, but the recorder might pick it up. We can only hope so anyway."

"Hope my ass," Shaundelle said. "With just the three of us out there, you'll be lucky if we don't start hitchhiking our way back to Clay Point."

"What about all that brave, 'I'm going to get it done' talk you gave us in the van?" Tatman asked.

"Shut up before I whack off your ponytail and use it as a broom," Shaundelle said.

Tatman's expression darkened, and Jack stepped in between them. "Okay, you two. Once we get inside and have the monitor set up, we'll pair up to work the area."

"There're five of us, Jack," Nonie said. "How do you split up five?"

"Yeah," Shaundelle said. "Didn't they teach you no 'rithmatic in school?"

Jack didn't bite on her bitch bait. "Tatman will stay near the monitors, so he can see what's going on in each room from the infrared cameras we'll set up in them. Shaundelle, since you're doing handheld cameras and Buggy digital recorders, you two stick together. I'll stay with Nonie and work the rest of the equipment. We'll set up the same way at the plantation, only there'll be more cameras to watch on the monitor because it's a bigger place. If you run across anything in either house, radio me." He handed each a walkie-talkie. "I'll come right away."

"And if I see something on the monitor," Tatman said, "in a room where y'all aren't, I'll radio you, too."

"Good, Tatman," Jack said. "Exactly what we need. Now let's get to work."

"You sonofabitch," Guy said softly. He was still lying underneath the van but had heard every word they'd said. "That's what you meant to do all along, you bastard, get Nonie alone. I knew it. I knew you were nothing but a lowlife. Well, if you want to see a ghost, Mr. Nagan, I'll show you one. You'd better leave my Nonie alone or I'll make sure that you never want to go ghost hunting again. Ever!"

CHAPTER TWELVE

As they gathered equipment in the driveway of the small house they were getting ready to investigate, Shaundelle suddenly slapped a hand on the side of the van, startling Tatman.

"Yo, Jack, I just thought of something," Shaundelle said. 'We gotta do this small house and then the plantation behind it. Are we gonna get paid for only one job since they're right next to each other or if we find something in both we get paid five hundred each?"

"Two different locations," Jack said, "So that'll be five hundred per house."

"Okay," Shaundelle said. "Didn't want to be wasting my time on a rush, you know?"

Jack looked back at her. "A rush?"

"Yeah, you know. When you get jacked out of something because you're so damn rushed into it that you forget to ask for details."

"Oh," Jack turned back with a grin. "No rush here, for sure."

Shaundelle leaned against the van. "So this could be a very, very lucrative night. This is a good thing. We should try to make two for ones every time we go out."

"We can certainly try," Jack said, "but the chances of finding two houses that are supposedly haunted side by side or back to back are rare. Guess it'll depend on how hard and fast we can work to find something like that."

"Oh, I'm all about hard and fast," Shaundelle said. "You can count on me. Like out in the wards in New Orleans, I gots a lot of my people who live out there. They've got creepy shit happening all the time. I bet we could do two or three in one night if we go out there. I'll call my cousin, Dashone and find out what's been hangin'. I'll get us some creepy shit. Don't you worry."

It was then Nonie noticed a gray Pathfinder pull up and park directly across from them on the street. A tall, lanky man with wiry salt-and-pepper hair got out of the SUV. He looked to be in his early fifties, wore Dockers, a button-down shirt the color of dirt, and black-rimmed glasses. He had a narrow, long face with a nose to match it.

"Stay here, Jack said. "That's Frank Richardson, the son of the woman who owned this house. I'll make sure everything's still cool, then we'll go in and get started."

As Jack got out of the van, Nonie inched toward

the front of the van to do a bit of eavesdropping.

Jack held out his hand when he met up with Frank, and the man took it and shook it enthusiastically. They stood in the middle of the street, chatting like they'd known each other for years.

'How're you doing, Frank?" Jack asked.

"Best as can be expected I guess. You know Mom was well into her nineties, so her dying didn't come as a huge surprise, but she had such a big personality, you'd have sworn she'd live forever."

"I'm sorry for your loss."

"Thanks, buddy. Look I'm not going to stand out here getting all mushy and hold you up. Here's the key to the house. Just a heads-up. There's a lot of . . . stuff in there. Mom never threw anything away. I've been packing up just the living room since she passed away and still have a good bit left to pack. At the rate I'm clearing out the house, I'll be lucky if we'll be able to start renovations by next Christmas. Anyway, the house itself was . . . Well, is pretty cluttered with boxes and the rest of her things. I haven't even touched the other rooms yet. Feel free to go through any room you like. All I ask is that you leave what's boxed in the living room alone. It's just souvenirs and things she collected over the years."

"You can trust me, of course," Jack said. "No one will mess with the boxes."

"Oh, I know. Wouldn't have given you the key otherwise. I'll give you a call sometime mid-morning tomorrow, and we'll meet up so I can get the key back. I'll be interested in hearing if you guys find anything in there tonight. Mom always claimed there was a ghost in the house. Called him Captain. She claimed most of the activity was in the kitchen and upstairs. Now upstairs is not a living area. She kept it as kind of museum of sorts because it served as a hospital during the Civil War. She has a couple of army cots up there with Confederate uniforms laid across them, and heaven only knows what else. You're welcome to go up there, just ask your people not to handle the antiques if you don't mind."

"No problem."

"Oh, and just so it won't take you by surprise," Frank said. "Mom has a sawhorse in the middle of the living room with a saddle on it. She used to ride, you know. Won that saddle in a riding competition. Very proud of it, too. I'm afraid you'll have to work around that along with the rest of the chaos."

"Not to worry, my friend. We'll be very respectful of her things. I just appreciate you letting us in to do an investigation."

As Frank and Jack shook hands, indicating they were about to part ways, Nonie hurried back to the other side of the van. If an old woman claimed that she had a ghost in her house, she either had a vivid imagination or it was the real deal, which made Nonie nervous. The spirit the old woman claimed she saw was either residual energy, like a shadow of a person from the past playing a role they'd played in life over and over again or an intelligent haunting, meaning that the spirit was able to communicate with the living. For all she knew, as attached as Frank's mother was to her home, she might very well still be hanging around inside. Nonie was concerned that if the spiritual activity in the house was intelligent, and she did see it, she was going to have to watch her reaction to it so the others, aside from Buggy, wouldn't discover her secret.

Jack hurried back to the van and dangled the house key in front of everyone. "Time to get to work. Everybody grab an equipment case. I'll open up the house and see what we have to work with."

"Hol' up," Shaundelle said. "That man just gave you them keys? Wasn't he afraid you or one of us might steal something inside?"

Jack shook his head. "I've known Frank for a long time. Knew his mom, too. They're good people, and they know I'm not a thief. Do I have to worry about any of you being thieves?" Jack said, eyeing Shaundelle since she'd brought up the subject.

"And have some ghost chasin' me all the way back home to get their shit back?" Shaundelle said. "Oh, hell, no. I ain't even gonna collect dust in that place. Pictures, remember? I do the pictures. No stealing here. No, and hell to the no."

"Good," Jack said. "Frank said the place was pretty cluttered with memorabilia that he's been trying to pack away for weeks. So let's be on our Ps and Qs and not touch anything. We'll just have to work around the clutter."

"Yeah," Buggy said. "Old people have a tendency to hold on to things forever."

"It's more than that," Jack said." Frank's mom was the first Miss Louisiana and also the first woman to win ribbons and trophies for barrel-racing quarter horses. He said she still has the saddle she won from one of the competitions in the living room. It's sitting on a sawhorse."

"Wow, Nonie said. "Impressive lady."

"Oh, she was," Jack assured her. "And she had the one of the most positive attitudes I've ever known in anyone. She was a pip."

Nonie chewed her bottom lip, getting more nervous by the minute.

"Because of the clutter, I don't think we'll have room to set up a command station with our cameras and monitor. So we'll each carry handheld equipment and go from room to room and see if we pick up anything. Nonie, you can still handle the Rem Pod, only take a camera with you, as well. Buggy, you can still bring a digital recorder, but I'll give you an IR camera to operate, too. I'll handle the rest of the gadgets with Tatman. We'll each have a walkie and they're already set up on channel one. If you run into a problem, all you have to do is depress the talk button and the rest of the team will hear you and come to where you are. And remember, no matter what kind of clutter you run into, don't move it. That was important to Frank, and I don't want to violate his trust."

"No problem," Tatman said.

"Got it," Buggy and Shaundelle said in unison.

"I won't touch a thing," Nonie said.

"I can't reiterate that strongly enough," Jack said. "Not only due to Frank's trust but I don't know if any of you have noticed, this is an historical site." He pointed at the front door of the house. A bronze plaque hung beside it that read; HISTORICAL SITE 1860. "That's another reason it's critical that we not touch anything or move it from its place. Everybody got that?"

"For heaven's sake that's the third time you've told us," Buggy said. "I won't touch a thing."

"As if I'd want to touch her old stuff," Shaundelle said.

"Hear you loud and clear, boss," Tatman said.

Jack looked at Nonie since she'd yet to respond. Her mind wasn't on what she could or couldn't touch. It was on who or what she might see once she got inside.

"Nonie?" Jack said, getting her attention.

"Huh?"

"Historical site, lots of memorabilia. No touching, okay."

"No problem," Nonie said.

"Piece of cake," Shaundelle reassured Jack.

Nonie looked over at Buggy whose eyes looked even bigger than they actually were. This was their first ghost scouting venture and she knew Buggy was thinking, "*Oh, my God, what if we do find something? What am I going to do? Run or record it?*"

Nonie took Buggy by the hand and squeezed it and mouthed. "It'll be all right. I'll be right there with you."

"Okay," Jack said. "Let's get set up. Everybody grab a case. I'll unlock the house."

At that moment, Nonie felt an electrical current run from the ground up to her feet, which typically meant there was a spirit nearby.

Trying to shake the feeling, Nonie went to the back of the van and grabbed a midsize carrying case.

While Tatman handed out cases to the rest of the crew, Nonie walked up the steps of the house to a wide wraparound porch. The house was indeed small and shotgun in style, but it was two stories tall.

Jack was fumbling with the key in the knob when Nonie reached the porch.

When Jack walked into the house, Nonie was right behind him. He stood in the doorway, flipped on a light, and said, "Sweet Jesus."

Nonie stood on tiptoe and peeked around his broad shoulders. There were boxes everywhere. They lined the entire length of the couch and were stacked three high. True to his word, there was a sawhorse in the middle of the living room with a saddle on it. There were pictures everywhere. Pictures of Mrs. Richardson with family and with celebrities. There was barely enough room to walk around the boxes and clutter that filled the living room.

"I was right," Jack said. "There isn't any room to set up a monitor. We're going to have to do everything handheld. Now, if I remember right, the kitchen is straight back that way." He pointed past the living room. The bedroom and bath are over there, on the east side of the house, and then we have upstairs to check out." He pointed to the narrowest set of stairs Nonie had ever seen. As thin as she was, she thought she'd have to walk up sideways in order to make it up into the attic.

As she wondered how Shaundelle was going to make it up the narrow stairs to take pictures, something odd caught her eye. Hanging on the wall at the base of the staircase was a picture of the Madonna and Child. Only their faces were warped. The Madonna's face looked squished in at the cheeks, causing her head to have an hourglass appearance. The Child she held looked like it had a large bubble head and narrow chin, huge eyes that looked nowhere. It gave her the creeps. She didn't know who painted the portrait, but she had no idea what possibly possessed the old woman to hang something this ugly in her house.

"Ah, I see you caught that," Jack said, walking up behind Nonie. "There's a story behind that picture. Frank told me about it five years ago. His mom had a friend who was a painter, and he kept having horrific nightmares of a demon night after night. The demon was always chasing him, meaning to possess him. Frank's mom suggested that he paint the creature. I guess she figured putting it on canvas might help remove it from his subconscious, and he'd be able to get a decent night's sleep. The problem was when he painted it, the sight of it on canvas freaked him out so much that he quickly covered the demonic image with the Madonna and Child. The painter claimed that at first, the portrait was perfect. The Madonna as beautiful as any he'd ever seen and the Child sweet and innocent. Then, over time, the picture of the Madonna and Child suddenly began to warp, like the demon beneath it meant to come through. Although the demon never fully manifested itself on the canvas the way it had when originally painted, the painter meant to burn the canvas. Frank's mom, though, was so fascinated by the portrait that she actually bought the painting from the painter and hung it at the foot of the staircase. Why? I have no clue, and, unfortunately, she isn't here for us to ask."

"That's the freakiest thing I've ever seen,"

Shaundelle said, crowding in behind them. "That thing needs to be covered with a black towel or something."

"I agree," Jack said. "But remember, we can't touch or move anything in the house. There's a reason it's there, and I guess it'll stay there until Frank decides it's time for it to come down. All we're going to do is investigate. We'll change the pairing I mentioned in the van. Nonie, you take the Rem Pod, and Buggy you take a camera and both of you go into the kitchen. Shaundelle and Tatman, grab a couple of digital recorders and a camera and go to the bedroom and bath area. Take some pictures back there, do some EVPs I'll stay in the living room and take pictures and do some EVPs myself."

Everyone nodded yet they were obviously

nervous because hands were shaking as they pulled equipment out of cases. They eyed one another as if ready to do whatever needed to be done, but not really wanting to do it.

Nonie and Buggy made their way into the kitchen, maneuvering around the sawhorse, tons of boxes, piles of bric-a-brac, odds and ends of memorabilia overloading a coffee table.

When they finally made it into the kitchen, they found much of the same hoarding, except for the sawhorse and saddle. There was an old metal kitchen table with a worn yellow Formica top and four metal chairs to match, each seat covered in plastic material the same color as the table.

Nonie placed the Rem Pod on the table, and the second she set it down, the lights went off and it began to beep.

"What the hell is that about?" Nonie said, backing away from it. "Take pictures, Bug! Take pictures of the lights."

"Maybe we should call for help on the walkies first," Buggy said nervously.

"Just take pictures for now while it's going off. That's evidence, right?" Nonie said. "Isn't that what we're here to get?"

"Do you see . . . uh . . . do you see anybody?" Buggy asked.

Nonie did a once-over of the kitchen, then said in a loud whisper, "If you mean do I see a ghost, no."

Buggy nodded slowly then put the camera lens to her eye and started shooting the Rem Pod that was still beeping and flashing lights. "How many do I take?" she asked."

"Just keep taking pictures," Nonie said. "I'll get

one of the digital recorders set up and we'll do an EVP session."

After Buggy had taken a dozen or more pictures, the Rem Pod finally stopped beeping and only a single green light remained on instead of the flashing parade of blue, red, yellow, and green.

Suddenly, from the corner of her eye, Nonie caught a familiar figure hiding behind an eight-foot-tall piece of cabinetry. She saw a nose and a chin, enough to make her grit her teeth.

"Never mind," she told Buggy, I know what set the Rem Pod off."

She marched around the cabinet, put a hand on her hip and demanded, "What the hell are you doing here?"

"What?" Buggy asked. "What are you talking about? Who are you talking to?"

"I'll give you two guesses and one doesn't count," Nonie said.

"Don't tell me he's here," Buggy said, looking over her shoulder, turning around in a circle. "Where is he?"

"Here," Nonie pointed to the side of the cabinetry. "Caught like a duck at a Christmas dinner."

Guy hung his head and walked out from behind the cabinet.

"I didn't want you to see me," Guy said.

"Well, no shit," Nonie said. But you'd have had to do a much better job than hide behind a set of cabinets for Pete's sake."

"What's he saying?" Buggy asked.

"Said he didn't want to be noticed."

"By you? Not possible."

"My point exactly," Nonie said.

Guy shrugged his shoulders. "I just wanted to protect you, Nonie. You know there are spirits in here."

"I would hope so," Nonie said. "Besides you. Look, let me tell you something, I need to be able to record what's really in this house. I don't need you pulling any shenanigans so that what we're recording is you moving shades, knocking over chairs. If you're going to hang around to keep an eye on me, then do just that. But stay out of my way and no funny business."

Guy took a finger and formed a cross with it over his chest. "I promise I will stay out of trouble, but trouble's already gonna find you. Just don't go upstairs, okay?"

"I have to go upstairs," Nonie said. "I have to

take pictures. Not many people in this group can fit up that narrow staircase. Even I'll have to probably go up them sideways."

"There's something up there that could hurt you," Guy said.

"I'll have to take the chance," Nonie said.

"Then I'll be up there with you," he said.

"What exactly is up there?"

"What's he saying?" Buggy asked, her voice shaky.

"That there's something up in the attic that we should be careful of because it could be dangerous."

"Oh uh-uh, I'm not going up there," Buggy said. "You can send Shaundelle up there, but I'm keeping my little white ass down here."

"How in the hell do you think we're going to get Shaundelle up those narrow steps?" Nonie asked.

"Yeah, but I'd have to pass next to that creepy picture and then make my way up into the attic, where Guy said there was something up there. I don't know, Nonie. This just isn't working out like I thought it would."

"You're going to come with me up there and record," Nonie demanded. "Remember, I'm the one who sees those freakazoid ghosts, not you. If there's something dangerous up there, we're out in a nanosecond."

Guy harrumphed. "It's not a matter of getting out of there, upstairs I mean. All of you should be getting out of here."

CHAPTER THIRTEEN

Jack had just finished an EVP session in the living room when he heard voices coming from the kitchen. He made his way around the clutter in the living room, went to the kitchen and saw Nonie and Buggy talking to each another.

"Did y'all come up with anything?" Jack asked Buggy then glanced over at Nonie.

"The Rem Pod went off," Nonie told him.

Buggy nodded. "I got pictures of it."

Jack's eyes lit up. "That's a good thing. Were any of you near the Rem Pod when it went off?"

"No," Nonie said. "We were on the other side of the kitchen. It just went off by itself." She threw a glance at Buggy. "Right?"

"Absolutely. Right." Buggy crossed her arms

over her chest.

"That's a positive sign. I'm glad you got pictures of it," Jack said. "Nonie, do you think you can handle the camera if I give Buggy an IR video camera?"

"What's an IR video camera?" Buggy asked.

"Oh, sorry," Jack said. "It's an infrared camera, which means it'll take pictures of whatever you're seeing, or in some cases what you're not seeing, in the dark. It doesn't require a flash."

"I guess it would have been cooler if we'd have gotten the Rem Pod going off with a video camera instead of one that only took stills," Nonie said.

Jack shrugged. "We've got pictures. That's what counts."

"You want us to try again?" Nonie asked. "You know, with a video camera?"

Jack shook his head. "Tell you what. I've just finished an EVP session in the living room. I didn't do a playback but I'll run the audio when we get back home. I have an audio editing suite on my computer that's able to take out the junk noise and pick up any viable EVPs."

"And what's an EVP again?" Nonie asked.

"Electronic voice phenomena. You may not be able to hear a spirit's voice but sometimes the recorder picks up their voices. It has something to do with sound frequency."

"What do they normally say?" Buggy asked. "What do they usually talk about?"

"Most of the time we get EVPs when they're responding to a question we've asked."

"What kinds of questions?"

"Did you die in this house? Did you live in this

house? Did anything traumatic happen to you in this house? Questions like that."

"Whew," Buggy said. "I hope I can remember all of that."

"He's just giving us an example of the types of questions we should ask," Nonie said, then looked at Jack. "Right?"

"That's right. We'll be running the IR camera. It has audio so it'll pick up any loud sounds, like knocking or banging, things like that. Sometimes it'll pick up an EVP or two, but most of the time we get those from our digital recorders."

"I'm getting confused," Buggy said, her brow furrowing.

Jack held up a hand. "Let's uncomplicate it then. You take the IR video camera, and Nonie will take the Rem Pod and the regular camera. Don't worry about doing any EVP sessions for now. I'll follow up wherever you've been and take care of the EVPs. Look, we're already off to a great start. The Rem Pod went off, and Buggy's got that documented. Now we're just going to see if we can find more. Sound good?"

"Works for me," Nonie said.

Buggy nodded.

"Great."

"Why don't the two of you go upstairs now? I'll take the kitchen." He took the video camera that was hanging around his neck off and handed it to Buggy. "It's really easy to work." He showed her the on and off button, the focus and zoom knob. "It's as easy as the regular camera. The only difference is you'll be videotaping the whole thing and Nonie will be snapping still shots." He turned to

Nonie. "All you have to do is set your Rem Pod down, and if it goes off, just start shooting pictures. You know how to operate the camera, right?"

"Just press the silver button here," Nonie said, indicating a fat round button on top of the camera.

"That's right. And it's an infrared camera so no flash needed. So don't be surprised if one doesn't go off. It doesn't mean it's broken. The camera will be able to catch things we can't see with our naked eye. Sometimes you'll catch a shadow of something that doesn't look like much but if you take a picture of it, you might be surprised by what you get. You just never know. That's what makes this so much fun."

"Fun . . . right," Nonie said and rolled her eyes at Buggy.

"Do we have to go upstairs?" Buggy asked Jack.

"That's where Mrs. Richardson always said Captain lived."

"Absolutely," Jack said. "From what Frank told me, nothing's been moved up there yet, so we might have a good shot of getting some kind of paranormal activity if Mrs. Richardson was right about the captain."

"Gives me the shivers just thinking about going up there," Buggy said.

"I know it's kind of creepy," Nonie said. "But we signed on for this gig and we've got to finish it . . . Miss I've Got A Great Idea!"

"Now you're just being a smartass," Buggy said and pouted.

"Just start the camera rolling as you walk up the stairs and keep it rolling while you're there," Jack said to Buggy. "Sweep it around the room slowly. If

Nonie happens to pick up anything on her camera . .
. Wait, Nonie, I'll tell you what, since you're just
operating a camera, I'm going to give you a digital
recorder, as well. Just turn it on and place it on one
of the cots in the room upstairs. Place the Rem Pod
in the opposite corner of the room."

"But what if I do something to piss that spirit off
whenever I ask a question?" Nonie asked.

"All you have to do is ask any spirits in that
room to speak into the silver rectangle that's on the
bed. Point to it. If there's an intelligent spirit up
there, it should understand what you're saying and
will go to the recorder then say what it has to say.
Let him or her know that by them doing so, we'll be
able to hear what they have to say. Ask questions,
and we'll see if we can get any EVPs up there. That
way we'll have video, still shots from Nonie, the

Rem Pod, and a digital recorder going at the same time."

"And what if the Rem Pod goes off?" Buggy asked.

"That's where you want to aim your camera. If it goes off, chances are there's an energy boost around it, and if that doesn't come from either of you, chances are it's from a spirit. I'm anxious to get into the kitchen and do an EVP session to see if we get anything, especially since the Rem Pod went off in there."

He handed the Rem Pod back to Nonie. "Now you have the pod, an IR camera and a digital recorder. Don't forget to set the Rem Pod and digital recorder at opposite ends of the room. And Buggy, you'll be working the IR video camera. Keep your eyes peeled."

"And what if we see something?" Buggy asked. "Do we have to simply stay there and work with it?"

"Absolutely," Jack said. "There nothing up there that's going to harm you."

"How can you say that for sure?" Nonie said. "Ever see *The Exorcist*?"

"You're talking apples and oranges. A kid was possessed in *The Exorcist*. If there is a spirit here, it's here because it probably doesn't know how to move on."

Nonie let out what seemed to be an involuntary snort. "What's with that anyway? When you die, isn't there supposed to be a light that comes to get you to lead you to where you need to go?"

Jack shrugged. "From what I've heard, yes, but I've never died before so I really can't verify that."

Nonie glanced over her shoulder, and she and Buggy drew in a deep breath at the same time. Both looked about as excited to go upstairs as they'd be at the thought of crawling through a vat of roaches.

"Look," Jack said. "When I'm done in the kitchen, I'll go upstairs and join you, okay?"

Nonie chewed on her bottom lip.

Buggy nodded.

Both left the kitchen almost robotically and headed for the stairs. Jack couldn't help but watch Nonie as she left. She looked to be twenty-nine, thirty at the most, stood maybe five foot-four and was slender. She had shoulder-length, curly, walnut-colored hair and the largest most beautiful blue eyes he'd ever seen. Her nose and ears were small in comparison to her full lips, which he'd give anything to kiss. Jack knew by her beautiful eyes that she was terrified to go upstairs.

All of them were since this was their first time at ghost hunting. He had to give them kudos for going through with it, despite their fears. Then Jack suddenly remembered something and called out to Nonie.

Nonie and Buggy were back in the kitchen in a heartbeat.

"Yeah?" Nonie asked.

Jack tilted his head, curious. "Earlier, when the two of you were in the kitchen, I heard the two of you talking. Did you see anything or hear anything? It almost sounded like you were responding to something that was being said. I mean, I heard you talking to Buggy only what was said in response didn't seem to apply to what you said. Make sense?"

Nonie glanced at Buggy and back at Jack. "Probably just talking to myself. Doing a little rundown on what I would tell a ghost if I saw one."

Jack could tell by the way she wouldn't look at him directly in the face that there was more to the story than that. And he planned to find out what it was but now wasn't the time.

He hesitated for a couple of seconds then said, "Okay, you two, upstairs. I'll take care of EVPs here."

When the girls left the room Jack placed a digital recorder on the kitchen table and walked around the small area. "Are there any spirits in this room that want to communicate?" Jack asked. "There is a device on the table that will record your voice if you have something to say. You can speak into it and we'll hear your voice."

"No!"

Jack jumped, he heard that word loud and clear, and it seemed to be coming from right over his left shoulder. He turned around, but no one was there. His heart started beating faster. He was thankful for the digital recorder because it would definitely pick up his question and the answer he'd heard audibly. In the ten years he'd been investigating that had only happened to him twice.

"Communicate with me," Jack said. The only sound he heard were windchimes that he assumed were hanging outside, near the back door of the kitchen.

"What's your name?" Jack pressed. "Are you male or female?"

"Man," the voice said loudly. Jack jumped again surprised he'd heard it so clearly. He was anxious to get the recording to the producers of WXRT so they could hear what he'd just heard.

"Is there something we can help you with?"

No answer came through that he heard, but that didn't mean he hadn't received an answer. It might have come through the recorder but he wouldn't be able to tell until he brought it home.

"Is there something that we can do to help you move on? Are you stuck here?"

"NO!"

The voice was strong and loud and sent a shiver up Jack's spine. If there was a spirit that strong in the kitchen, it was no wonder that Nonie's Rem Pod had gone off earlier.

"Do you have a message for anybody in this house?"

No response.

"Is there anybody in this house or outside of this house that you want to communicate with specifically? If it's outside of this house, we can bring a message to them. If it's inside of this house, your message can be related to them."

No response.

"What has you so quiet now? Why won't you talk to me?"

Still no response. Nothing that he could hear with his own ears anyway.

"If you want me out of this room, you'll have to show me a sign, give me some kind of sign that you want me out! Otherwise, I'm not leaving." In that moment the cabinet door right above Jack's head swung open with enough force to whack him on the forehead before slamming shut.

"Shit," Jack said. He knew better than to provoke

any kind of spirit that tried to manifest itself, but he'd done it anyway, and he deserved the goose egg he felt already forming on his forehead. His vision was a little blurry, so he stood for a moment, waiting for it to clear.

Then he left the kitchen and went into the bedroom and bathroom where Shaundelle and Tatman were working.

When Shaundelle spotted Jack, she did a double take. "What the hell happened to you?"

"Guess we've got a spirit around here that doesn't like our company," Jack said.

"What?" Tatman said. "What happened?"

"I did what I knew I shouldn't have done. I was getting some good EVP's, even picked up some words I heard with my own ears. I told the spirit if it didn't want me here to show me. That's when one of the cabinet doors flew open, one right above my head, and the knob popped me on the forehead."

"Oh, uh-uh," Shaundelle said. "I'm not gonna be no place where no ghost is gonna be knockin' nobody upside the head. I'm outta here. I'm not going to take no chances that some ghost is gonna mess up this pretty face."

Tatman grabbed Shaundelle by the arm. "Take a picture of Jack's face. You're the one with the camera. Take a picture of his face so that the knot on it will be more proof." He turned to Jack. "Do you have any film of the cabinet door opening?"

"No, I didn't have anything with me but my digital recorder. I was going to just get EVP's. But still, Shaundelle, take a picture of this goose egg so I can put the story together for the producers."

With shaky hands, Shaundelle did as she was

asked. As soon as she was done, she started to hightail it out of the bedroom. Jack caught her by the arm.

"We need you here," Jack said to Shaundelle. "We have five of us to work with. One short is going to leave us in a bind when we get to the plantation. How are we going to hunt that big place and keep someone watching the monitor?"

"I ain't gonna have no ghostesses punching me upside the head," Shaundelle said. "If they are pissed off here, they gonna be more pissed off there 'cause it's a bigger place."

"We don't know that," Jack said. "And besides, I'm the one who provoked the spirit in the kitchen. That's why I got whacked by the cabinet door. Just don't provoke. Don't say something like, 'You come out and get me you big ugly sonofabitch,' because they just might."

"Do I look stupid to you?" Shaundelle said. "I guarantee you I ain't gonna be provoking nothing."

"Shaundelle, we really need you," Tatman said. "You're an important part of this team. This gig is already a given. That's five hundred dollars in your pocket. You gonna just throw that away?"

Shaundelle gritted her teeth and huffed. "All right, all right. But if something all googily comes after me, I'm outta here, y'all understand? I wasn't expectin' all this shit to come down."

"You'll always have somebody with you," Jack said. "I'll make sure you're not alone. Just remember, you're the one who's alive. They're dead."

"Yeah, I can see how that works considerin' that big-ass knot on your forehead, "Shaundelle said.

"Just because they're dead doesn't mean that can't cause you any harm."

"I told you it was because I provoked it," Jack said. "All you have to do is keep your questions simple and don't provoke. It won't have reason to attack you."

"Hell I sure ain't gonna provoke shit," Shaundelle said. "All I'm going to say is 'Happy birthday,' 'How's your mama?' and 'What was your favorite meal when you were alive?' I'm not going to be asking anything that's going to piss them off. You can count on that. If I'm going to keep this up, you'd best watch my back," she said to Tatman.

"And, Jack, you provoke again and you'll deserve another knock on the head," Shaundelle said adamantly. "You tellin' me not to provoke, then you best listen to your own self. 'Cause it looks like whatever's in here don't want us here. Now where is Nonie and Buggy?"

"I sent them upstairs," Jack said.

"By themselves?" Shaundelle all but yelled. "Nobody told them not to provoke anything. Suppose they start spouting off at the mouth, trying to get a ghost to respond? What then?"

"Nonie's not the type to provoke," Jack said.

"But Buggy is," Shaundelle said. "If she gets pissed off enough, she's gonna speak her mind and speak it loud and clear."

"Then I'll just go up there and make sure they don't," Jack said. "By the way, did you guys pick up anything in the bedroom or bathroom?"

"Not even a blip," Tatman said. "It was as quiet as an empty church back there."

"Okay, then you and Shaundelle take your turn in the kitchen and living room, and I'll go meet Buggy and Nonie upstairs and give them a heads-up on provoking," Jack said. "Though I doubt either one would do it, I guess it's better to be safe than sorry. I don't want to take any chances."

"You better not take any chances with my girls," Shaundelle demanded. "Either of them come back with so much as a scratch on 'em, I'm going to take that lump that you got on your forehead and add another one to the bottom of your chin. Got that?"

"Oh, I've got it," Jack said. "You're the one I'm a bit concerned about provoking. Your temper sometimes jumps out of your mouth before it goes through your brain."

"Yeah, but I know when to let it flare and when to keep it in check, and when it comes to ghostesses, it's checked, double-checked, and triple-checked. It's gonna be like Walmart, show me your receipt. I'm gonna be the nicest thing them ghostesses have ever seen."

Jack nodded and headed upstairs, where Nonie and Buggy were working, hoping he wasn't already too late to warn them.

CHAPTER FOURTEEN

Nonie took the staircase leading to the attic sideways, keeping her back to the wall mostly to avoid having to look at the freaky Madonna and Child portrait that hung at the foot of the stairs. Just looking at it gave her the creeps so bad it made her shiver. Had she seen it or stared at it any more than she already had, she'd have lost her nerve and not made it up the stairs.

Alongside of her, Buggy clung to Nonie's shirt, taking the steps sideways like Nonie. She was certainly small enough to take them head-on, but evidently chose to follow her friend's lead.

As Buggy held on tight and concentrated on Nonie's footsteps, the one thing she didn't realize was that Guy was following up the rear, a look of worry on his face. He stayed two steps below Buggy so she wouldn't pick up any sense of him. Nonie had to give him kudos for doing exactly as she'd asked him to do. Watch over them but not get in the way and create any shenanigans.

When Nonie made it to the top of the stairs the opening looked like any regular attic door opening, except it had no door, just a wide maw, wider than an average attic door. The last step allowed her to walk into the room and that's when she saw them. She nervously held out a hand to help Buggy up the final step,

When Guy made it into the room, he said, "Holy shit."

There were three old army cots lined up side-by-side in the attic. Two of them had Confederate uniforms laid out on them without bodies. The third held an old gentleman with a white beard. His eyes were closed and he lay on his back. Nonie could tell by the way his right leg was bandaged that he'd lost part of his leg from the knee down.

When all three were up in the attic, the old man opened his eyes.

"Who dares interrupts me at this hour?" the old man said, then rolled over onto his side. A gun appeared in his right hand. Nonie was no expert on guns except this one looked like the type that used musket balls for ammo. He aimed it at her.

"I said who comes in and dares bother me at this hour? Can't you see that I am recuperating from a dire injury?"

Nonie told Buggy to start rolling camera on the beds. She turned her digital recorder on and placed it on the fireplace mantel that sat against the east wall of the room. Nonie started flashing pictures with her camera. The old man sat up, put his eye to the sight of his gun and aimed it at Nonie's head.

"You dare walk into this room without permission? You dare walk into this house without permission? You will die. You are a Yankee aren't you? Only Yankees have no courtesy. Southerners are the only ones who would have enough sense and courtesy to ask, to knock, to see if anyone was home, to see if it was convenient for anyone home to have visitors."

"Oh, Captain, leave the poor dear alone," an old woman's voice said, sending Nonie spinning on her heels. Near the back of the room on the opposite side of the fireplace Nonie saw an elderly woman that she could virtually see through. There was enough matter to her to make out what she looked like, though. Short and bow-backed, a little chunky in the gut. White hair tightly permed. She wore a pink housedress decorated with white and yellow flowers and had pink slippers on her feet. The glasses on her face kept sliding down her small nose.

"Can't you tell a Southerner when you see one?" the old woman asked Captain. "These women aren't Yankees. They're from around here."

"How do you know," Captain said, his voice booming.

"I've been listening to their accents since they came into the house."

"Did you invite them here?" Captain asked.

"No, but my son did and whatever my son wants he gets, so leave it be. It's none of your business. Go back to recuperating. You're not going to shoot anybody today."

With a harrumph, the Captain lay back on the bed and placed the gun on his right side.

"Hello, dears," the old woman said. "My name's Helen. I'm Frank's mom."

Nonie nodded.

"Do you have trouble speaking?" Helen asked.

"No ma'am," Nonie finally answered.

"What?" Buggy asked. "Do you see somebody?"

"A couple of somebodies," Nonie said in a stage whisper. "I'm talking to an old lady right now. Her name is Helen."

"That's the first Ms. Louisiana!" Buggy said. "That's Frank's mom."

"I know. She just told me that. Look, I want you to record just past the fireplace, and aim the IR Vid in that direction." Nonie pointed to where Helen stood. "See if it picks up anything."

"Do we mind if we take pictures of you?" Nonie asked Helen.

Helen tapped her permed hair. "Oh, dear, I'm certainly in no condition for photographs, but I'll allow you one or two."

Nonie held the IR camera, looked through the viewfinder. All she saw was a shadowy silhouette. She took pictures of it regardless.

"Now how can I help you?" Helen asked.

"We're with a scouting team," Nonie said, And we're looking for haunted locations. There's a film crew that wants to put the most haunted locations on television. A program called Something's Out There. "

"I'm picking up moving shadows," Buggy said, her voice shaky.

"Keep filming," Nonie said. "Hopefully we're getting her conversation on the recorder."

"Oh, my goodness," the old woman clapped her hands. Nonie saw the motion but didn't hear the clap. "I would love to be on television. Can you set it up so that I can be?"

"I don't know if anyone would be able to see you."

"Why can you?"

Nonie shrugged. "I have since I was a little girl. See the dead I mean. As for you being on television, I can't promise anything. All we have to do is bring enough evidence to the producers, and they decide whether or not to send a film crew out here."

The old woman pursed her lips, then said, "Okay, what kind of proof can I give you?"

Nonie thought for a second, long enough for

Buggy to nudge her and ask, "What's going on?

"Can you make something move?" Nonie asked.

The old woman laughed. "Make something move? Oh, my dear, I'm quite adept at doing that since I passed on. My arthritis is completely gone."

"What's she saying?" Buggy asked.

"I'll fill you in later," Nonie whispered.

"I take it your friend there can't see or hear me, right?"

"Right."

"What about the young man standing beside you?"

At the mention of someone standing beside her

Nonie flinched and glanced in the direction the old woman indicated. Guy stood next to her grinning like a kid who'd stolen a bag of chips from a vending machine.

"Yes, he can see and hear you. He's passed on, as well, just hasn't made it to the other side yet," Nonie said, giving Guy a hard look.

The old woman nodded her head. "I know where he's coming from. The light came for me, but I wasn't ready to go. Have been in this house with all my memorabilia for way too many years. All the stuff my son is trying to pack away means the world to me. It should be left alone so people who come to visit the house can enjoy it."

"Is that why you're still here?" Nonie asked. "Have you tried communicating that to your son?"

The old woman tsked. "He can't hear or see me. I've tried leaving obscure messages around the house, like unpacking boxes he's already boxed, but he's not really a believer in such things. I want to talk about the television thing again," Helen said.

"How does this work for you?"

"Can you make something move?" Nonie asked.

"Of course, my dear," Helen said with a chuckle. With that she walked over to one of the empty cots that held a Confederate uniform. As she headed that way Nonie told Buggy to aim her video camera in that direction. As soon as the camera was pointed in that direction, one of the cots flipped over on its side.

"Quit showing off," the captain growled.

"Oh, hush, you old coot," Helen said. "I want to be on television." With that she sent the second empty cot sailing across the room.

"Holy crap," Buggy said. "Who's doing that?"

"Mrs. Richardson," Nonie said. "She's determined to be on television."

"How was that?" Helen asked. "Do you think

it'll get their attention?"

"Oh, I'm sure it'll get somebody's attention," Nonie said with a laugh.

"What else can I do?" Helen asked.

Nonie couldn't have asked for a Christmas present that would've made her happier. "See that silver machine on the other side of the mantel?"

"Yes, I saw you put it there."

"It's a digital recorder. If you go near it and speak, it'll pick up whatever you say."

"Buggy," Nonie said. "Aim your camera at the fireplace, where the digital recorder is."

Helen hurried over to the fireplace, her slippers shuffling across the floor. She leaned over to the digital recorder. "Hello, my name is Helen Richardson, and I'm a ghost, but I'm speaking to you now on this machine so I can be on television.

My house is a historical site. It's very old and part of it used to be a hospital during the Civil War. There were many men that came here to be doctored on and sent back to the field. Some, bless their hearts, didn't make it. Me? I just died of old age, right downstairs in my recliner. I guess my body parts just got old and shut down. It wasn't painful, though. Now I feel better than ever. I can come and go where I please and right now I would be pleased if you'd send your film crew over to my house and put me on television. I used to watch the Ed Sullivan show all the time. I think being on television would be the greatest thing ever."

Helen looked over at Nonie as if to confirm that she'd said enough. Nonie nodded. "I can't thank you enough for your help, Mrs. Richardson."

"Call me Helen, please."

"Okay, Helen. Thank you again for your help."

"You're very welcome. Oh, and just so you know, Captain has one of his legs. But his spirit has both, and occasionally he'll go stomping around the house. You had a friend downstairs earlier, snooping around which made Captain angry. So the voice your friend heard downstairs belonged to Captain, and I'm afraid the lump on your friend's head came from Captain, too."

"Who's the young man beside you?" Helen suddenly asked. "Oh, I see, you're one of us." She turned to Nonie. "And you did introduce us before." She tapped a finger against her right temple. "Every once in a while this old clock up here forgets to click to the next second. I apologize for that."

Helen looked at Guy. "My name is Helen. What's yours?"

"Guy Skinard."

Helen lifted a hand to shake his but their palms simply passed through each other.

"Does she see you, as well? Helen asked referring to Nonie.

"Every day," Guy said.

"What a blessing it is to have someone to talk to every day. And what about your friend, the one with the video camera. Does she see anything at all?"

"Nothing," Guy said. "Bug can't see anything but she knows that Nonie can. You know what's odd? If people paid close enough attention, I'd bet anyone could see us if they really tried hard enough. I think some are just too scared and that may be—"

"You said her name is Bug?" Helen asked. "Odd name for a girl."

"It's Buggy," Guy said. "Her real name is

Beatrice, but she'd rather be called by her nickname. Anyway, that may be Buggy's problem. She's just too afraid to see. I'm sure she's fine being afraid and just leaving well enough alone."

"Well, if you don't mind," Helen said with a yawn. "It's way past my naptime. It's been a pleasure meeting all of you, but I think it's time that you leave now. The later it gets, the grouchier Captain gets. I think it's his leg. It's like ghost pains. I think it really starts hurting him. I wish there was more I could do to help him, but, unfortunately, he never went to the light when it called to him. He was too angry over his troops being killed on this property during the war. He wanted to stay around, hoping to be healed so he could find them. I tried to explain it to him that that's not going to happen, but the poor dear won't listen to me. A little hard in the head, if you know what I mean."

"And you're still here because you don't want your son to renovate the house?" Nonie asked.

"Oh, no," Helen said. "He can turn it back to its original splendid glory. In fact that would be wonderful. I just don't want him taking all of my trophies and pictures, all the things I worked so hard for out of the house. I want them to be showcased."

"I know," Nonie said.

"Know what?" Jack asked, suddenly appearing up in the attic.

Helen disappeared in the blink of an eye. Captain remained on his cot, giving Jack a hard, cold look.

"To try to get the EVPs and pictures we need for the production crew," Nonie said. She figured a half lie wasn't as condemning as a balls to the wall lie.

"I heard all kinds of banging going on up here. You two okay?"

"Fine," Nonie said.

"Yeah," Buggy said. "Two cots moved on their own. One flipped over and look . . ." She pointed to the cot on its side on the other side of the room. "That one got thrown."

"We've got pictures of that," Nonie said. "We also did a fairly long EVP session, so I'm sure we'll come up with something."

"Great job," Jack said.

Nonie saw Guy get up and move between her and Jack. He edged closer to Jack until they were nearly nose to nose.

Jack shivered. "Did it suddenly get cold in here, like twenty degrees or something, or is that my imagination?"

"Not that I noticed." Nonie said.

"Maybe we shut it down here for the night," Jack said. "The house isn't that big, and I think we've got plenty of pictures and EVPs to go over to see if we've caught anything."

"You mean besides the lump on your head?" Nonie asked, giving him a half smile.

"Funny."

"What happened?"

"Long story. I'll tell you later."

"Okay, so let's move onto the plantation," Nonie said with a shrug.

"Not until you answer my question," Jack said.

"What question is that?"

"I said it sounded like you were talking to someone other than Buggy. I could hear you all the way downstairs near the hallway."

Nonie shrugged. "We could have been role playing in case we did see someone. You know, figuring out the questions we'd ask, things like that. Maybe that's what you heard." She wasn't very good at lying and knew it.

From the look on Jack's face, he didn't fully believe her either. His eyes were narrowed and suspicious. There was a moment of silence before he said, "Fine, let's move onto the plantation. I'll get Tatman and Shaundelle and let them know."

"Sounds good," Nonie said.

After gathering up the equipment, Jack started down the stairs of the attic with Buggy following right behind. Guy followed after and Nonie pulled up the rear.

When they reached the living room, Jack turned to Buggy and said, "You mind going to get

Shaundelle and Tatman and tell them we're heading for the plantation now. I'll make sure all the equipment down here is rounded up.

"Sure," Buggy said, and hurried off to the kitchen.

Jack turned to Nonie. "You saw something up there, didn't you? You see them don't you?"

"If you're talking about the cots, yes, I saw them move."

"I'm not talking about that."

"What are you talking about then?"

"The dead. You were talking to somebody other than Buggy. I know it as sure as I know my name."

Nonie raised an eyebrow. "I don't know what you're talking about."

"If you can see them, then we'll see them on camera." He held up the digital recorder she had used upstairs. "Better yet, that conversation will be picked up on this recorder, and I'll be able to tell who you were talking to. Buggy or someone else. That's why I'm asking you directly now, so I don't have to question you later."

"You're being a jerk," Nonie said, folding her arms across her chest.

"No, I'm not. I'm just trying to get the truth. If you can actually see these ghosts then that's a huge plus for us."

"All I see is a man trying to force me say something I don't want to say."

"Fine," Jack said. "Have it your way. But I have a feeling we'll be having this discussion again very soon.

A cold sensation suddenly ran up the back of Nonie's spine, and it had nothing to do with a drop in temperature. Realization froze her to one spot for a moment. The recordings. The digital recorder and the camera. If they picked up any of Helen's conversation and the sound of the cots moving, undoubtedly they picked up her voice, too. Her saying she'd seen the dead since she was a little girl. Her responding directly to Helen's questions. She'd screwed up royally. She'd gotten so caught up in the moment that she'd forgotten her deal with Buggy. Nonie was supposed to signal her if she saw a ghost. Not talk to it! Now Jack had the recorder. She'd be busted as surely as a raccoon rummaging through garbage.

CHAPTER FIFTEEN

The plantation house stood approximately seven hundred feet behind the Richardson home and looked creepy as hell. Nonie was anything but excited about having to investigate it.

When they'd wrapped up at the house, Jack went to the back of the van and grabbed more flashlights. He handed one to each person on the team.

"Use them only if absolutely necessary," he said. "The plantation will be great for our IR vid camera and full spectrum camera. Both will get great pictures without any light, which is a good thing since the plantation has no electricity."

"Crap on a saltine, that figures," Shaundelle said, and threw her hands up. "No electricity? Are you kidding? We won't be able to see nothin'"

"That's why I gave all of you flashlights."

"Yeah, but you said not to use them unless it was necessary," Shaundelle fumed. "I consider using a flashlight when I'm walking into an old, creepy joint like that without electricity a necessary."

"Maybe it's not as bad as it looks," Nonie said. "We'll turn the flashlights on when we first get inside. You know, to get a lay of the land."

"Right," Jack said. "Soon as we decide who'll investigate what area, flashlights go off."

"We're not like each going to do a room by ourselves, huh?" Shaundelle asked.

Jack pursed his lips thoughtfully. "It's definitely big enough for us to do that. We could cover more territory—"

"Oh, hell to the hell-no," Shaundelle said. "I'm not goin'—"

"Let him finish," Nonie said, then suddenly saw Guy appear between Jack and Tatman. He scowled at her.

Nonie gritted her teeth to keep from lashing out at him.

"Like I was saying," Jack continued. "It's big enough for each of us to take a different area, but since all of you are new to this, we'll stick to pairs."

"Now you're talkin,'" Shaundelle said.

"Thank G-o-d," Buggy said.

Even Tatman looked relieved, like he'd just passed a pent-up bubble of gas.

The plantation stood two and a half stories tall with a pair of dormers resting on the edge of the roof, facing the front porch. By flashlight, it looked like the building had once been painted white with green shutters. Now most of the paint on the clapboard structure had either curled up, chipped off or had bowed to naked wood.

Nonie aimed her flashlight at the multiple windows from the first floor up to the dormers that had center panes. She didn't see one that hadn't been shattered.

Four large, round pillars, also in desperate need of paint, were attached to the roof's edge that hung over a sagging porch. Chipped and dirt-covered brick steps led the way up to a wide porch.

"H-How do we get inside?" Nonie asked, feeling sweat form at the nape of her neck despite the cool November night breeze. As angry as she'd been moments ago when she'd spotted Guy and he'd vanished, she wished him back.

"Through the front door," Jack said. "It's not locked."

Shaundelle shook her head vigorously, dreadlocks flying. "Breakin' and enterin'. Breakin' and enterin. We gonna wind up in jail."

"No we're not," Jack said. "Remember, I told you I spoke to the cops, to the city, and as long as we don't take anything from the house, they've allowed us access."

"Yeah, but what if some rookie shows up," Shaundelle said. "And he don't know squat about who you talked to. We gonna wind up in the back of a squad car for sure."

"Trust me," Jack said. "That won't happen. I promise."

"Let's get this over with," Nonie said. "It's getting late, and I've got a funeral to work in the morning."

"I thought you said your mom and Margaret gave you the day off tomorrow?" Buggy said.

Nonie eyed her for ratting her out. "Yeah . . . well . . . Let's just get this over with."

Jack aimed his flashlight at the porch as they made their way to the front door. "Be careful climbing up here. The porch is sagging badly, and there're a few broken boards."

"Aren't we going to get the equipment?" Tatman asked, following up the rear as they entered the house.

"Yeah, but I want to make sure we're not facing another Richardson hoarding before we started unloading everything."

The front door gave an ominous creak as Jack turned the knob and pushed it open. Everyone stepped inside huddled together.

"I don't like this place," Nonie said, her ghost radar on high alert. It felt like a low-voltage electrical current running through her body.

"Ditto that, girl," Shaundelle said.

A short foyer opened up into a large sitting room. Two old, dusty rockers sat against one wall and an even dustier piano sat against the opposite wall. Aside from that, the room was void of everything, including light. Jack led them to a room off to the left, where an old wooden dining table, large enough to seat ten stood in the middle of the room. No chairs surrounded it. A soot-covered fireplace sat against the west wall. One could only assume this used to be a dining room.

The plantation seemed to be one big square, like a large box with walls separating rooms for general purposes. Jack aimed his flashlight at the doorway to the right of the dining room. The room behind it held a fireplace, similar to the one in the dining room, yet nothing else. They followed Jack's flashlight to the right, into another doorway, which led to a large, dusty, empty room.

As they continued in what seemed like a ceremonial circle, the next door led to what appeared to have once been a sitting room. A ratty, old, cloth-covered couch sat in the middle of the room. One more doorway led them into what appeared to have been a bedroom. Someone must have attempted an upgrade, however, for where a bed should have been, stood a wall with a toilet behind it.

The last room in the circle of doorways was the kitchen. It held a hearth, rat feces on the wooden countertops, chipped ceramic sinks, and an old icebox. Out of all the rooms they'd covered so far, this one seemed to be twenty degrees colder than the rest.

"We've got plenty of room to set up a command center," Jack said.

"Aren't you going to check out the upstairs before you set anything up?" Nonie asked.

"We'll start setting up down here, then do a walk-through upstairs and see how many rooms we have to cover. I may not have enough cameras to cover both floors at one time, which is why I suggest we start down here."

"While you set up, mind if Buggy and I check upstairs?" Nonie asked.

Buggy went wide-eyed. "Are you crazy? All we have are flashlights. And look at those old creaky stairs. Half the banister is gone. You've got a death wish or what?"

"Then I'll take Shaundelle with me," Nonie said, determined to get upstairs. She'd hoped it would have been Buggy because she wanted to call out to Guy and see if he was around.

"This black girl ain't goin' nowhere right now," Shaundelle said. "Jack said we'd check it out later. I don't know why you want to go up there now. To find trouble?"

"Just curious," Nonie said, frustrated. She couldn't ask Tatman because Jack needed him to set up cameras and the main monitor.

Nonie shrugged. "Fine, I'll go alone."

"Stop trippin', Nonie. You're not going up there alone," Buggy said.

"Then are you coming?"

Buggy let out a loud sigh and clicked on her flashlight. "Yeah, okay, I'll go, but you're gonna take the lead, and I'm hanging on to your shirt for dear life. So if something pops up, don't count on me to save you 'cause I'll be hauling ass back downstairs."

"Just a quick run-through," Nonie said, trying to signal Buggy with her eyes that there was a direct purpose for her wanting to leave the group.

Buggy didn't catch the signal. Instead, she grabbed hold of the back of Nonie's shirt, and said, "If we're going to do a run-through, then you best get to runnin' before I chicken out."

As soon as they hit the landing and were out of earshot, Nonie whispered in Buggy's ear. "He's not here."

Buggy's eyes grew wider. "He who?"

"Guy."

Buggy let out a relieved breath. "I thought you were going to say a demon or some weird crap like that. Where'd he go? You'd think he'd a least be here watching your back."

Nonie flashed her light about. "Earlier, when I told Shaundelle to give Jack a chance to finish what he was saying, you should have seen the eyes Guy gave me. You'd have sworn I'd kissed Jack right on the mouth in front of everyone."

"Well, that's not hard to figure out," Buggy said. "Guy's jealous. If he thought you were taking sides with Jack, it probably pissed him off."

"Pissed off I can understand," Nonie said, "but what if he shows up and starts acting stupid because he's mad? You know, throwing things around, moving through different rooms as a shadow?"

Buggy shrugged. "All we can do is document what we see. I don't think the producer is going to care what or who it came from. As long as we get activity on camera, we're golden."

"When he saw how upset I was, he faded out. I think he's still in the house. I just don't know where."

Buggy gave her a stern look. "If he jumps out of some hidey-hole and scares me, I'll bash in what little brains he's got left."

"No brain bashing," Nonie said. "Besides, no matter what you threw at him, it'd just go straight through his body. He's a ghost, remember?"

"All this talk about ghosts is giving me the willies," Buggy said with a shiver. "Let's go back downstairs and see what room we've been assigned to."

"Wait, there's worse."

Buggy gulped.

"Remember back at the Richardson house? The recorder and camera upstairs?"

"Yeah."

"I forgot to give you signals like we talked about at the funeral home. I blabbered all up in those recorders talking to Helen."

"Shit."

"I know, right? Now Jack's got the recorder. He's going to hear everything I ran my mouth about."

"Double shit."

"That's what I'm saying."

"What're you going to do?"

Nonie sighed. "Lie my ass off I guess. I don't know."

Buggy blew out a breath. "We'd better get downstairs before someone comes looking for us."

With a nod, Nonie headed down the short set of steps from the first landing. She'd barely made it to the second step when something pushed her hard from behind, and she tumbled to the floor.

"Are you all right?" Buggy asked, hovering over her.

Groaning, Nonie got to her feet. "Yeah, but why did you push me like that?"

Buggy's face turned ashen. "I never touched you, Nonie. I was following one step above you when I suddenly saw you go ass over teakettle, onto the floor. Thank heaven that was a short landing!"

It was then Nonie heard a giggle, a deep-throated giggle with malice laced through it.

"Who's here?" Nonie asked, holding onto the banister. "Guy?"

No response.

"Why would he push you that way?" Buggy said. "You could've broken a hand or a leg."

"Because I don't think it was Guy. Someone else is here."

"Can you see them?"

"No."

"Let's get the hell out of here," Buggy said. "Meet up with the group."

Shaken, Nonie simply nodded her head and headed towards the voices coming from the room with the hand-hewn wall and toilet.

Shaundelle gave both a double-take when they walked into the room. "Where've y'all been? And why do both of your faces look so white it looks like you've put flour on them?"

Not wanting to scare Shaundelle even before they started, Nonie came up with a bold-faced lie. "We went to the first landing to check it out, and when we were heading back down, I tripped and fell down the last two steps."

"Shouldn't have been up there alone," Tatman said.

"Yeah, that's what you get for wondering around on your own like that," Shaundelle said. "You're lucky you didn't break something."

"Are you okay?" Jack asked Nonie.

"A little sore, but I'll survive."

As Jack and Tatman unrolled wires and set up the monitor on top of the piano, Jack glanced at Nonie. "See anything while you were up there?"

"Nothing," Nonie said, opting not to mention the shove. And she hadn't lied to him. She hadn't seen anything. "But we only went up to the first landing of the staircase. None of the rooms."

Jack continued to study her face for a moment longer as if knowing something had happened, but allowing her to reveal it in her own time.

"So how are we breaking this up down here?" Nonie asked in an attempt to shake her concentration away from his lips. His full, luscious lips. Just staring at them started a fire burning in her belly.

"Tatman and I are going to get my small generator out of the van since there's no power here. The cameras operate on batteries, but not the monitor. After that, Shaundelle and Tatman will take the room that looked like it was once used as a dining room. I'll take the other two rooms and you and Buggy will take the kitchen."

At the sound of "kitchen" Nonie felt like a block of ice slid down her spine. Of all the rooms they had to investigate down here, for some reason, the kitchen was the last one she wanted.

"How about we switch," Nonie said to Shaundelle. "Buggy and I will take the dining room and you and Tatman the kitchen."

Shaundelle's eyes narrowed. "Is there something in that kitchen we should know about?"

"I don't know," Nonie said. "We haven't been in there yet."

Shaundelle pursed her lips and looked over at Tatman who shook his head.

"Nah," Shaundelle said. "We'll stick with the dining room. More room to run the hell out of there if we do catch something."

"Why don't you want the kitchen?" Buggy asked. "Seemed pretty innocuous to me. I mean, it is, right?"

Not wanting to set off any alarms, Nonie shrugged. "Just not fond of rat turds everywhere." But something was bothering her. She hadn't seen any spirits when they'd gone into the kitchen, but her gut told her otherwise. Sure, one of them could have been Guy, and she hoped it was. But something else lurked in the dark corners of that room. And it was angry and disgruntled that they were there, and planned to get rid of them as quickly as possible. She hadn't seen it yet, but knew it would reveal itself once she and Buggy were alone in the room.

Jack handed Nonie the full spectrum camera and a digital recorder. This time he gave Buggy the Rem Pod and an IR camera.

As he handed out more equipment to Shaundelle and Tatman, he reminded them about the plan. "Lights on for just a few seconds so you can get a handle on what's in the room and won't trip over anything. Then lights off. You'll be able to see the room through the camera. The colors will be different, though."

"Where's them walkie things?" Shaundelle asked. "I want to be able to get hold of somebody if anything weird goes down."

"Was just about to hand them out," Jack said, then gave everyone a walkie-talkie. "Only use them if there's a problem. No chitchat about who'll be doing what next Saturday night, okay?"

"Gotcha," Shaundelle said. "But like me and Tatman can talk between each other, right?"

"Sure," Jack said. "Just keep the chatter about the case and keep it to a minimum. If you don't, you might miss something."

"Like what?" Shaundelle asked, bug-eyed.

'Voices, banging sounds, whispers. Things like that."

"Crap on a saltine—you mean we could hear whispering and banging?" Shaundelle said.

"I'm saying just in case. You don't want to be talking a blue streak and miss out on anything relevant that could be recorded. Now all of you stay put for a bit, Tatman and I have two more cameras to set up down here and get the generator, then we'll be ready to go live."

As soon as the guys left to finish up the camera work, Shaundelle asked Nonie, "How come you wanted to switch rooms earlier?"

Nonie shrugged and stuck to her story. "Too many rat turds on the counter. Creeps me out."

"So you'd rather I stick my hand in the turds than you?"

"No, no," Nonie protested. "I-I kind of freak out with stuff like that, and you're a stronger woman than I am."

"Hmm," Shaundelle said, then went over to examine the piano.

As she clunked on the keys that were so far out of tune she might as well have been playing a ukulele, Buggy asked Nonie, "We're going to be in deep shit in there, aren't we?"

"Where?"

"The kitchen."

"I don't know about deep shit, but I think it's going to get messy."

"So why don't we just back out now?"

"Five hundred bucks, that's why. It won't be anything we can't handle, but the cash I can definitely handle."

"You'll give me a thumbs-up if anything shows, and I can't see it, right?

"You have my word."

Buggy studied her face for a moment. "For some reason that gives me absolutely no comfort."

CHAPTER SIXTEEN

The one thing Guy Skinard did best when he was bored was snoop, which was exactly what he was doing while, Mr. Know-It-All Jack, was giving everyone instructions downstairs. Since Nonie had been assigned the kitchen area, Guy figured it best if he check it out before she went inside. That way, if anything out of the ordinary was running about, he could let her know about it—and hopefully get back in her good graces.

Dodging his way from room to room so Nonie wouldn't spot him, Guy finally made it back downstairs and into the kitchen—and wished he hadn't.

There, standing near a fireplace where he assumed most of the cooking had been done years ago, stood a large black woman with a thick neck. She looked to be about thirty-five-years-old, was taller than he was by an inch and outweighed him by at least a hundred pounds. She wore a faded pink and white kerchief wrapped around her head, a brown dress that looked like it had been made out of burlap, and stood barefoot. She held a flat iron skillet in her right hand.

"What you think you doin' here in my kitchen, white boy? I sure as hell didn't give you no invite." She slapped the flat of the skillet against the palm of her hand as if to illustrate the sound it would make pinging against his head. Her eyes were squinty, her lips huge, and her nostrils flared from cheek to cheek. He could see through the woman to the wall directly behind her. "I think it be about time you gets to steppin'."

Guy held up his hands as if in surrender. "We were given permission to come here," he said. "Sort of."

"What you mean sorta?" She took a step toward him, then stopped and cocked her head to one side. "You playin' games with me or are you for real? I can see the cabinets on the other side of you. You one of us?"

"If you mean dead, yeah," Guy said. "Look, my girlfriend and some of her friends were told by the state that no one lived here and hadn't for over ten years. They said as long as they didn't take anything from the house—not that there's much to take— they could do an investigation."

"What kinda investigation?"

"They're looking for ghosts."

The woman let out a loud belly laugh. "Your girlfriend got one up her nose and don't even know it?"

"She knows."

The woman took a step closer, her expression morphing from anger to curiosity. "How she know?"

"She sees me."

"She see all the dead?"

"Not all of them, but some. More than me if that's what you're asking."

The woman slapped the flat iron against her palm again. "What's your name, boy?"

"Guy Skinard. What's yours?"

"Tiana Lewis. How long it's been for you?"

"How long has what been?"

"Since you been dead, idiot. What you think I mean?"

"A little over nine years."

Tiana twirled the handle of the skillet in her hand. "Me? Not sure. A hundred, hundred twenty-five years I suppose."

"You don't look old enough to have been here that long."

"Boy, don't you know nothin'?" Whens you die, you stay stuck at the age you died. I was fifty-two back in the day."

"So why are you still here?" Guy asked. "Didn't the light come for you when you died? Didn't you see it?"

"Oh, I seen lights alright, but they was torchlights. White men, carrying torches. Hung me and my man out on that big oak tree out back. My eleven-year-old boy, too."

Guy felt his jaw drop. "I'm. . . I'm sorry that happened to you."

Tiana nodded slightly and slapped the skillet hard against her palm again.

"What happened afterward?" Guy asked quietly. "Didn't you see another kind of light? A bright, welcoming one?"

She pursed her lips and lifted her chin. "Yeah, I seen it. My man and boy went right to it."

"What color was that light?"

"Blue. Why you ask? Don't you know the color? Ain't you seen yours?"

"Yes, but mine was purple."

"Hmm," Tiana said. "Purple. That be my favorite color."

"Why was yours blue and mine purple you think?" Guy asked. "I hear other lights are white. Why the color difference?"

"I look like Gawd to you?" Tiana said. "I don't know the why part. You can ask Him when you decide to move on your ownself. That's all Gawd's doin'."

"Why didn't you follow your light?" Guy asked.

"And leave them men here to get away with what they did? Not me. Huh-uh. Somebody gotta make them pay."

"But you've been here so long. Don't you think they'd all be dead by now?"

A cold, steely look crossed Tiana's face. "Maybe. Maybe not. That's why I here. Waitin'."

"For what?"

Before Tiana could answer, Guy heard voices in the hallway that led to the kitchen. They belonged to Nonie and Buggy.

Tiana's lips turned into a hard, straight line and her eyes narrowed. "Who's that?" she demanded. "Them people you say wanna find a ghost?"

Guy nodded. "A couple of them. Two women. I recognize their voices. One's my girlfriend, the other is a close friend of hers."

Scowling, Tiana said, "This close friend got the eye her, too?"

"The eye?"

"You not too bright for a white boy, huh? The eye, boy. Can she see you like your lady friend can see you?"

"Oh," Guy said, feeling stupid for not catching on the first time. "No, she can't see me. But she's going to see that skillet you've got floating around in midair by itself. You might want to put that down for now."

Tiana twirled the skillet handle in her hand again. "This here ain't goin' nowhere 'cept where it's at."

"If they see it, they'll take pictures and video it moving around in thin air. You want that?"

"What's that a video?"

Guy shifted nervously from foot to foot as he heard Nonie and Buggy drawing closer to the kitchen. "It's sort of like a camera only it takes constant pictures of things and people as they move around."

"A camera?"

Blowing out an exasperated breath, Guy mimed holding a camera and made clicking sounds as he pressed his finger against an imaginary button. Then he mimed holding a camcorder and made whirring sounds, trying to mimic the sounds it made while recording.

Tiana frowned, looking utterly confused.

Hearing Nonie's voice ever closer he held up his hands and said to Tiana, "Look, they're going to be holding boxes that have lights on them."

"They bes' not be bringing no boxes with lights up in here," Tiana declared, holding up the skillet like a tennis racket.

"No, no!" Guy said. "The boxes can't hurt you. Nobody here is going to hurt you."

"You gots that right!"

Suddenly a loud gasp then a short scream came from the kitchen entryway. Guy glanced over his shoulder. It was Nonie and Buggy, both standing with mouths agape, staring in Tiana's direction at the skillet twirling in midair.

"Everything all right back there?" a man's voice called from somewhere else in the house. By the tone of it, Guy guessed it to be Jack.

"Uh-no," Buggy wheezed.

Nonie poked her with an elbow, her eyes flitting between Guy and Tiana, then called out. "Fine. Everything's fine."

Evidently her assurance wasn't required because Tatman abruptly popped his head around the kitchen entryway. "We've got power, so I'm gonna set up a stationary . . . fuck a duck!"

Guy grimaced, figuring Tatman's response to seeing an iron skillet swinging in midair was about as appropriate as it got.

The camera Tatman held in his right hand shook as he aimed it at the skillet. He shouted at Nonie and Buggy, "Use your cameras for damn's sake! Turn on the Rem Pod, the recorder, hell y'all do something!"

Buggy fumbled with the Rem Pod, and when she finally managed to turn it on, the circular puck let out a shrill squeal that remained constant, and its lights began to flash like Christmas tree ornaments gone awry.

As Nonie scrambled to get the digital recorder working Tatman, breathing hard and uttering "Damn . . . damn . . ." every couple of seconds tried holding his shaking camera straight while he yelled over his shoulder, "Jack, ya need to get in here now!"

Guy couldn't help but grin. He'd tried to get Tiana to lose the skillet, mostly for Nonie's sake. But now, maybe the skillet wasn't such a bad idea. If Tatman was this shaken up by what he saw, for all Guy knew, Jack might witness it and go running for the hills. He could only hope that would be the case. He'd love nothing better than for Nonie to witness Mr. Hunk turn into Mr. Chicken.

CHAPTER SEVENTEEN

Nonie blew out a frustrated breath. She had the digital recorder running in one hand and was trying to hold the full spectrum camera steady in the other. She clearly saw the large black woman swinging the skillet as easily as she saw Guy standing not far from her. With Tatman in the room, however, she couldn't directly address Guy or the woman. All she could do was stand there and look as astonished as everyone else. She heard footsteps rushing towards the kitchen.

"Are you two getting this?" Tatman asked breathlessly. "I mean—I mean . . . holy crap!"

"What's going—" Jack's flashlight beam crossed the threshold only seconds before he did. Evidently he wasn't used to seeing inanimate objects twirling in midair because he pulled up short and his mouth fell open, dropping his words in midsentence. He glanced from Tatman to Buggy then Nonie before his eyes zeroed in on the skillet again.

Nonie saw Guy arch a brow at the large black woman.

"I told you to put it down," he told her.

The woman harrumphed. "I ain't gots to do nothin' I don't wants to do, boy. Them days of people telling me, Tiana do this, Tiana don't do that is long gone."

"Yeah, but look at what it's caused," Guy said. "Now you'll never get rid of them."

A grin spread over the woman's face. "Oh, I can gets rid of 'em. That be for sure."

Jack trained the camera he had hanging around his neck on the skillet. "You catching this, Tat?"

"Hell, yeah," Tatman assured him.

"Nonie, is the recorder running?"

Nonie nodded, then realized Jack wasn't looking her way. He was too busy snapping still shots of the skillet action. "Yep, it's on," she said. "I've got the full spectrum running, too."

"Anything showing up on the FS?" Jack asked.

She looked over at the screen and saw a large shadow shaped just like Tiana, swinging what looked like a flat iron from hand to hand. "Big shadow. Shaped like a woman."

"Let me see," Jack said hurrying over to her side.

Nonie handed him the camera. It wasn't as if she'd lied to him. Through the lens of the full spectrum, Tiana was seen as a shadow. She just hadn't revealed that she knew for a fact that it was a woman because she saw her with her own eyes in Technicolor standing only a few feet away.

"Oh, man, this is excellent!" Jack said. "Hold the recorder out in the direction of the skillet, Nonie."

When she did as asked, Jack said loudly, "Whoever's here, can you tell us your name?"

Nonie saw Tiana look at Guy. "Why he wants to know my name for?"

Guy shrugged nonchalantly.

"Are you a man or a woman?" Jack asked.

Tiana snorted. "I be a woman, fool."

"You've gotta remember he can't see you," Guy said. "Only one of the people here can. My girlfriend."

"Which one she be?"

Guy pointed to Nonie. "That real pretty one. Longish brown hair, big eyes, small nose."

"What her name be?"

"Nonie."

"What she got in her hand?"

"It's called a recorder. You talk into it, and it plays back what you said."

A look of astonishment crossed Tiana's face. "Even if the person talkin' be dead?"

"The dead are different. Sometimes it picks up our voices. Sometimes not."

"Why some and not all?"

"No idea."

Tiana stilled the swinging skillet and took a few steps closer to Nonie and the recorder she held out in one hand.

Everyone in the room, except Nonie, gasped as the skillet moved closer to them.

Tiana looked from Nonie to Jack to Buggy to Tatman before turning her attention back to the recorder. She leaned over and said loudly. "My name be Tiana Lewis."

"How old are you?" Jack asked.

Tiana gave Guy a quizzical look. "That machine didn't say what I said. How come?"

"They have to rewind it in order to hear what was said," Guy told her.

"Well, what they waitin' for? I wants to hear what I said."

Nonie heard a loud *clunk* from another part of the house, then Shaundelle yelled out, "Where the hell'd everybody go?"

"In here!" Tatman shouted back, not taking his eye off his camera's screen.

Heavy, quick footsteps made their way to the kitchen. Shaundelle stomped her way inside and propped her hands on her hips. "Why you left me back there by myself, dude. Ain't we supposed to be sticking together? What the hell all y'all doin' in here anyway?"

Tatman glanced over at Shaundelle, then stepped to one side, giving her a bird's-eye view of the floating skillet.

For a moment, Nonie thought Shaundelle's eyes were going to pop out of her head. "I—I—Oh, lawd Jesus of Nazareth." Obviously in shock, her voice was barely audible. She took a step back, then another.

"She belong to y'all?" Tiana asked Nonie.

Unable to answer, Nonie shot Guy a look.

"Her name's Shaundelle," Guy said. "And she doesn't belong to anybody but herself."

"Say what?" Tiana asked. "Who be her master then?"

"She doesn't have one," Guy said. "It's not like back in your day, Tiana. Slavery's been done away with a long time now."

Tiana gave Nonie an astonished look. "You mean all y'all white people here ain't got no slaves? Y'all gots to do y'all own cookin' and cleanin' and everythin'?"

Nonie gave a slight nod of her head, hoping everyone's attention was still on the skillet and not on her.

"What's the matter with you woman? She too uppity to talk to me?" Tiana asked Guy.

"The others don't know she can see you or me, and she doesn't want them to know," he said.

"How come? Aw, never mind, I knows how come. They'd be all over her all the time, right? Nonie can you see my dead mama. Nonie can you see my dead sister. Nonie, Nonie, all the time Nonie, right?"

Nonie gave another slight nod.

Tiana tsked. "See, I knows."

"I'm gonna . . .uh . . ." Shaundelle took another step back, then another. "I'm gonna . . .uh . . . wait in the van. Yeah, that's what I'm gonna do . . . wait in the van!" With that, Shaundelle turned on her heels and hightailed it out of the kitchen. Seconds later Nonie heard the front door of the house slam shut.

"We've got some great shots with the full spectrum," Jack said. "With any luck, we'll get some class A EVPs."

Tiana looked over at Guy. "You know, them is some boring ass people if you ask me. They get all excited about seeing my fry pan, then ask dumb questions. I think I'm gonna stirs them up a little."

Nonie didn't particularly care for the twinkle she saw in Tiana's eye.

"Don't you think we have enough evidence?" Nonie quickly asked Jack. "Tatman's been shooting with his camera, the Rem Pod has been going off nonstop, and we've got stills of a pretty decent size shadow. Maybe it's time we go. Leave the rest for the film crew."

"Are you kidding?" Jack said. "Look at that skillet still floating over there by itself. That's got to mean something's holding it. If we hang around long enough, maybe do a little coaxing, we might catch a full-bodied apparition."

"Oh, uh-uh," Buggy said. "No full-bodied anything for me thanks. I've seen enough with just that pan."

"Do you mind that we're here?" Jack asked, questioning the floating skillet once more. "If you want us to stay, can you move that pan? Lift it higher?"

Tiana scowled at Jack like he was a kid too bored to do anything but play in a mud hole. She kept the skillet still.

"If you want us to leave, can you move the pan lower, maybe put it on the floor?" Jack asked.

Tiana winked at Guy then slapped the bottom of the skillet hard against the palm of her hand. It made a thunking sound that made all of them, including Guy, jump.

"I'm tired of all they mess," Tiana finally said, then raised the skillet over her head and took three quick steps toward Jack and Tatman. She swung the pan once, missing Tatman's head by inches.

Tatman let out a gasp and both men stepped back a couple of feet.

As the men chattered amongst themselves, Buggy grabbed Nonie by the shirt and leaned into her and whispered softly, "What's she doing?"

"Looks like she's about to bounce that pan over somebody's head if you ask me," Nonie said, keeping her voice barely audible.

"W-We should leave now," Buggy said. "I think we pissed it off."

"Right, yeah," Tatman agreed, backing up until he reached the threshold of the kitchen archway. "I'll start pulling in cables. That work for you, Jack?"

Instead of answering, Jack took the recorder from Nonie's hand and stepped closer to the offending skillet. "What's your name? Did you die in this house? Do you own this house?"

Tiana's expression went from one of amusement to aggravation. She gave Nonie a quizzical look. "How come you with them busybodies anyways, askin' all them questions like any of it's their business?"

Nonie pursed her lips and gave Tiana the slightest shrug, hoping neither Jack nor Tatman noticed.

Snorting out a heavy breath from her nose, Tiana suddenly charged Jack like a bull who'd been teased one too many times.

"Shit!" Jack quick-stepped backward. "Okay, we'll leave."

Tiana pulled up short, but started twirling the skillet in her hand.

"Pack it up, Tat," Jack called out to Tatman, who'd already hurried out of the kitchen. "Nonie, Buggy, grab your equipment and go to the van."

Not needing to be told twice, Nonie and Buggy collected the equipment they'd been assigned to, including the recorder, which Nonie plucked out of Jack's hand and hurried out of the kitchen. Neither of them looked back until they were outside and had made it to the van. The night was starless, cool, yet seemed to be charged with electricity. It only made things seem more ominous. They both grabbed for the rear door handle and pulled but it wouldn't open.

Shaundelle's face suddenly appeared in the passenger window, eyes bugged, mouth agape.

"Unlock the doors," Buggy yelled. "Let us in."

"Them boogities follow you?" Shaundelle shouted back.

With her hands full of cameras, Buggy turned to one side and kicked the van door. "Open the frigging door. It's just us!"

In that second the door slid open, and Shaundelle motioned for them to get in quickly. "Hurry up before something comes sneakin' in here with y'all. Where's Tatman and Jack?"

With a loud clatter, the back doors of the van flew open, and Tatman all but threw cameras and cable into the cargo area.

"Get in so I can lock the doors again," Shaundelle told him.

"Can't. Gotta go get the monitor," Tatman said. He slammed one of the back doors shut and left the second one open. "Jack's pulling in the rest of the equipment. Y'all need to come help."

"You lost your head?" Shaundelle said incredulously. "I ain't goin' back in there!"

"No way, Jose," Buggy said. "Jack said come to the van, so we're in the van."

"I'll come," Nonie said, and opened the passenger door. Just as she turned to get out of the van, Buggy grabbed her arm and pulled her back inside.

"Stay," Buggy said, looking Nonie right in the eye. "Stay put." By the look on Buggy's face, Nonie knew she wanted to say a hell of lot more than she was saying but kept her words to herself.

She shook free of Buggy's grasp. "I'll be okay. No problem."

"No problem?" Shaundelle said loudly. "What's wrong with you, girl? Didn't you see that pan floating around all by itself? How can you say no worries? There's for sure boogities up in that house. Y'all got it on film, on recorder, now it's time to get the hell outta here."

"Won't be but a minute," Nonie assured them, then amidst Buggy and Shaundelle's loud protests, hopped out of the van and hurried back.

After doing a quick hop, skip and duck onto the porch, she rushed into the house. "What else do you need out of here?" she asked Tatman who was hurriedly wrapping cable around the base of a large monitor.

"This is all that's left down here," he said, glancing nervously over his shoulder toward the kitchen. "Jack's upstairs collecting the last two stand-alone cameras."

They heard a loud clopping sound coming from the stairway and both Tatman and Nonie stood at attention. So did every hair on Nonie's arms.

"What the . . .?" Tatman began.

Jack came swinging past the last landing and bounded down the creaky staircase. "Got them," he said, holding up two cameras like they were trophies from a last-man-standing contest. "Let's go."

Without so much as a second glance toward the kitchen the three of them hurried for the front door with Nonie and Jack squeezing through it at the same time. Tatman followed so closely behind he might as well have been their shadow.

Once the rest of the equipment was loaded into the van, the three of them jumped inside, Jack at the wheel. It took him all of two seconds to turn the engine over, slap the gear shift into drive and stomp on the accelerator. The van lurched, then shot out of the driveway like it had been infused with rocket fuel.

CHAPTER EIGHTEEN

For the last twenty miles, no one spoke a word. Jack drove with his eyes locked onto the road but his mind was filled with everything that had happened at the old plantation. In all the time he'd been doing investigations, never had he witnessed anything so—overtly paranormal.

The moment they'd left the plantation, everyone in the van seemed to give a collective sigh of relief, then began to talk all at once. They started to recount everything they'd seen or heard from the Richardson house and the plantation. Tatman had kicked off the conversation, then Shaundelle chimed in along with Buggy, each talking over the other. Jack had added his own two cents, but he'd been more interested in what the others had to say as they'd witnessed more than he had. He couldn't help but notice how quiet Nonie was, however. She only offered a comment or two when directly addressed but didn't offer a recall of her experiences at all.

Jack had kept an eye on Nonie from the rearview mirror. She looked distracted, as if wishing everyone would talk about something else for a change. The only time she'd truly interacted with the group was when a small argument broke out between Tatman and Shaundelle.

"Man, oh, man, we made some moolah tonight!" Tatman had said. "Right, Jack? Those producers can't deny some of the things we picked up in both houses?"

"I just hope it shows up when Jack reviews the footage on the cameras and the audio on the recorders," Buggy said. "Suppose we went through all of that tonight and nothing shows up on film?"

"Stop being such a party popper," Shaundelle said.

"You mean a party pooper," Tatman corrected.

Shaundelle batted a hand at him. "Whatever. We caught some good stuff. Better than what those guys on TV get when they go ghost hunting. Me? I think we're gonna wind up being stars."

Tatman snorted. "A falling star maybe. You ran out of that plantation so fast, a comet couldn't have caught up with you."

Shaundelle tsked and flipped her hair away from her shoulder with a hand. "I just wasn't prepared for that skillet thing. You gots to be prepared for weird shit like that."

"You've got to be prepared for anything no matter where we go," Tatman shot back. "It's not like somebody gives us a what-to-expect map for any of these places. All we know is that they're supposed to be haunted then get some evidence if it is. You didn't stick around long enough at the plantation to get anything but a rash from running out so fast. With all the evidence we got, I think they should split your five hundred between me, Nonie, Buggy, and Jack. You didn't hang around long enough to get jack-shit."

"Hey, dude, don't you be messin' with my money. I was in the house, saw that pan hangin' in the air like it was a balloon. That's enough evidence. My own two eyes." Shaundelle scooted to the edge of the backseat and tapped Jack on the shoulder. "Ain't that right, Jack? I get my green for the plantation, right?"

Not wanting to further the argument, Jack agreed that she'd get paid. He hadn't counted on any of them running out if they were confronted with an entity. In truth, the fact that Shaundelle had run off without collecting any evidence and would get paid the same as everyone else didn't feel fair. But he hadn't established any rules from the get-go, which could have clarified a situation like that. So, to make sure he didn't forget in the near future, he established it right then and there.

"From now on, though, if anyone leaves a site without helping to obtain evidence, they'll have to be excluded from pay. It's just not fair to the rest who stick around."

"Yeah, but what if that evidence can cause danger to one or all of us?" Nonie asked. "You can't just make us stand there like fools, waiting to get blasted by some pissed-off ghost. There's got to be some safe word, some sort of protocol if shit starts getting deep. Money's not worth putting any of us in danger."

"That's different," Jack said. "If a situation looks or feels dangerous, anyone has the right to get out."

"Well, why you think I hauled my butt out that place?" Shaundelle said. "If a floatin' around frying pan don't look dangerous, then I don't know what do."

"She's right," Buggy said with a hearty nod.

"I'll give you that," Jack said, remembering how the skillet had wound up chasing them all out of the house. If anything, Shaundelle might have been smarter than all of them put together because she'd left before the entity threatened to attack.

"Let's just agree to stick together. No one left floating around a location alone, okay?" Jack said. "That way if something comes up and gets out of hand, we'll all make the call to bail."

"Sounds fair enough," Tatman said.

"Yeah," Shaundelle said. "'Cept I ain't gonna be waitin' for the rest of you to wise up about what is or ain't getting' out of hand. I can see with my own two eyes. The way I sees it, if a spook gets up in our face, we out the place. Now see that? I made a motto for our Krewe. Spook in the face, get out the place. What y'all think?"

"Works for me," Buggy said.

"Sure," Nonie said quietly, staring out the passenger side window.

"Work for you, Jack?" Tatman asked before offering his two cents.

"Yeah," Jack said, then gave all of them a quick glance. "Just remember that we don't get paid unless we're able to bring back evidence. So sometimes things may get a little spooky, but we've got to get that on film, audio, doesn't matter. Dangerous is different. No amount of money is worth getting hurt over."

They rode in silence until Jack pulled into Tatman's driveway and stopped the van. "I'll be going over all of the recordings we did tonight to see if we got any class A EVPs and also all the camera work. See if we might have picked up more than we actually saw. Then I'll bring everything over to the producer."

"When'll we get our money?" Shaundelle asked.

"I'll push for tomorrow," Jack said. "The next day at the latest."

Evidently satisfied with Jack's answer, Tatman grinned and opened the front passenger door. "Can't wait. Hey, y'all don't have to stay cramped up back there," he said to Shaundelle, Nonie, and Buggy. "Somebody can ride shotgun."

"That'd be me," Shaundelle said. "Since I'm the next drop-off."

Once Shaundelle moved from the back of the van to the front seat and everyone had bid Tatman good night, Jack took off once more. He only had three more stops to make, only he wanted to make sure Nonie's was the last one. He wanted a chance to talk to her alone.

By the time he dropped Shaundelle and Buggy off at their respective houses, and he'd coaxed

Nonie into the front passenger seat, she let out an expansive yawn.

"Sorry," Nonie said, glancing at the clock illuminated on the van's dash. It was three minutes to one in the morning.

"Long night, I know," Jack said. "That's one of the challenges with investigating. Sometimes you have to wait for hours before anything makes itself known. Luckily that wasn't the case tonight."

Nonie nodded, offered him a small smile, then glanced over the seat toward the back of the van.

"Is something bothering you?" Jack asked. "You were pretty quiet on the ride back here. Even now you seem a little . . . I don't know . . . jumpy maybe?"

"No," Nonie said a bit too cheerfully. "Guess it's just from being tired. Had a big funeral before we went out tonight. Still haven't regrouped from that yet."

They rode in silence for a minute or two before Jack worked up the nerve to say, "Do you mind if I ask you a couple of questions?"

He chanced a glance in her direction and caught her staring at him. Even in the dark, it was easy to make out her small nose, her full, beautiful lips and eyes that could send any man to his knees. Her expression was one of genuine curiosity but the way she lowered her eyes when he looked directly at her tattled on her nervousness.

"I guess not," she said hesitantly.

By this time Jack had already made it to Nonie's duplex. He stopped the van near her side of the building, behind her Acura, killed the engine and turned in his seat to face her.

She looked down at her hands which were fidgeting in her lap.

Jack stared at her for a moment, unsure of how to phrase either question, which felt odd to him. He knew himself to be a straightforward kind of guy. If something needed to be said or done, he was the man for the job. Right now, though, wasn't about what he could or couldn't do. He saw Nonie as a slightly wary fawn, one who might bolt at any moment, and he didn't want that to happen.

Jack cleared his throat. "Tonight . . . Well, tonight there were a couple of times I could have sworn that I heard you talking to someone other than Buggy. I say that because you'd ask a question or make a comment and Buggy wouldn't answer. At least I didn't hear her answer. Now that everybody's gone, and it's just the two of us, I have to ask . . . Do you see spirits, Nonie?"

She looked up at him sharply, then just as quickly turned her head so she stared out of the windshield. The fawn was about to bolt.

Jack reached out and put a hand on her arm. "I'm not trying to be nosy or have you talk about something you'd prefer to keep to yourself. I mean, if you could see them, spirits I mean, I can easily understand why you wouldn't want anyone to know. I probably wouldn't admit it to anyone either. I'd be concerned people would think me crazy or worse."

"What's worse than people thinking you've got moths in your pantry?" Nonie asked.

"Moths?"

Nonie twirled a finger near her right temple. "Bats in the belfry, screws missing from the toolbox, a shank short of a full cow. You know."

"Yeah, right . . . crazy. Worse, to me anyway, would be people always after you, wanting to know if you see their dead father or mother, sister or aunt. Never giving you a moment's peace."

Nonie nodded. "Yeah, I can see that being a problem."

He cocked his head to follow her gaze. "Look, I'm really not asking simply to get tangled into your personal business. The reason I started doing paranormal investigations was to answer questions for myself. Questions about the afterlife. Like *was* there an afterlife. Over the years, I've seen and heard things I can't explain, but nothing that ever gave me a concrete answer to that question."

"So you think if I see or hear the dead, you'd get that answer from me," Nonie said matter-of-factly.

Her words caused Jack to sit back in his seat. The way she put it made him feel like he was using her, and that's the last thing he'd ever want her to think.

Seeing her staring out the windshield again, Jack gently cupped her chin with a hand and turned her head so she'd look at him. He saw worry in her eyes.

"It's okay," Jack said releasing her chin. "Forget I asked, okay?"

Nonie looked at him for a long moment then nodded ever so slightly. She turned as if to grasp the door of the passenger door, then turned back to him. "You said you had two questions for me. What's the second?"

Jack grinned, happy that she remembered. "The second question should have been the first if I hadn't been so crass and nosy."

"You weren't crass," she assured him. "I think curious is a better word for it. Nosy, yes."

He smiled.

"Well? The question?"

Jack drummed his thumbs softly on the steering wheel. "Would you . . .I mean, could I take you out to dinner sometime?" Even at thirty-seven-years-old, awaiting her answer made Jack feel like a schoolboy who'd just asked the most popular girl in class to the prom.

Nonie glanced nervously toward the back of the van, as if double-checking to make sure no one was seated behind them. She looked back at him. "I-I'd love to," she said quietly, then opened the van door and scrambled out. As she closed the door, she gave him a soft smile then hurried off to the duplex's porch.

Jack waited until she was safely inside before starting up the van. He inched his way around her Acura, all the while considering the wonders and mystery that made up Nonie Broussard. It was more than her beauty, her quick wit and intelligence. There was a shyness about her, but not to such a degree that it kept her from saying what was on her mind. Nonie reminded him of an exquisite piece of art that had been cut into puzzle pieces. As one got to know her, you got the gist of the picture, but you longed for more pieces to be put into place so the work of art would be made whole. He suspected Nonie purposely hid some of the puzzle pieces, like the fact that she was a medium, in order to protect herself. He'd bet his life on that, but he could also appreciate her desire to hold that piece of her close to the vest. It didn't take a brainiac to figure out the challenges that might present in her life if that information went public. Despite what secrets Nonie held close, Jack wanted to uncover each one. He wanted to understand her. Protect her. Be with her. And, as far as he was concerned, whatever it took, he planned to do just that.

CHAPTER NINETEEN

Nonie closed the door to her apartment and leaned against it with her eyes closed for a moment. She could still feel the smile on her face. Jack had asked her out to dinner. Asked her out on a date. And she'd said yes.

Oh, God . . . She'd said yes!

Nonie's eyes flew open. She expected to see Guy standing inches in front of her, demanding to know what this date thing was all about. Instead, all she saw was her couch, television, over-stuffed chair— everything normal and in its place. Except for Guy. The last place she'd seen him was at the plantation with Tiana. Nothing after that. Something was off. If anything, staying true to form, Guy would have been standing in front of her blabbering, "I told you so, I told you so," referring to his warning to her about ghost hunting. Tiana had done her best to give everyone a good scare.

Wondering where Guy might have gone off to, but glad he wasn't around to bust her hump, Nonie felt her shoulders finally relax. It was nearly 2 a.m., and she desperately needed a shower and sleep.

Just as she pushed away from her front door and turned to lock it, Nonie heard a loud crash come from the kitchen. The crash was quickly followed by pinging and clanging, rustling noises and more crashes, like dishes being smashed against the kitchen wall. She hurried to the kitchen to see what was causing the ruckus and pulled up short when she caught sight of her trash can sailing over the snack bar. Old newspapers, junk mail, an old bologna package and an empty milk carton scattered throughout her living room. From across the snack bar she saw her refrigerator door open and an egg carton come sliding out as smoothly as a skater on ice. She watched as the carton opened, then an egg came floating out of the carton, hovered for a second or two, then went flying towards her stove and smashed against the wall behind it.

Another egg pelted the snack bar, then another, both spreading into a lake of yellow goo. Thankfully there was only one left, but it was one too many for the last one took out her coffeepot.

For a while, all Nonie could do was stand like an openmouthed mannequin and watch the disaster unfold before her. As her coffeepot tipped over and rolled off the kitchen counter and onto the floor with a loud PING! fury suddenly sparked her into action. She planted two fists on her hips and shouted, "Guy Philip Skinard, stop that this instant!"

The egg carton dropped to the floor with a plop.

"Where the hell are you?" Nonie said, fuming.

Like a mirage in an overheated desert, Guy suddenly wavered into view. Smokey, silhouette at first, then he solidified. He wore the same clothes he always wore, only his hair was wildly mussed, and his nostrils flared with anger.

Nonie marched over to the snack bar and faced him. "What the hell is your problem?"

"You!"

"Me?" Nonie spread her arms out indicating the mess he'd just created. "What's with all this? When did that start? I thought you couldn't pick up material things."

"Surprise, surprise," Guy said and lifted his chin.

"Quit being a smart-ass."

Guy gave her a nonchalant look, then yawned as if discussing the matter bored him. "I've been able to manipulate matter for about a week now. Been practicing."

"Why didn't you tell me?"

He scowled. "I tried. Remember the other day when you were setting flowers up in the viewing room and I told you I had a present for you?"

Nonie chewed on her bottom lip vaguely remembering him telling her. "Yeah, okay, so?"

"That was my present."

"And you show me by trashing my apartment? If you can throw it out there you sure as hell better be able to straighten it back up," Nonie declared.

"Don't get all self-righteous on me, Nonie Marie. You're the one responsible for the mess."

"What the hell are you talking about?"

"You told that investigator dude that you'd have dinner with him, didn't you?"

Nonie felt her shoulders slump. She hadn't seen Guy in or around the van the entire time she'd sat alone in there with Jack. How did Guy know? Even when he didn't materialize, she'd always felt him around before. Had he been in the van, anywhere within earshot, she'd have known it.

"Didn't you?" he prompted again.

Nonie glared at him. "So what if I did. It's not like you and I can walk into Landry's Steak House and order dinner. And how did you get that bit of information anyway? Where were you hiding?"

Guy smirked. "In plain sight."

Nonie blew a stray hair away from her face and scowled. "Where in plain sight? I didn't see you anywhere. I didn't even feel you lurking around the way you do when you go all invisible on me."

"Doesn't matter where I was. All that matters is that I heard the two of you."

"That's eavesdropping,"

"So."

"That—that's just wrong," Nonie said and bent over to pick up a piece of old newspaper that had been dumped out with the rest of her trash. When she straightened up, Guy was in the living room, standing about ten feet away from her.

"Tell me you won't go out to dinner with that man," Guy said.

Nonie felt a twinge of guilt pinch her heart, but she lifted her chin defiantly. "Look, I have to eat anyway, right? What does it matter if I have something to eat with Jack? He's just a guy—Guy."

Guy's eyebrows knitted together. "Aw, come on, I know you're not that blind, Nonie. Jack Sprat wants to share a hell of a lot more with you than a meal, and you know it!"

Nonie cocked her head to one side. "Don't even think about getting loud with me, mister man."

"I don't want you going out with him," Guy shouted. Before Nonie knew it, he was standing right beside her and shouted into her right ear. "Don't do it!"

"Now that's about the saddest thing I've ever seen," a woman's voice said from behind Nonie, causing her to whirl about.

On Nonie's couch sat Helen Richardson. She wore a pink housedress with slippers to match, and her hair was a cap of white, tightly permed curls. She looked exactly as she did when Nonie had first seen her upstairs at the Richardson house, along with her gun-toting mascot, Captain. The only difference between then and now was that Nonie could see through Helen. She wasn't as solid as she'd been during their first encounter.

"M-Ms. Helen?" Nonie leaned forward and squinted, making sure her eyes weren't playing tricks on her. Unfortunately, they weren't.

"Yes?" Helen said, then smiled sweetly.

Nonie licked her bottom lip. She suddenly felt dehydrated. "W-why . . . what—what are you doing here?"

Helen patted her hair with a hand. "Because, dear, like I told you back at the house, I want to be on television. I figured it would be best if I came

here to make sure you wouldn't forget about me."
She tugged her housedress primly over her knees.
"You know, back in the day, I was known as a go-
getter. I wasn't the kind of woman who let grass
grow under her feet, if you know what I mean. That
hasn't changed just because I'm dead. I want to
make sure I'm one of the first in line for your
television show."

Nonie looked at Guy who looked at Helen.

"Why can I see through you now?" Guy asked
Helen. "Before, you looked as solid as Nonie."

Helen swatted a hand his way. "It's all about
energy, son. I hadn't been out of my house since the
day I died. Traveling out this way zapped quite a bit
of my energy. I guess that's why I'm a little . . .
foggy maybe."

"How did you find your way here?" Nonie asked.

"I followed him," Helen said, motioning to Guy. "As soon as y'all left my house, I hooked my energy onto his and there you go."

"So you were with us at the plantation?" Guy asked. "I didn't see you there."

"Like I said," Helen reiterated. "Energy. I was a bit weak in the knees, having left my house and all. Wasn't quite sure what to do with myself. Felt a bit wonky. So I hid in corners most of the time, out of the way, until I could get my feet under me. Felt a bit more whole, you know?"

"But if you latched onto me then and all the way here to Nonie's," Guy said. "I would have felt you, seen you, right?"

Helen shrugged. "I don't have the answers to everything, son. I'm just like you where death is concerned. A lot of unanswered questions. All I can do is try things every once in a while and see if they work. I guess it's a matter of how important things are to you. You know what I mean? The more important something is to you, the more energy you'll put out to take care of it, get it. That sort of thing. For me, being on television is important." Helen held up a hand as if to stop traffic. "But wait a minute, we got off track here. I was saying that this was the saddest thing I'd ever seen."

"What's sad?" Guy asked.

"You're giving this young lady here a hard time about going on a date with a live man. Son, you're dead. What's she supposed to do with you in that condition? You've got to let her move on with her life."

Nonie heart thudded in her chest. As much as she loved Guy and would always love Guy, she'd wanted to tell him that very thing so many times. Nine years was a long time to mourn and having him around all the time never allowed her to completely go through the mourning process. She'd been on dates before, but nine out of ten times they'd been interrupted by Guy. And he did it out of sheer jealousy. Sex had become a once a year event, if she was lucky. It usually happened when she and Kyle, Lyle's twin brother, accompanied Buggy and Lyle to their annual beach vacation either in Biloxi or Pensacola. For some odd reason, Guy never followed her out of state. She wasn't sure if it was because he didn't want to or couldn't, and she wasn't about to ask him. Not that the sexual experience with Kyle was any huge treat. A Romeo he was not. His sex education ran more in line with his work as an offshore operator. Drill in, clear out. After a few experiences with him and sensing nothing was going to change . . . for the better, Nonie figured some things were better tended to on her own.

Aside from those vacation days, Nonie was always holding her breath, waiting for Guy to pop up whenever another man came near her. There were occasions when he'd go on sabbatical for two or three days, to where she wasn't sure. She'd asked him once or twice, and his response was always some smartass remark like, "Oh, just doin' a walkabout." Like he was from Australia or something. Guy didn't even know how to find

Australia on a map. He never offered more of an explanation than that.

Nonie glanced over at Guy, whose face had clouded with anger.

"Nonie is my girl," he said. "That's why I didn't go into the light when it came for me after I died. I wanted to be here for her. To protect her, look after her. We swore we'd always be together, get married, have children. Maybe some of that can't happen now, but I can still be with her, protect her, like a man is supposed to do for his woman."

"Son," Helen said with a shake of her head, "you being with her all the time stops her from living life. From living the life she was meant to live after you passed on. You should have gone to the light when it came for you. That would have been the best thing for you and for her. Now, though, she's stuck.

I can feel from her heart that she loves you. She'll always love you, but that doesn't mean that there isn't room in her heart to love someone else. Someone who's alive who can give her some happiness."

"How can you tell me what I should or shouldn't do when you didn't go to the light either?"

"My situation's different. It involves my house, not another human being. My husband, Charlie, has been gone for many a year now. He took to the light right away, Lord bless him. As soon as I get my house situation under control, I plan on finding me that light again and my Charlie. That's where the forever after part comes in."

Guy glanced down at the floor for a moment, then looked up at Nonie. "Don't I make you happy?"

Nonie peered over at Helen, hoping the woman might chime in about now. Helen just gave her a quizzical look.

After clearing her throat, Nonie said to Guy, "What can I say? Of course you make me happy. But she's right Guy, I can't move on with my life if you're always around."

"You'd rather I go? You don't want to see me anymore?" The hurt look in Guy's eyes made Nonie fidget.

"I didn't say that," Nonie said. "Don't start getting all melodramatic. I'm just saying that every time I try to go on a date like a normal human female, you're all up in my stuff, in my face, telling me to leave. And heaven forbid if somebody tries to kiss me goodnight! Look at what happened this evening when you found out Jack wanted to take me to dinner. You trashed my place. How's a living person supposed to deal with all of that?"

Nonie watched Guy's expression crumble into one of sadness. It hurt her heart, and she wanted to take back everything she'd just said.

"So what is it?" Guy asked. "What do you want? Me to stay or leave you forever?"

Nonie put a hand to her heart. "I want you to understand that I love you and will always love you, but you've got to quit trying to control every part of my life. And you need to accept the fact that I'm the one still alive here. There's a life I have to live. I don't know where it'll lead me or who it will lead me to. But if you're always standing there in front of me, I'll never have answers to those questions. I'm not saying any of this to hurt you, Guy."

"Of course she doesn't want to hurt you," Helen chimed in. "Look how there's so much sadness on her face. You should be ashamed of yourself, my boy, for making her hurt that bad when all she's trying to do is tell you how she feels."

"Yeah, but how about what I feel?" Guy said. "Nobody seems to be taking that into consideration."

"You're giving her an ultimatum," Helen said, "and that's not fair."

"But what am I supposed to do?" Guy said. "I love her."

"I know that, too," Helen said. "So what y'all got to do is compromise. If Nonie wants to go on a date, you let her go on the date and stay here at the house. When she comes back, she'll be with you. At least that would give her some chance to live her life without you always in her face. You can't stay stuck here forever. That's not what this is all about."

"Then why are you still here?" Guy asked. "I know you said you wanted to make sure your house was okay before you left with the light, but suppose it never gets right? Suppose your son turns it into a rental house or winds up selling it? What are you going to do then? Stay here until that changes?"

"I think it's going to change for the better with me and the house being on television," Helen said. "I'm counting on that. Once that happens, all I've got to do is wait for the light to come back and get me, and I'll be ready."

"Suppose . . . suppose the light doesn't come back?" Guy said quietly. "Suppose you had one chance to go to it, and if you didn't, you can't anymore?"

Helen let out a deep sigh. "Son, you about the most negative thinking little man I've met. Get your head out of that stupid place and think positive. That light is love, real, down to your soul love. That's all it's about. That kind of love doesn't leave you here high and dry. It'll be here when you're ready."

Motioning to Nonie, Helen asked, "So, you going to put me on television or what?"

"It's not up to me, Ms. Helen. It's not up to any of us who were at your house. We have to review the pictures, video and audio we took, and if we captured anything, we bring it to the producers of the television show. They're the ones who'll be making the decision on which location will be on the program. Now you do know that you yourself won't be on television, right? As far as I know, I'm the only one who can see you. What the television crew will be looking for is evidence like your voice again on their recorders or your body showing up as a shadow on film."

"Oh, I know I won't be on television in my body," Helen said. "And it's not about me, like I said. I want to stop my son from redoing the house and trying to sell it. If people think it's haunted, everyone will want to come and see it. He could rent it out to people who like to sleep in scary places, like a haunted hotel, you know? And people could see my saddle and all the pictures I have with celebrities and other important people. Everybody watching the show will see my collection and think, 'now that must have been one heck of a woman.' That way they won't forget me, you know? That's all I really want. Is for people not to forget."

Nonie heard the loneliness in Helen's words, and it tugged at her heart.

"But we should have some good captures from when y'all were there, right?" Helen said. "I spoke right in your machine like you told me to."

"I haven't heard anything yet from Jack, who's reviewing the material, but as soon as I do, I'll make sure you know. But you've got to remember, Ms. Helen, if they want to film your house, you're going to need to be there. The producers are going to be expecting the film crew and the cast of investigators to get some evidence. So you need to be there to make that happen."

"I may be old, but my mind's all collected. I know I got to be at my house when they come. Until then, though, if it's okay with you, I think I'm going to hang out here with y'all. That way I can find out firsthand when they give the okay for television. I know they will. I just know it."

"Hang out here?" Nonie echoed, trying to hold back a moan. Her apartment was already too crowded with Guy. Now another ghost wanted to take up residence?

"Just until we find out," Helen said. "You have any idea when that's going to be?"

"Jack, the tall guy with the dark hair—"

"That big good-looking fella?"

Nonie nodded and resisted glancing over to see Guy's reaction. "He's reviewing all the data tonight. When he's done, he'll take whatever he finds to the producers, and they'll make the decision. Until then, all we can do is wait."

"Good then," Helen said. "I'll just wait here until we find out, then I'll go back to my house and make sure those producers get their money's worth. I'll make sure they get a good show."

"Why do you want to wait here?" Nonie asked. "Can't you wait for the news at your house?"

"I like being close to the action," Helen said with a grin. "I could have followed Jack to his house but he doesn't have a dead person following him around. Not like you've got. I had to hitch a ride where I could find it. I'm not going to be any trouble. I promise you that. You'll hardly even know I'm around. For sure I'm not going to pitch no hissy fit like he did. As far as I'm concerned you can go and come like you want."

Nonie lifted a brow. "Appreciate that." She scrubbed a hand over her face. Great, that was all she needed. Another ghost in her house watching her every move.

CHAPTER TWENTY

The next morning Nonie woke with a start. She'd been dreaming about Tiana Lewis and her skillet. Only this time, instead of chasing Jack and Tatman like she did at the plantation the night before, Tiana chased Guy and flattened his head with a skillet. Immediately, Guy's head expanded back to its normal size, then he faded out of sight. As soon as he vanished, Tiana had turned towards her.

Nonie glanced at the clock on her night stand: 9:05 a.m. She groaned, stumbled out of bed and went into the adjoining bathroom. She hadn't gotten much sleep last night. Guy and Helen had had a talkathon in her bedroom. And although she'd asked them repeatedly to quiet down or go into another room, she could still hear them whispering. All night. They'd talked about how they died, about their families. Helen talked a lot about the future and what it might hold if she was able to get back to the bright light that had originally come for her.

If Nonie had gotten three hours of sleep, it had been a lot. She felt grumpy, in need of coffee and a shower, but most of all she wanted to get out of the house and away from Guy and Helen. She hadn't seen them when she woke and wasn't about to call out and get their attention now. Wherever they were was better than here.

She turned the shower on, letting the water run a little cooler than she liked, hoping it would alert her body to wakey-wakey. She undressed and stepped into the spray. The water got her eyes open and heart pumping. She quickly soaped up and washed her hair. As she stood under the shower, rinsing her hair, her thoughts roamed over to Jack. She replayed the scene of when he'd asked her out to dinner. How his hazel eyes had taken on a soft green tint. How the muscles in his arms strained against his shirt sleeves when he'd leaned toward her. Though she'd never say it aloud, Guy had been right. More than dinner had been desired in that moment. Only that desire had come from her.

When Jack had touched her, had cupped her chin with his hand to turn her head towards him, she'd felt a spark of heat rush through her body, like someone had lit kindling meant for a bonfire.

Frustrated, Nonie lifted her head and let the spray hit her full in the face. She opened her mouth, let it fill with water, then spat it out against the shower stall. All of this ghost business was driving her crazy and she needed to talk to someone about it. She thought about Buggy, but her friend didn't get off of work at Meemaw's Café until three, and she'd be too busy to talk at work. Her Uncle Fezzo came to mind. Although he'd said seeing the dead ran in the family, she thought it might be worth testing the waters with him and sharing some of what she'd been going through. What she *was* going through. She had to do something. She was collecting ghosts like some people collected baseball cards. The only difference was card collectors *wanted* more cards. And the last thing she wanted was more ghosts. Thankfully Tiana hadn't shown up . . . yet. Nonie could only cross her fingers that the large, angry woman would stay at the plantation and wouldn't suddenly catch the "television" bug that had Helen so firmly in its grip.

After turning the shower off, Nonie peeked

around the shower curtain to make sure she was

alone. Seeing neither Guy nor Helen, she hurried

out of the shower, quickly dried her body and hair

off with a thick white towel, then dressed in a pair

of jeans and a white, pullover shirt. She gave her

hair a quick whoosh with a blow-dryer, then

debated on whether or not to put makeup on.

Suddenly remembering that Inez Trahan's viewing

was today, she took off her jeans and exchanged

them for black slacks. If she showed up at the

funeral home in jeans during a viewing, her mother

would stroke out. Following that train of thought,

she swiped on some mascara, added a bit of lip

gloss, then left well enough alone.

After slipping on a pair of black sneakers, Nonie

hurried out of her duplex, looking over her shoulder

every couple of seconds to make sure Guy and Helen hadn't reappeared. She never thought she'd see the day that she'd be rushing to get to the funeral home on a day off, but she needed to get out of the house before Guy and Helen reappeared. She wondered where they'd gone off to. Guy couldn't read her thoughts but she wasn't sure about Helen. For all she knew, they might be heading over to the funeral home right now as she planned her big escape.

Nonie was locking her front door when Dora Arsemont came out onto the duplex's porch.

"Good morning, cher," Dora said. "How you doin' today?" She wore a pink shift with blue floral designs across the bodice, white patent leather flats and black-rimmed, cat-eye glasses. A haphazard line of red lipstick traced her thin mouth, which held her ever-present dangling cigarette. A white patent-leather purse sat in the crook of her right arm.

"Fine, Ms. Dora," Nonie said, forcing a smile.

Dora eyed Nonie's outfit. "You don't have work today?"

"No, ma'am. I've got the day off."

"Aw, mah, dat's too bad. I was going to the funeral home, me, to see poor Inez. You know we used to play bingo together at de bingo hall down by Thibodeaux's Ranch."

"I'm sure your attendance will be appreciated, Ms. Dora. Now if you'll excuse me, I've got some errands to run."

"Oh, okay, go run you errands," Dora said, ashes falling onto the porch from her cigarette. She suddenly held up a hand. ""Wait, wait. Did somebody come to you side of de duplex early dis morning? Like one, two in de morning?"

Nonie frowned. "No. Nobody."

"'Cause I heard all kinds of noise coming from you place. Dishes breakin', like somebody was cat-fightin' in dere. You sure dere was no problem? No boyfriend you was fightin' wit'?"

"Positive. There wasn't a problem," Nonie lied, remembering Guy's hissy fit.

"Hm," Dora said, then puffed on her cigarette and blew smoke out of the left side of her mouth. "Mah, maybe I was dreamin' den. No, no wait . . . It wasn't a dream 'cause it woke me up. I remember dat. It was a crash dat woke me up."

Nonie shrugged and took a step off the porch.

"Ah, well," Dora said. "Maybe it came from Sarah and Michael Doucet's house across de street.

You know how dem two is always fightin'. He comes back late from work drunk, and she gives him hell. Broke his nose one time wit' a ironing board. Can you believe dat?"

Nonie shook her head in a display of disbelief and took another step down from the porch.

Dora shook a finger, her eyes not totally focused on Nonie. "But you know, dat racket sounded too close for it to be from across de street."

Inching her way away from the porch, Nonie waited for Dora to snap back to attention.

"Ah, well," Dora said, hitching the handle of her purse back to the crook of her arm. More cigarette ashes plopped onto the porch. "If you say it wasn't you, den I guess it wasn't you. I'm glad you okay."

Holding in a sigh, Nonie shook her car keys and smiled. "I'm just fine, Ms. Dora. I've got to run those errands now."

"Yeah, I got to go me, too."

Nonie hurried over to her car, unlocked the door and jumped inside before Dora had a chance to start on another rant. She shoved the key into the ignition, started the car, and tires squealed as she pulled out onto the street.

In the ten minutes it took Nonie to drive from her place to the funeral home, she thought about the investigation they'd done the night before. She was curious as to whether they'd captured anything on video or audio, and if so, was the evidence going to be anything close to what she'd experienced firsthand. More importantly, if they did get evidence, that meant a sweet thousand-dollar check for everyone in the group. She'd save that money until she got a handle on how regular the investigations would be. If they were often enough and produced enough to warrant a regular check, she'd let her father know she would no longer be on the funeral home's payroll. Until then, she'd squirrel away the money. A thousand dollars a weekend was nothing to sneeze at, but the investigations came with no guarantees. They'd lucked out getting two in one night. Even luckier getting two active ones in one night. That might not always be the case. Of course, she had to consider the fact that she'd collected an extra ghost in the deal. That was something she definitely hadn't counted on. Nonie couldn't help but wonder if that was going to be an issue with every investigation. One thing she didn't need was ghosts following her everywhere, all wanting something from her. Like Helen wanting to be on television. There was only way to find out, though. Keep doing investigations and see what happened.

Still pondering the ghost situation, Nonie arrived at the funeral home, spotted the hearse parked under the side portico and three or four cars parked in the visitors' lot. She drove around to the back of the funeral home and parked near the garage.

It was nearing 10:30 a.m., which meant a half hour left before they moved Inez from the funeral home to St. Anthony's. After that, the place would be relatively free and clear for an hour.

Nonie got out of her car and went into the garage and through the side door that led to her father's office. Normally his door would have been locked from the inside, but he left it unlocked during funerals so Fezzo could move easily from the garage to the embalming room without going all the way around to the front entrance.

She stuck her head inside the office, relieved to find it empty, then tiptoed into the hallway and saw Fezzo alone in the coffee room, sipping on a cup of brew. His eyes lit up when he spotted her.

"What you doing here, mon petite?" he asked. "You were supposed to have the day off, no?"

Nonie kissed her uncle on the cheek, then went over to the counter, grabbed a Styrofoam cup, and filled it with coffee. "Just needed to get out of the house," she said. "Buggy's working at Meemaw's right now, so I figured I'd stop in here, see what was going on." She sat down next to Fezzo. "Got a minute?"

"I've always got time for you, mon petite," he said.

Nonie sipped on her coffee and asked, "Where's Mom and Dad?"

"Your mama's not here. Guess she figured since Ms. Inez's funeral was going to be small that your daddy, Margaret and me could handle what needed handling. Your daddy's with Inez's family right now. Poor old soul, her. She's only got three or four people dat came see her. Margaret's out by de front desk and Butchy, him, is in de embalming room. There's not too much going on right now. Me, I'm waiting until it's time to put Inez in de hearse and bring her to de church."

Nonie nodded and sipped on her coffee again.

Fezzo sipped on his coffee, as well, eyeing her. He put his cup down on the table. "So how was you night?"

"It was different," Nonie said, unsure of how much to tell her uncle.

"Different den what?"

"Well, we went to two houses, and I think we caught some things on our cameras and recorders. You know, this whole thing is for a television show some people from New Orleans are putting together."

Fezzo's brows arched. "You gonna be on TV?"

"Not me. We're just scouts. We check on locations that are supposedly haunted, and if we find one, other people will go back to that place with a film crew. They're the ones who'll be on TV."

Fezzo frowned. "Don't seem to fair if you ask me. Y'all find a place but somebody else gonna get de credit for finding it?"

Nonie shrugged. "Pretty much. But we get paid for scouting, which is good. I don't really care about being on television."

Fezzo studied her for a moment. "What made you want to do dis scout thing?"

Nonie drank more coffee, feeling a little embarrassed about the real reason she started scouting. "The money," she said finally. "If we get evidence on film or audio, we get paid five hundred dollars each."

"Poo yi, that's some good money," Fezzo said. "What kind of stuff y'all have to get on dat film and audial? It's got to show a real live ghost or you got to hear voices on the recorders like de kind you hear on dem scary shows?"

"It's not as much as what you see on television. Not all the spooky sounds you see in the movies. It's more lights, shadows, a word or two on the recorders, maybe a sentence if we're lucky."

Fezzo eyed her. "How come you look like you about to jump out you skin? What you got to talk to me about? Something happened last night? I don't think it was no light or shadow. I can see dat from you face. Was it bad?"

"I guess it depends on who you ask," Nonie said. "It wasn't bad for me. Just weird." Before he could ask anything more, Nonie plowed ahead with the real question she wanted answered. "Uncle Fezzo, what made you think . . . or know that I could see . . .uh . . ."

"Dead people?" he finished for her.

Nonie nodded.

Fezzo drew in a deep breath and worked his coffee cup in a circle on the table with a thumb and finger. "Because your grandma, me and you daddy's mama, could see de dead."

"I know. You told me."

Fezzo nodded. "Yep. But you know she never talked about it wit' anybody but close family. When her mama and daddy passed, she'd see dem at de house all de time. And she'd tell us dat."

"Did you or Dad ever see anything?"

"Non, neither one of us. I guess it skipped a generational, 'cause it got you like it did your grandma. So you see, it's not something I'm a stranger to. I see in you face sometimes dat something's not right. Not normal. For a while, I could figure out what was de matter. I thought about to ask you, but didn't want to stick my nose in you business. Den I remembered. De look on you face when you bothered wit' dead people is de same look my mama used to carry on her face."

Nonie swiped a hand through her hair, not sure of how to take this latest news. "But if Dad knew his mama saw dead people, how come he got upset when I told him and Mom that I saw Grandpa, Mama's daddy, the day after his funeral."

Fezzo shrugged. "I guess he didn't want you to have to carry dat burden like our mama did. Maybe he thought if he told you that you was dreamin' or made a mistake in what you saw, dat whatever makes you see would go away. You understand?"

"I think so."

Fezzo cocked his head slightly and studied her. "You see you boyfriend, Guy, huh? He's around a lot?"

Nonie felt tears sting her eyes and wasn't exactly sure why. She glanced down at her cup. "Yes, I do. Almost every day." When she didn't hear Fezzo respond, she glanced up at him. He was nodding slowly.

"I figured dat, me. Now what about last night. You saw something?"

"Yeah." Nonie pierced a little arch in her Styrofoam cup with her thumbnail. "I saw an old lady at the first house and an old man."

"They was dangerous or no?"

"The old lady wasn't. The old man was more grouchy than dangerous. Now the second house we went to, things got a little bit crazy."

Fezzo arched a brow at her, but didn't say anything.

"I saw a large, black woman there that went after two of the guys that were with us with a big iron skillet."

Fezzo let out a little gasp. "Aw, mah, no. And you don't think dat was dangerous?"

"Well, she didn't come after me. And from what I saw, I don't think she was going to really hit any of the guys with that skillet. I think she just wanted to scare them good because they wouldn't shut up and stop asking her questions."

"What dey did when she took after dem wit' de skillet?"

"The leader of the group told all of us it was time to go. He didn't want any of us to get hurt."

"Smart man."

Nonie nodded. "He is."

Fezzo rubbed his chin briskly. "So is dat's what's botherin' you now? What happened last night? Or is it you boyfriend? Is he here now?"

"No, I haven't seen him yet today."

"Then what's got worry lines on you forehead?"

Nonie blew out a short breath. "Remember I told you I saw an old woman in the first house we went to?"

"Yeah."

"She sorta followed me home. Well, actually, she followed Guy to my house. He's there most nights. The woman's name is Helen, and she said she latched onto Guy's energy and came home with us because she wanted to be on television."

"How she knew about de television thing wit' you?"

"She asked me what we were doing there, and I told her."

"Poo yi," Fezzo said again. "And what about de one wit' de skillet. She came back with you her, too?"

"No. Her name was Tiana Lewis. As far as I know, she stayed where we left her, back at an old plantation." Nonie chewed on her bottom lip for a moment. She'd told Fezzo so much already yet there wasn't one speck of incredulity in his eyes. His expression was serious, and she had his full attention. "I'm not quite sure about what to do with Helen, the ghost that followed me home."

"Well," Fezzo said, sitting back and scratching the side of his neck. "From what my mama used to tell me, if a ghost follows you it's because dey want something from you. From what you tol' me, dis ghost wants to be on de television. Is dat something you can give her?"

Nonie shook her head. "I'm not the decision maker on whether or not they send a film crew to her house. That's the producer's decision."

Fezzo frowned. "Wait up. She can't be on television anyways. She's dead."

"I know, and she knows that, but she wants her house on television. She thinks if people know her house is haunted they'll want to come and see it. Her son is trying to renovate it right now. She's afraid he's going to try and sell it, which is something she doesn't want."

"Mah, why she didn't just ask you to tell her son not to sell her house?"

Nonie gave Fezzo a wary look. "Suppose a stranger came up to you and said, 'Uh, Mr. Broussard, your mama doesn't want you to sell her house,' what would you do?"

"Hm, dat's a good point."

They sat silent for a moment, each finishing off the last of their coffee.

"Well, mon petite, I don't know what I can tell you that would help. I'm afraid dat Helen's gonna leave when Helen's ready to leave."

"Great."

Fezzo laid a hand on her arm and patted it. "Look, I know you went to do dis thing wit' de ghost because de money was good and because you don't want to work here."

Nonie started to object, but Fezzo held up a hand to stop her. "I don't blame you for dat. It's hard, workin' around so much sad all de time. You got so much life in you. You don't need to be in a place like dis. I know dat, and deep down I think you daddy knows dat, too. Now me, I'm old, so being here don't make me no matter. When I was younger and out in de swamp alligator huntin', I faced danger every day. I don't have to do dat no more. Working over here, I face the sad every day, but you just gotta know how to put it in its place. I can do dat me 'cause I'm old. It's different for you right now. De only thing is you have to be careful about what you chose to do. What you gonna do if everywhere you go you wind up bringin' a ghost home wit' you?"

"I don't know. That's my problem. I don't know how long I'm gonna be stuck with Helen."

"Well, my baby, all I can tell you is once you get to dat bayou, den you cross de bridge dat goes over to de other side. Dat's all you got. Until den, we just guessin'. This Helen ghost, is she nice?"

"Oh, yes, very," Nonie said. "But I don't want her following me around for the rest of my life."

Fezzo chuckled. "I wouldn't want dat me either."

"Last night Helen and Guy talked all night long. I hardly got any sleep."

"You grandma used to have de same problem. Sometime she'd say de ghost would talk and talk and keep her awake all night. And it would stay dat way until she figured out a way to help dem get past their troubles. She never had no peace, God rest her old soul. But you know, mon petite, what you got is a gift. And when de good Lord gives you a gift you have to use it. Dat's why he put you here on dis earth. Sometime it's gonna be to help a soul cross over to de other side to meet him. If dat's what you gotta do, den dat's what you gotta do. You can't just keep collecting de dead. You gonna have to find a way to take what you got and work wit' dat."

"But if it's a gift, and I'm supposed to help, is it bad that I get paid to do it?"

Fezzo gave his head an adamant shake. "Not in de least. Not everybody can do what you do. Like wit' me. You think just anybody can go out to de swamp and alligator hunt?"

"No."

"Dat's right. You got to know what you doin' or you gonna wind up being alligator bait. So you see, huntin' dem alligators was my gift, and I got paid to do it. I got paid. You get paid. No difference. With you, though, you get two good things out of it. You get paid and you get to help a poor soul find its way back to where dey supposed to be, wit' God." Fezzo patted her arm again. "You got to promise you old Uncle Fezzo, though, dat you gonna be careful. Always keep you eyes open. If you see something dat's dark, don't mess wit' it. Just turn around and leave. De dark ones, you can't ever tell what dey gonna do."

"Oh, Guy's already warned me about that," Nonie said. "He didn't want me to do these investigations in the first place."

"Mah, you boyfriend might be dead, but he's not stupid. He's already passed, so he sees all dat's on de other side."

"Not all of it, I think," Nonie said. "He didn't cross into the light when it came for him. He said he wanted to stick around here to make sure I was safe. He didn't want to leave me."

"Well, you know dat's something you gonna have to work out wit' him. He's not supposed to be here all de time like dat. He's supposed to go to dat light. Either way, it's gonna all work out okay, mon petite. De good Lord don't give you a gift without showing you what to do wit' it. Sometimes he don't show you all at one time. It might take a little while to catch on."

Nonie took Fezzo's hand from her arm and gave his palm a quick kiss. "Thanks, Uncle Fezzo. It felt good to get all of that off my chest."

"Anytime," Fezzo said with a grin. "Dat's why I'm here."

"Hello? Hello? Is anyone back here?" a woman called from down the hallway.

Fezzo got to his feet. "We in here," he said, making his way to the door to see who it was. Before he reached the doorway, Clara Grubbs, the woman who'd been with Anna Mae Turner, Mayor Fontenot's mistress, rushed into the room. She wore a plain brown skirt with a beige blouse and black flats. Her white-blond hair was mussed like she'd just woken from a nap and forgot to brush it out.

"Oh, Mr. Broussard," Clara said to Fezzo. "I saw your brother out front and talked to him and Margaret. Both said I should come and ask you, that you might know."

"What I might know?" Fezzo asked. "What's wrong? How come you look so upset?"

"I can't find Anna Mae. After the funeral, after that big mess that happened, she never came back home. We came here in separate cars because I had to get groceries after the funeral, and she wanted to go to Lafayette to see her brother instead. I talked to him. Her brother I mean. She never made it there and never came back home."

Nonie got up from the table. "Did you try calling other relatives?" she asked. "Maybe she went back to Alabama or Georgia. Where was she from again?"

"Alabama," Clara said. "I called the entire family. No one has seen or heard from her. No one in town has seen her. Not that she'd show her face around Clay Point right now. Not after that big fight at the funeral. She was so embarrassed. I don't know what to do. I was hoping one of you might have seen her."

"No ma'am," Fezzo said. "Not hide or hair."

"Neither have I," said Nonie.

Clara swiped a shaking hand through her hair repeatedly. "I don't know what else to do."

"Have you gone to the police?" Nonie asked. "Maybe you should talk to Sheriff Buchanan or Deputy Lopez. They might know something."

"I've already talked to them," Clara said. "They haven't seen Anna Mae, and they claim they can't put file a missing person's report yet because it's too soon. They said she was certainly old enough to go wherever she wanted to go. Said she could have gone to Florida for all we know to get away from town for a while. Let folks get over the scuffle she had with the mayor's wife. I don't believe that, though. Anna Mae would have told me if she'd wanted to leave town. She wouldn't have just left. And all her clothes and makeup are still at the house. She wouldn't have left without that. No clothes, makeup, shoes. She wouldn't have gone out of town like that. I told that to Sheriff Buchanan, but he didn't want to listen. All he kept saying was there was nothing they could do about it right now."

"Did they offer any help?" Nonie asked.

"All they said was that they'd ask around town. See if anyone has seen her. That's nothing different than what I've already done." Clara put her hands over her face and sniffled. "I truly don't know what to do now. I'm so worried that something might have happened to her. It's just not like her to leave that way."

"Ms. Clara, why don't you come and have a seat," Nonie said. "Let me get you some coffee."

Fezzo nodded and took Clara by the shoulders, gently leading her to the table he and Nonie had been sitting at. He pulled a chair out for her.

"You want cream and sugar in your coffee?" Nonie asked, already at the urn.

"No just black. Just like Anna Mae would have taken it. Black." Clara sniffled again. "Why would she disappear like that? I don't understand."

Suddenly, T-boy stuck his head into the coffee room. "Hey, peanut," he said to Nonie.

"Hi, Dad."

"Y'all helping out, Ms. Clara?"

"Not too much we can do," Fezzo said. "Neither me or Nonie seen Anna Mae."

T-boy tsked, then said, "Fezzo, can you get the hearse started? We're ready to head to the church."

"I'll be right there, brother."

T-boy nodded and disappeared from the doorway.

"If you'll excuse me, Ms. Clara, I have some business to tend to," Fezzo said.

"Oh, please don't let me interrupt anything," Clara said and started to stand.

"No, no," Fezzo said. "Stay and have some coffee with Nonie. Have a little chat, maybe calm down a bit before you get back on the road. You don't need to be driving all nervous like dat." He gave Nonie a little nod as he left the room.

Clara sat back down and took the coffee Nonie offered her.

Nonie didn't have a clue what to tell the woman to comfort her. "I'm sorry you're going through this, Ms. Clara."

"Thank you."

"I wish I could help you. Have you gone to Meemaw's Café? A lot of people in town go there for breakfast and lunch. Maybe somebody there has seen Anna Mae."

"I've been there twice. No luck." Clara took a sip of coffee, then looked around the room as if to assure herself they were the only two in the room. She leaned closer to Nonie. "And you know what else?"

"What?"

Clara sighed deeply. "I don't know why I'm telling you this because I haven't told another living soul."A worried look crossed her face. "Since Anna Mae left, there are all kinds of strange things happening at my house," she whispered.

"Like what?" Nonie asked.

"Sometimes I'll go into my kitchen to get something to eat or drink and all my cabinet doors are open. I'll go in my bathroom, and the shower's running. Weird stuff like that. This morning I woke up and found my washing machine running. I sure didn't turn it on, unless I walked in my sleep and didn't know it. I mean that machine was running like it had a heavy load of clothes washing. Kept making a *kathunk kathunk* sound. I turned off the washer and checked inside. Nothing in it."

The hair on the back of Nonie's neck stood at attention. She didn't care for what crossed her mind in that second. Strange things were happening at Clara's house, and that sudden prickly feeling at the back of her neck was usually a sign that a ghost was nearby. She couldn't help but wonder if Anna Mae might be the one causing the poltergeist activity. If that was the case, it meant Anna Mae was dead. In light of the embarrassing fight at the funeral home, could she have taken her own life? Nonie quickly discarded the thought. Anna Mae had been too full of life and self-righteousness to commit suicide.

"That really does sound strange," Nonie said to Clara, not knowing what else to say.

"I know," Clara said, still whispering. "It's just another thing I don't know what to do about. I'm really kind of afraid to go back to my own house, and I should be there in case Anna Mae calls." She looked down at her coffee cup then back up at Nonie. "Would . . . would you mind coming with me to my house and taking a look around? See if you see anything strange going on? Maybe see if you find anything I might have missed that would give me a clue as to where Anna Mae might have gone?"

Nonie tried not to flinch. She'd been expecting the question. "I don't know if my going there would do you any good, Ms. Clara."

Clara rested her cup on the table and took one of Nonie's hands in both of hers. "Please come with me. Just check things out. I'm really scared to go back there by myself."

"I don't—" Nonie began, and Clara squeezed her hand tighter.

"Please, please, just come and check things out," Clara begged. "You don't have to stay. I've been gone since early this morning, and I'm afraid of what I might find when I go back home. It could just be me going off my rocker because Anna Mae's gone missing. Another pair of eyes would help me so very much."

"All right," Nonie said finally. "If you'll wait until after Uncle Fezzo is finished with Ms. Inez, I'll ask him to come with us. We'll have a look around, see if there are any clues that might lead us to Anna Mae."

"And if there's anything weird going on?"

"We'll check that out, too. Make sure there isn't a logical explanation for it."

Clara blew out a breath. "Thank you. Thank you so much. The police didn't even come to my house to look around for clues about Anna Mae. Is that sad or what?"

Nonie gave a little shrug, not wanting to comment one way or the other.

"Any idea how long it'll take Mr. Broussard to finish with Inez?"

"It may be a while," Nonie said. "Uncle Fezzo has to drive the hearse to the church, then wait until they're done at the cemetery in back of the church."

"Okay. Then I'll go and visit Anna Mae's brother in Lafayette, see if he's heard anything new. I'll leave you his phone number. If you don't mind, when y'all are done, give me a call, and I'll hurry back here. It should only take me thirty minutes or so to get back."

"No problem," Nonie said.

"Oh, and if you don't mind, please don't tell your uncle about the weird things going on in my house. If something happens while the two of you are there then it happens. But if nothing is out of sorts, then I don't want him to think I'm crazy."

"No problem, Ms. Clara. As soon as Uncle Fezzo is done, I'll give you a call, and we'll meet up at your house." Nonie got to her feet, hoping it would signal Clara that it was time for her to be on her way.

Clara stood up, went over to Nonie, and gave her a hug. "Thank you again. It's hard when you're carrying something so big inside of you and nobody wants to listen to what you have to say. Know what I'm saying?"

More than you know, Nonie thought. *More than you know.*

CHAPTER TWENTY-ONE

Guy didn't like the fact that he was hiding out in Helen Richardson's attic along with her sidekick, the grouchy Captain. But he'd owed her one. At this very moment Helen's son was downstairs packing up her memorabilia, which she planned on unpacking as soon as he left. She'd asked Guy to come with her to help. He hadn't wanted to leave Nonie's side, but Helen had taught him to blip, which he found to be a huge time saver. Since he already knew how to manipulate objects, she'd asked for his help in unpacking. Helen's hope was that if her son found what he'd packed unpacked enough times, he'd finally get the idea and leave her stuff alone and in its rightful place.

The blip she'd taught him, how to transport from one place to another in the blink of an eye, took awhile for Guy to get down right. Helen had told him that all he'd needed to do was close his eyes and concentrate on the place he wanted to be the most. Then she warned that a warm, fuzzy feeling would churn in his gut and that he wasn't to open his eyes until that feeling passed. This would get him to where he wanted to be in a blink instead of him having to hide in the back of vans or sneak around buildings or through rooms so Nonie wouldn't spot him, especially if she was pissed.

The first few times Guy tried the technique, he didn't quite make his mark. Once he envisioned being in Nonie's bedroom and wound up in her bathroom. Another attempt and he'd found himself at Meemaw's Café. Finally, Helen had taken him by the hand, walked him through the concentration it took to blip, then described her house in the minutest detail. The attic, all the army cots, Captain and the details of his features, the Confederate uniforms that lay on the cots in the attic. She painted a picture so vivid that when the warm and fuzzy feeling churned in his gut he waited for it to dissipate, then opened his eyes and found himself along with Helen standing in the middle of her attic.

"You see," Helen had said. "All it takes is true concentration. You have to get your mind off of that girl and on wherever it is you want to go. The location, not the person in the location. If you're going to get anything accomplished while you're stuck here, you're going to have to concentrate on more than her."

"But she's the reason I'm here," Guy argued.

"I told you, you've got to let that girl live her life."

"But she's my girlfriend."

"She *was* your girlfriend," Helen said. "I hate to be so black and white about it, but that's the truth. She *was* your girlfriend. She can see you, you can see her, and that's what makes it so hard for both of you to let go. If she didn't have the ability to see the dead, you'd be the only one doing the seeing, and she'd have moved on with her life by now. But because she can see you, she's stuck. The same way you're stuck. I know she loves you. I can feel it in her. But she's locked between what she feels for you and the desire for more. What did you say, it's been nine years since you passed?"

"Yes."

"That's a long time to keep someone waiting."

"She's been on dates. It's not like I'm suffocating her."

"Did you interrupt those dates by chance?" Helen asked, then suddenly threw up a hand. "Aw, listen to that. I heard the sawhorse downstairs move. He's trying to pack my saddle. I'm glad you're here to help because that would be a bit heavy for me to move by myself."

"But don't you move things with your mind?" Guy asked.

"Yes, but I can only move with my mind what I could physically move when I was alive. In other words, if it was too heavy for me to move when I was alive, my mind can't seem to compensate for the weight. I can make it move, but not that much. I don't know why I can't get through to my son when I got through so easily to your girlfriend. He can't even feel when I'm right next to him. It's sad really."

"You see, you even called her my girlfriend," Guy said.

"As a point of reference. You know what I'm talking about. I'll call her Nonie from now on. Just Nonie. Lord, listen to all that racket downstairs. I wish he'd leave everything alone. I know he wants to renovate the place, and I don't want that to happen. I want it to stay the way it is. Have people come through the house and see my pictures with famous people, my saddle, and all the things I collected over the years. Why he'd want to pack that all away is beyond me. I can't get him to hear me, get him to understand that the house would be more valuable if he left it as it is."

"Maybe he just wants to sell it and be done with it," Guy said.

Helen gasped. "I didn't think of that. You need to help me stop him. We're just going to keep unpacking everything he packs."

"But I can't stay here with you, Helen. Every time your son comes here, he'll pack again, and it looks like he comes every day. I can't stay with you to help with the unpacking every day. My job here is to take care of Nonie."

"This would be a good diversion for you," Helen insisted. "Help wean you off Nonie. Think of it like that."

"I don't want to think of it like that. She's the reason I didn't go to the light when I died. I wanted to protect her, to be with her. We were meant to be together forever."

"Maybe so, but that's when both of you were alive. It doesn't work that way now that you're dead. Think about it. How would she marry a ghost? How would she have children with a ghost? You're not being fair to her."

"She's the one not being fair," Guy said. "I'm the one who stayed behind for her."

"My boy, that was your choice not hers. You can't blame her for that and you can't expect her to live in gratitude because you didn't move over into the light. I keep telling you that what you're doing is hindering her, but that message doesn't seem to be sinking into your thick head. I don't mean to be ugly, but you're not listening to what I've been telling you." Helen suddenly clapped her hands. "Oh, listen . . . The front door closed. Let's go see how much damage he did this time. Now remember, we don't have to go down the attic stairs to get to the living room. We can blip ourselves there. That'll give you some practice. Do you want some help doing it again?"

"Maybe so. I might wind up at Roy's Grocery back in Clay Point."

Helen took him by the hand. "Okay, concentrate on my living room and everything in it. My pictures, the sawhorse and saddle, the sofa with the blue afghan, all of it. You've got it in your head?"

"Yes."

"You've got the warm and fuzzies?"

"Yes."

"Okay, give my hand a squeeze when the wfs start to go away and we'll blip into the living room."

Guy opened his eyes. "The wfs?"

Helen tsked. "Oh, for Pete's sake, the warm and fuzzies."

"Oh, okay." He closed his eyes again, and as soon as his stomach felt the wfs begin to wane, he gave Helen's hand a little squeeze.

In a nanosecond, Guy found himself standing in Helen's living room. In that same moment, they heard the lock click into place on the front door.

"We could have simply stayed downstairs while your son was here. It's not like he would have seen us."

"I know, but I didn't want to take any chances. I get upset when I see him packing, and when I get upset sometimes things have a tendency to go a bit wonky. You know, ceramics flying off the mantle, dishes rattling in the kitchen. I don't want to scare him like that. He means well, my son I mean. He just doesn't know what else to do. He doesn't know what my wishes are. He's only doing the best he knows how. I'm hoping that the continuous unpacking will give him the message somehow. He knows it's not a burglar doing it because nothing's missing. Now help me move this saddle back on the sawhorse."

The saddle had been placed on the couch and covered with a blanket. Helen took the blanket off the saddle and grabbed the horn while Guy grabbed the backend of the saddle, and together they jostled it back onto the sawhorse. Then they busied themselves unpacking the boxes her son had packed, with Guy asking every other minute, "Where do you want this? Where do you want that?"

After what seemed to be an eternity of unpacking pictures, bric-a-brac, medals, books, and putting them back just so, Guy suddenly got a gnawing sensation in his gut. It was a Nonie alarm.

"Something's going on with Nonie," he said to Helen. "I need to get back to her. She's either in trouble or about to get into trouble."

"But you promised you'd help me with this mess."

"I did. I've been helping. Look I know you taught me how to blip, but I'm still not sure of myself, and I could use your help. Something's going on with Nonie, and I have to get to her. I'm sensing some kind of danger around her. I need your help to make sure I get to her right away and stop her from going there."

"Going where?"

"I'm not sure yet, but it's someplace she's not supposed to be. I have a feeling she's going to wind up seeing something she doesn't want to see, shouldn't have to see."

"You're not making any sense," Helen said.

"You're going to have to trust me like I trusted you with this whole blipping thing," Guy said. "I know Nonie. I feel her. And she's about to do something that she needs to stay away from. I've got to convince her of that. Look, I'll come back here with you when we're done with Nonie, but please, help me get to her."

With a nod, Helen took hold of Guy's hand. "Remember, we have to concentrate on a place, not a person. Do you know where she is right now?"

"I suppose her apartment. She had the day off of work today. But I don't feel like she's there."

"Do you have any feel for where she might be?"

"I'm not sure."

"Well, then let's concentrate on her apartment. Even if she's not there now, she'll eventually go back there, right?"

"I suppose so. Everything's so scrambled in my head. I usually have a pretty good bead on where she is most of the time. Not right now, though. Maybe it's the blipping that has my radar off."

"Okay, stop freaking out, and we'll start with her apartment," Helen said.

Guy nodded and closed his eyes. He soon saw in his mind's eye Nonie's dinette set, her kitchen, her beige Naugahyde couch, the brown, overstuffed chair, her television set that sat on an oak, pressboard stand. He focused on the scent of her apartment, a mixture of lavender and cinnamon, just like Nonie.

As the wfs went cold in his belly, Guy heard a slight whooshing sound. He opened his eyes and found himself standing in the middle of Nonie's apartment. Alone.

CHAPTER TWENTY-TWO

By two that afternoon Jack labeled the last segment of his Pro Audio Editing program. His head was pounding. He'd been watching video and editing the audio to clean up the white noise since nine that morning. He'd only stopped once to grab a slice of bologna and a Coke from his fridge. They'd picked up so much evidence, both on audio and video, he didn't know where to start placing things on a jump drive to show the producers. Without a doubt, the two locations they'd investigated were prime for *Something's Out There.* He wanted to make sure he had all of the camera shots cleaned and audio marked on the exact segments so he could loop the EVPs they'd collected.

One thing that amazed him was that every EVP they'd captured had been a class A, which meant a word or two came through clear and precise. One didn't have to strain an ear to make out what was said, as was often the case with many paranormal investigation programs now on television. He'd never heard any this clear before. It was a rare find, like waking up on Christmas morning to find the one present you'd always wanted under the tree.

The video and stills had contained some remarkable evidence. At the Richardson place, there were stills of ectoplasm, which were white wisps of smoke with red and green streaks running through it. He'd found at least four with arcs of mist and streaks. He ran the photos through an editing program to make certain that what they'd captured hadn't been light fragmentation or equipment malfunction. All had checked out perfectly.

He'd found video of what looked like a shadow figure, its form defined well enough to identify it as female. That had been captured upstairs, where the Confederate uniforms had been laid across three cots that had been used during the Civil War. Along with the female shadow, they'd also captured a darker shape on one of the cots. It looked like a man lying on his back, and at one point, you actually saw it roll to its side. Neither of the shadow figures had facial features that could be identified, but there was little question they were human . . . or had been.

The EVPs he had collected himself had produced a few class B, a woman whispering,

"Hi," at the Richardson's, and another one from the old plantation that seemed to ask a question but all he heard was the word, "Who . . .?" The EVPs that Nonie had collected, however, were all Class As.

As he listened to the recordings through the editing suite, he heard Nonie speaking to someone. Buggy had been up in the Richardson attic with Nonie, but the response picked up on the recorder wasn't Buggy. There were quite a few places where it sounded like Nonie was having a conversation with someone. Her voice came through clear, but oftentimes what followed was dead air. On occasion, a single word came through that didn't quite make sense. Not in relation to what Nonie was discussing anyway. Nonie's EVPs picked up words like, "television" and "I want." They'd even gotten a complete sentence— "What's your name?"— which was rare in electronic voice phenomena. Usually a spirit had enough energy to produce a word or two, but one who spoke complete sentences had to be drawing extra power from something . . . or someone.

What stuck with Jack the most, though, was his question regarding who Nonie had been talking to. In his gut, he just knew that she was speaking directly with a spirit. That she could see them. In his years of investigating, he'd worked with a few mediums, some real, some phony. With the mediums who were the real deal, he'd always hear a one-sided conversation. The medium speaking to the spirits. He always questioned their validity, however, until he picked up a corresponding EVP.

Nonie sounded so sincere in her conversation in the Richardson attic, and her responses so direct, that there was little question in his mind that he might be working with the real deal where Nonie was concerned.

Buggy had hardly spoken a word during the recordings, so Jack knew Nonie hadn't been speaking to her. So who had she been speaking to? What had she seen up there?

If he was right and Nonie could see the dead, of course it meant the group as a whole had a leg up as far as the producers were concerned. On one hand he thought that to be a positive thing but on the other it made him feel guilty for even thinking that way. It made him feel like the group would be using her in order to get real evidence they needed to get paid. But she was the one who came with the group. It wasn't like he'd encouraged her to join. The group had already been put together when his uncle had contacted him about leading it.

If Nonie could see the dead, what effect did that have on her personal life? Did she see them everywhere she went? Did they keep her from sleep? Did she ever have a moment's peace?

He couldn't help but worry about her. Whoever had talked her into joining the group had to have known about Nonie's ability. Did it make Nonie feel used? Did doing these investigations and seeing more ghosts have any kind of negative impact on her?

There was only one way he'd be able to get answers to those questions and that was to ask her directly. He'd tried to twice before, but she'd avoided answering.

Even more amazing were the EVPs and pictures they'd captured in the plantation. No one, not even a hard-core skeptic could deny the oddity of a floating iron skillet. The EVPs captured were those of a woman saying things like, "Get," and "What do . . ." When Jack had asked specific questions of the entity holding the skillet, he'd received direct responses, like, "Who . . ." and "make them . . ." The responses came across as angry and frustrated, which could have explained why the entity had taken after them with that skillet.

The pictures and film they captured of that floating skillet were as uncommon a find as happening upon a blue diamond in the middle of the Sierra Desert. An inanimate object moving on its own volition was often associated with poltergeist activity. But that skillet had been the only thing to move. No cabinet doors banged open and shut, no windows opened or closed on their own. Just the skillet. This made Jack lean toward the belief that they were dealing with an intelligent spirit with enough energy to manipulate inanimate objects. That was some pretty powerful stuff.

Jack would bet his entire investigative history that Nonie had been able to see who had been holding that skillet. He'd caught her shrug on one occasion as if responding to something someone said, although no one in the group had addressed her.

The full-spectrum camera had picked up a large, dark shadow attached to the skillet. Judging by the shape and size of the shadow, Jack figured it to be that of a large woman. Had it not been for the shape of breasts it would have been difficult to identify the gender of the shadow because it didn't appear to have hair.

No doubt all of this evidence would blow the producers away. Hopefully, getting the money that the Boo Krewe earned would encourage them to continue with more investigations, given what they'd experienced with the skillet woman. Most of all, he hoped it would encourage Nonie to trust him enough to tell him what she'd seen.

That way they could work in tandem instead of her having to hide her abilities.

It was obvious to him that Buggy knew about Nonie's talent. If she didn't, Jack didn't think Nonie would have so openly communicated with the entity while Buggy was nearby. He didn't want to approach Buggy behind Nonie's back, though. Back door gimmicks weren't his style.

Jack dropped the evidence from the stills, the video, and audio onto a jump drive, closed his laptop, and packed everything away in a carry case. With that done, he went into his bathroom, stripped, and stepped into the shower.

He had a meeting with the producers and his uncle in an hour, and he knew they would be more than pleased with their finds. Although he expected head honcho platitudes, Jack couldn't help but feel a bit guilty and awkward about presenting the evidence. Had it not been for Nonie, they might not have gotten anything at all. She was the one who seemed to instigate most of what they picked up on audio and video.

Jack needed to talk to Nonie in order to shake away the guilt and awkwardness. He wanted to make sure she was good with all of this. But he was dealing with a chicken-and-egg theory here. He either talked to Nonie first, before the evidence was released to the public, or he got the money they'd earned, thus building some semblance of trust with the group. For most people, money spoke a hell of lot louder than a bunch of meddling questions. Considering that, he'd take the evidence to the producers, get the money for the Krewe, then call everyone together for a meeting. He'd show the entire crew the evidence, give them their money, then try to get Nonie alone to talk to her about what weighed so heavily on his mind.

Jack knew he'd be more than ready to give up this entire gig if any of it hurt Nonie in any way. And the only way he could make sure was for her to tell him. She'd agreed to have dinner with him, and for a moment he thought that might be a good time to question her about her abilities. Then he thought better of it. He wanted to have dinner with her to get to know the real Nonie, not so he could drill her about what she could or couldn't do when it came to the dead. He wanted the dinner to be special. Just him and a beautiful, intelligent woman, each getting to know the other. The ghost stuff had to be separate. He wouldn't discuss it during dinner unless she did, which he doubted would happen since she'd dodged his questions on so many fronts before.

He was anxious to know the real Nonie. The one that didn't have to hide. If anything, he wanted to be a safe place for her, where she felt at ease enough to share whatever was on her mind with him. He'd never felt that way about another woman before. It wasn't like he was a prude because he dated often enough, but rarely the same woman more than twice. It was difficult for him to find someone who held his interest for very long. Nonie was different. She was a little quiet and introspective, but when she spoke, he seemed to hang on her every word.

Jack couldn't put his finger on what it was about Nonie that had so captured him. All he knew was she was special, and it had to do with much more than the fact that she possibly saw ghosts. What attracted him to her was Nonie simply being Nonie. With her beautiful curly brown hair, large gorgeous eyes, and her slender body. What captured him most, however, was her smile. It lit up a room and seemed to pull something out of him that made him automatically want to smile back.

As Jack stood under the shower and thought of Nonie, he had to turn the spray to a cooler setting and started working geometric equations in his head. He didn't think it would be cool to meet with the producers and his uncle with a bulge in the front of his pants.

CHAPTER TWENTY-THREE

When Nonie and Fezzo arrived at Clara Grubb's, they found her pacing in her graveled driveway. Clara lived off of Grainger Street, which held an eclectic neighborhood. Some homes were old clapboards in need of paint and lawns that needed serious attention. Other homes were made of brick, a few with manicured lawns. Clara's house was a cottage style set on piers. It was beige with white shutters and the front windows held planters with foliage overflowing in them. To Nonie, the foliage looked more like weeds than plants that might produce any flowers. But she was no horticulturist.

"Thank you so much for coming," Clara said, when Nonie parked and opened her car door.

The woman stood there wringing her hands.

"What are you doing out here?" Nonie asked, getting out of the car. Fezzo followed her lead. "Did you lock yourself out of your house?"

"No, no. I thought I'd wait for the two of you to get here before I went inside." She gave Nonie a knowing look. "You know, I just thought I'd wait."

Nonie knew Clara didn't want to say that she was afraid to go into her house alone in front of Fezzo. If anything weird was going on in the house, she hoped they'd witness it firsthand.

"I'm not sure why you needed us to come here, Ms. Clara," Fezzo said. "To make sure nobody was in your house?"

"Well . . ." Clara blushed. "That would be nice, given that Anna Mae has disappeared. You never know who might be lurking around. If someone took Anna Mae, they might be looking for me next. I'd also like for y'all to take a look around the house to see if you can find anything odd. A clue maybe as to where Anna Mae might have gone."

Fezzo raised an eyebrow. "Dat's for de police to do, no? I'm not no detective, me. I'll be glad to check in you house, though, to make sure nobody's in there waiting to get you."

"The police didn't even come to the house to check on anything," Clara said. "I've been looking at things inside over and over again. I hoped a fresh pair of eyes might make a difference."

Fezzo shrugged. "Mah, den we'll take a look."

Nonie had told Fezzo the reason for coming to Clara's back at the funeral home. He evidently wanted to hear the reason directly from the horse's mouth.

Clara led them to the front door of her house, opened it and motioned them inside. "Please, come in."

Judging from the furniture in Clara's living room and the wall color, Clara was really into beige. Beige walls, beige couch, a couple of ladder-back wooden rockers. A television set in a mahogany entertainment center. Across from the living room was the kitchen. Beige Formica countertops, white cabinet doors. Except for a saddle sitting atop a sawhorse, Clara's house reminded Nonie a little of Helen Richardson's house. Bric-a-brac was everywhere, pictures of her family, her children and grandchildren, dogs and cats. A collection of ceramic birds sat in a curio cabinet against the far left wall of the living room.

There were blue jays, sparrows,

canaries, cardinals, lining the top of shelves of the

curio. The bottom shelf held crystal

butterflies, at least a dozen. Large and beautiful, a

myriad of colors so brilliant they matched those of a

rainbow.

Clara motioned them to the kitchen. "Would

y'all care for something to drink? Coffee, a

soft drink maybe?" She walked into the kitchen

hesitantly, glancing over her shoulder every so often

to make sure Nonie and Fezzo were following her.

"No thank you, Clara. I'm fine." Fezzo said.

"Same here," Nonie said. "Nothing for me."

Clara nodded, her eyes flitting about the kitchen

nervously. "Where . . . Where would y'all like to

start looking?"

"Well," Nonie said. "Did Anna Mae have her own bedroom?"

"Yes. It's down the hall, second door on the right. Oh, and if y'all need the restroom, it's the first door on the left. At the end of the hall is my bedroom. Y'all are welcome to look in there, too, if you think it'll help." Clara folded her arms across her chest and shifted her weight from one foot to the other.

"Aren't you coming with us?" Nonie asked.

Clara looked over her shoulder toward the kitchen cabinets then back at Nonie and Fezzo. "Yes, I guess I'll come with you."

She led the way down the hall and into the bedroom on the right, where Clara flipped on a light switch. Inside was a queen-size bed neatly made, with a homemade quilt folded across the foot of it, a dresser, a small desk with a rolling chair and a vanity table with a tri-fold mirror on top of it, along with various makeup products, and a small, pink cushioned chair in front of it.

"You see what I'm saying?" Clara said, pointing to the vanity. "All of Anna Mae's makeup is still here. She would have never left without taking it."

Clara went to the closet door, which was to the right of the dresser, and opened it. It was filled with clothes, all neatly hung in a row. "And all her clothes are here." She turned to the dresser and opened the top drawer. "Not to be ugly or nothing, but you see this? It's her underwear drawer. Not a thing's missing from it. It's like she just vanished in thin air. I mean really, how are you going to go anywhere without fresh underwear, makeup or extra clothes? You see what I'm saying? Something's very wrong here."

Nonie looked around the room and tried to see it through the eyes of Anna Mae. If she was going to take a trip, surely she would have brought her stuff with her. Could she have been kidnapped? Or had she been so embarrassed over what happened at the funeral home that she decided to simply skip town and planned on buying all new clothes and accessories wherever she landed?

Nonie voiced her thoughts to Clara. "Suppose she was so embarrassed over the whole town seeing the fight at the funeral home that she just decided to skip town? Did she have her own car?"

"Yes," Clara said. "A red Mustang."

Nothing like flash, Nonie thought.

"I haven't seen the Mustang either since the funeral," Clara said. "Remember, I told you we came in separate vehicles because we each had things to tend to after the funeral. That car isn't easy to miss. If she'd been in town, I'd have spotted it by now."

"Maybe she decided to leave town instead," Nonie said. "Then figured she'd buy new clothes and makeup when she got to wherever she was going."

"She wouldn't have done that without talking to me first," Clara said. "We were pretty close."

As Clara spoke, Nonie watched Fezzo walk about the room, examining a hairbrush from the vanity. He sniffed a perfume bottle.

"Suppose she was embarrassed for you, too," Nonie offered. "She could have left to save you the embarrassment of having her around."

"I'm telling you," Clara said. "She wouldn't have done anything like that without contacting me. She knows how much of a worrywart I am. No matter what happened at the funeral home, we're cousins. It's not like I would have ever turned my back on her. I mean, I didn't agree with what she did, you know, with the mayor and all, and, in fact, I tried to stop her. But when Anna Mae got her mind set on something, she'd follow through with it or die."

"Well, maybe that's the case here," Nonie said. "She got her mind set on getting out of town and will probably contact you once she gets settled someplace."

Clara seemed to mull that over for a while. "Well . . . maybe. But it's her leaving all her stuff here that has me stumped. If she did make up her mind to leave and planned on contacting me once she got to wherever she planned to go, she would have packed her belongings."

"Let's look at it this way," Nonie said. "For the sake of argument, let's say she was too embarrassed to face you after that fight and decided to head out of town. Left everything behind so she wouldn't have to deal with that."

"But—" Clara began.

Nonie held up a hand. "For the sake of argument, let's run with this scenario. She leaves because she doesn't want to face anyone. The police could be right. Let's give it a day or two and see if she contacts you. If she doesn't, then the police have more to work with. They can file a missing person's report."

At that moment a loud banging sounded from the kitchen. Clara ducked as if expecting something to come flying at her head.

"You have somebody else in you house?" Fezzo asked.

"No, it's just the three of us," Clara said, her eyes wide.

"Okay, y'all stay here," Fezzo said. "I'm gonna go check it out."

As Fezzo limped out of the bedroom, Nonie followed closely behind him and Clara behind her. Even though Fezzo had told them to stay put, Nonie was too curious to leave well enough alone.

When they walked down the hallway, the banging in the kitchen grew more frequent and louder. BAM! BAM! BAM! It sounded like cabinet doors being slammed shut with great force.

As they turned right at the end of the hall and faced the kitchen, Fezzo said, "What the heck is dis?"

Nonie and Clara piled up behind Fezzo each looking over one of his shoulders. The cabinet doors below her kitchen sink were flapping open and slamming shut again and again. Fezzo's comment seemed to agitate whatever had taken over the cabinets because the utensil drawer to the right of the stove suddenly opened on its own then slammed shut. Another drawer that contained dishtowels was yanked out so far it hung by the end of its runner.

"You see, I told you," Clara said to Nonie with tears welling up in her eyes. "I told you there were strange things going on in the house."

Fezzo held his arms out and stepped back, pushing Nonie and Clara back with him. "I don't know what's going on here, but I don't think it's too good," he said. "I think we should leave."

"Where am I supposed to go?" Clara said. "This is my home."

"I don't know," Fezzo said. "But you may want to call a priest. I sure don't know what to do with doors that open and close by themselves and drawers hanging out all wonky. I could hunt a alligator back in my day, but dis, huh, dat's way over my head." He turned around and looked at Nonie. "You notice anything . . . different?"

Nonie knew he was asking her if she saw any ghost doing the cabinet clatter, but the sad fact was she didn't see a thing. "Nothing more than what you see," she said to Fezzo.

Abruptly the cabinet doors held still, and in the sudden silence, Nonie heard two people whispering in the living room. She glanced over her shoulder and saw Guy and Helen Richardson standing in front of Clara's entertainment center, huddled together, whispering and motioning to the kitchen.

When Guy and Helen spotted Nonie looking at them, both smiled and waved. Nonie gritted her teeth. She wanted to ask them what they were doing here, but couldn't with Fezzo and Clara standing nearby. She glared at Guy. They had enough trouble in this place. If there was another entity in this house, Nonie couldn't see it, which concerned her.

Something strong enough to slam cabinets should have held enough energy for it to be visible to her. But nothing, not even a shadow.

Guy signaled for her to come over. She shook her head slightly, indicating that she couldn't.

"Mah, it stopped just like dat," Fezzo said. "Dat's the strangest thing I've ever seen to my whole life."

"I'm really scared to stay here by myself," Clara said. "But I don't have anywhere else to go. With Anna Mae gone and this weird stuff happening in the house—"

"You mean dis has happened before to you?" Fezzo asked.

"Yes," Clara said. "I talked to Nonie about it when I went to the funeral home. I wanted y'all to come here to see if you might pick up a clue I might have missed regarding Anna Mae's disappearance, but I also wanted to see if anything weird would happen while y'all were here. For a while, I thought it was just me losing my mind."

Fezzo frowned at Nonie. "You should have warned me dat this kind of stuff might was gonna happen."

"I didn't know it was going to, Uncle Fezzo," Nonie said. "Clara was so desperate for help in finding Anna Mae, hoping we'd pick up a clue or something that I agreed we'd come. I wasn't expecting all of this."

Clara chimed in. "It's not her fault. I asked Nonie not to tell you about the weird stuff going on here because I didn't want you to think I was crazy."

Fezzo's brows knitted together. "Don't get me wrong. It's not like I'm scare or nothin', but this is something completely different than looking for clues about Anna Mae. I don't blame you for not wantin' to stay to you house. I wouldn't want to stay, me, neither if this was happening to my house."

A tear slid down Clara's cheek, and that one tear seemed to be the catalyst for a floodgate of sobs to open, tears she'd probably held in check for some time. Between sobs, she hiccupped. "I-I don't-don't know what to do. I-I don't know-know where to go. I can't take this anymore."

"How long dis has been going on?" Fezzo asked.

"A day, day and a half maybe," Clara said, then sniffled. "Since the funeral. I don't know how long ago that was. I'm losing track of time. I can't eat, I can't sleep. I'm worried about Anna Mae, all this stuff going on in my house. I feel like I'm losing my mind."

"Can't you go to your sister's?" Nonie asked. "Doesn't she live in Ville Platte?"

Clara shook her head. "She's got a husband and two teenagers. She's got enough on her plate. She doesn't need to be dealing with me."

"I tell you what," Fezzo said. "You come wit' me. I'm going to talk to T-boy, you know, my brother dat owns the funeral home? They got a nice big house wit' a extra bedroom. I'll talk to dem about you stayin' wit' dem a couple of days 'til we can figure out what's going on here."

Clara put a hand over her heart. "Oh, no, really. I wouldn't want to impose. I couldn't."

"Don't worry yourself," Fezzo said. "I'm gonna talk to my brother. It'll be fine."

Nonie looked at Fezzo like he had broccoli growing out of his nose. Her mother, Rita, taking in Clara Grubbs for two days wasn't going to happen without a hissy fit being thrown somewhere.

To stave off an impending family feud, Nonie jumped in. "Ms. Clara you can stay with me. I live down on Norman Circle, ten minutes from the funeral home. You can have my bedroom and I'll bunk on the couch."

"Oh, no," Clara said, wringing her hands. "There's no way I'm going to put you out like that. You having to sleep on your own couch? That's just not right."

Fezzo blew out a breath. "Mah, the only other thing I can think of is for you to go to Lafayette and get a hotel room. There's no hotels in Clay Point, but you already know dat."

Clara nodded enthusiastically. "That's a good idea. A hotel. I'll go to a hotel for a couple of days, make phone calls to other family members to see if anyone's heard from Anna Mae. And I'll call the priest, too. The one at St. Anthony's. Ask him to come bless the house." She blew out a sigh of relief. "Tomorrow maybe. I'll do that tomorrow when I'm feeling a little bit better."

"Now you talkin'," Fezzo said.

"I've got to pack some clothes, though. Things to bring to Lafayette." She looked at Fezzo with doe-like eyes. "Would you please follow me . . . you know, just in case something else goes crazy? I don't want to be back there by myself."

"Maybe it would be bes' if Nonie went wit' you since you packing girl stuff," Fezzo said.

Nonie, still stealing glances over at Guy and Helen who seemed to be conspiring about something, said to Fezzo, "If you don't mind, would you please go with Ms. Clara and just stand in the doorway of her bedroom while she packs. I'll be there in a few minutes."

Fezzo looked at Nonie, and after a long pause, he said, "Okay, den, I'm gonna stand guard at de door while you pack. Then I'll take you to the hotel myself."

"Thank you so much," Clara said, relief washing over her face.

"No problem," Fezzo said, then followed Clara down the hall to her bedroom. He glanced over his shoulder at Nonie once and frowned.

Nonie knew her uncle had at least twenty questions he wanted to ask her. He probably sensed there was something going on that she couldn't talk about in front of Clara so he'd played along.

As soon as they were out of sight, Nonie marched into the living room and confronted Guy and Helen.

"What are the two of you doing?" she whispered. "We've got enough problems over here. Didn't you just see what happened in Clara's kitchen?"

"Hello, dear," Helen said and smiled as if she hadn't heard a word Nonie had just said.

"Yeah, we saw," Guy said. "And we know who did it. We know why it's happening. You don't need to be here. You're going to wind up in a lot more crap than you bargained for if you don't leave."

"What are you talking about?" Nonie demanded.

"You okay, mon petite?" Fezzo called from the back room.

"Fine, Uncle Fezzo," Nonie called back. She turned her attention back to Guy and Helen and lowered her voice a notch. "Both of you need to go. I can't afford for Clara and Uncle Fezzo to see me talking to you."

"Honey, you need to leave this house," Helen said to Nonie. "You don't need to get involved in this."

"Involved in what? Anna Mae? Whatever or whoever's slamming cabinet doors that I can't see?"

"Yes," Guy and Helen said in unison.

"Well, which one is it?" Nonie asked, frustrated.

"Both," Guy said. "We saw who was slamming those doors."

When he didn't comment further, Nonie wanted to tap him in the gut with a fist. "Stop playing games, will you? Who was it? What's the big secret?"

"Nonie you really couldn't see who was slamming those doors?" Guy asked in a whisper.

"I already told you I couldn't. What are you talking about? And why are you whispering? Nobody can hear you but me and Helen."

Guy cleared his throat. "Yeah, you're right," he said loudly. "They can't hear us."

Helen held a hand out to Nonie. "Dear, you really should leave this house. This isn't a place you want to be."

"I know," Nonie said. "Both of you have already told me that, but you're not telling me why."

"Because police will get involved," Guy said matter-of-factly. "And then you're going to get tangled up in an ugly mess."

"What are you talking about?"

"Just trust me. When Fezzo and Clara leave, you need to make sure you leave with them," Guy said. "In fact, you should go now."

"Why dammit?" Nonie said. "You're not giving me anything to work with here except warnings that make no sense."

"You want sense?" Guy said. "Here's some sense for you. The person who's slamming those cabinet doors . . . is Anna Mae Turner. She's not missing, Nonie. She's dead."

"What?" Nonie said a little too loudly.

Guy nodded. "Check the backyard, you'll see."

"Yes," Helen chimed in. "The backyard."

"Nonie Marie, you okay?" Uncle Fezzo called out again.

Nonie heard footsteps hurrying down the hallway toward her. Within a minute, Clara and Fezzo appeared in the living room, Clara's face ashen.

"What's wrong?" Fezzo asked Nonie.

"Nothing, why?"

"We heard you yell, 'What?' just a minute ago," Clara said. "Scared the heck out of me."

"Oh, I'm sorry," Nonie said, trying to keep her eyes away from Guy and Helen who were gesturing for her to get out of the house. "Just thought I saw something out of the corner of my eye. It was nothing."

Nonie gave Fezzo a fleeting glance, then said to Clara. "Ms. Clara since we're still here, do you mind if we take a look at your backyard? That's the only place we didn't look for clues to Anna Mae's disappearance."

"I haven't been back there in weeks," Clara said. "What with my quilting and me having to run the bingo hall on Monday, Wednesday and Friday nights, I haven't had a chance to take care of anything back there. I'm sure the lawn will look horrid. Anna Mae isn't one to sit out in the sun much less take to yard work. Her skin is too sensitive for that."

"Do you mind if we take a look before we leave?"

"Be my guest," Clara said. "Just excuse the mess if there is one back there."

Clara pointed to a door to the left of her stove. "You can get to the backyard from there."

Nonie followed Clara's direction and went to the white wooden door. She opened it and found herself stepping down onto a small patio with two lawn chairs and a wooden table that held two ceramic cherubs. Surrounding the patio, and setting it apart from the rest of the backyard, were large gray stones placed neatly in a row. Beyond the patio was the backyard, which was maybe fifty by a hundred feet and surrounded by a white privacy fence. Two pecan trees stood at the back corners of the property.   Between the trees was a clothesline stretched between two metal poles. Clothes pins hung from the line like small beige claws. All of it was back-dropped by clouds rolling in from the west, turning the afternoon sky a smoky gray. It added to the eeriness of the place.

Nonie spotted a garden hose wound to a hose reel attached to the back of the house and a small metal shed about ten feet away. A mound of cement sat a couple feet from the shed. It rose about a foot off the ground and was about three feet in circumference. It was light gray save for the section nearest the ground, which was a much darker shade of gray. A ceramic blue jay sat on top of the mound.

Clara and Fezzo were standing behind her when Guy and Helen suddenly appeared near the cement mound. A chill ran through Nonie, and it had nothing to do with the temperature. She sensed trouble on its way.

Guy pointed to the cement mound. "She's in there."

Nonie felt her mouth drop open.

Fezzo, who was still standing behind Nonie asked, "Mah, Clara, why you got some cement sitting on the ground like dat? Did you tap a well there?"

Nonie turned around in time to see Clara shrug.

"I've never seen it before," Clara said. "I don't know what that is. Anna Mae liked to sculpt and work with ceramics, but I've never seen her work with concrete. It looks horrible there. Who would have done such a thing?"

Nonie walked over to the concrete and moved her hand across the mound. The top section was hard, but as her fingers moved closer to the ground they came back tacky, where the cement had not quite dried.

Nonie turned to Clara. "Do you have a shovel?"

"A shovel?" Clara said, seemingly taken aback by the question. "I-I think there's one in the shed."

Nonie gave Fezzo a look that said, "Just play along, okay," and hoped he caught on.

"Uncle Fezzo, would you mind getting that shovel from the shed? Maybe we can help flatten this out for Ms. Clara so it doesn't look so bad. Would you like that, Ms. Clara?"

"Oh, yes, but . . . I mean I wouldn't want you to go through all that trouble. I can hire somebody to come and take care of it. I'm-I'm so embarrassed. It looks horrible just sitting there, like I don't even care about my own lawn."

"No need. It shouldn't be that big a job," Nonie said. She stuck a finger into the doughy part of the concrete. "See? Not all of it has dried yet. If you wait much longer, though, you'll need to get someone in here with a jackhammer to break it apart. We can take care of it now while it's still curing."

Fezzo came out of the shed with a shovel. "I can take care of dat if you want me to," he told Clara.

"Well . . . yes, thank you. Y'all have done so much already."

"No problems at all," Fezzo said.

Suddenly Guy started waving his arms out in front of him and mouthed, "No, no!" Evidently forgetting that no one could hear him but Nonie.

Nonie looked at him quizzically.

"Don't let him start digging," Guy said. "You can't let Clara see what's under there."

By this time, Fezzo was already teasing the shovel blade around the base of the mound.

"Uncle Fezzo, maybe we should wait," Nonie said quickly.

Not looking up at her, Fezzo said, "No, you was right. If we wait, this concrete's gonna be too hard to handle wit' just a shovel. Clara's gonna wind up havin' to get someone in here to bus' it up with a sledgehammer. With everything Clara's going through, we can at least give the poor woman some peace of mind about her backyard."

With that, Fezzo took the ceramic bird off the mound and handed it to Clara, then he started chipping away at the ridge of concrete where dry met wet. Before long, he was able to get a thin layer of concrete off of the top. Nonie saw Fezzo suddenly shiver, and he turned to her. "You. . . uh, you see anything strange about dat concrete other than the concrete?"

"What are you talking about, Mr. Broussard?" Clara asked.

"No, not yet," Nonie said. "But I don't think it's a good idea for you to go any deeper. I think we should leave it as is."

Fezzo looked at her and pursed his lips. "Nah," he said. "Sometimes there's a reason for stuff like this. You know, concrete on the ground where there's not supposed to be concrete on the ground. I think we need to find out what it is." With a nod of his head, he continued to dig, only slower this time, much more carefully. He gave one grunt and a large chunk of the hardened concrete fell over to the side of the mound.

Two gasps rang out. The first one came from Clara, the second from Fezzo. One moment they'd been looking at a mound of concrete, and now they were staring at two human feet. They were crossed at the ankle so that the tops of the feet faced each other and rested toe to toe.

"Oh, sweet Jesus of all dat's holy," Fezzo said, and took a step back.

Suddenly Clara let out a scream that could be heard to the next parish. Nonie hurried to her side.

"Oh, dear, oh, dear," Helen said. "What a mess this is going to be."

Guy shouted, "I told you to leave it alone, Nonie Marie, didn't I? I told you not to get involved. Now look at what you did!"

"You stop being so mean to her," Helen snapped at Guy. "Can't you see the poor dear was just trying to help that woman?"

"Help her?" Guy said, furious. "Who's going to help Nonie now?"

Nonie took Clara by the shoulders and turned her toward the house. "Ms. Clara, why don't you go inside and call Sheriff Buchanan. Tell him what we found and have him send someone over right away. Can you do that?"

"It can't be," Clara said, and broke away from Nonie's grasp and turned back to the concrete mound. Visibly shaking, she took a step closer to the mound. "C-can you m-move some of the dirt a-away from the f-feet so I can see th-the toenails?" she asked Fezzo. She started to sob. "I-I j-just need to s-see the toe-toenails. Please?"

Looking about as reluctant as a grave robber shoveling into a grave at high-noon, Fezzo did as she asked. He leaned over, brushed dirt and concrete chips away from the feet, then pulled one foot slightly away from the other so the toenails could be plainly seen. Bright pink painted toenails.

"Oh, my God, oh, my God, oh, my God," Clara said, then clapped a hand to her mouth before dropping to the ground face-first in a dead faint.

Nonie grabbed her cell phone out of her back pocket and tossed it to Fezzo. "Call Sheriff Buchanan while I see about Ms. Clara."

Fezzo caught the phone and immediately started to dial.

Nonie dropped to her knees, rolled Clara over and put her head in her lap. She patted her cheek gently. "Ms. Clara? Ms. Clara, are you okay?" To Nonie, the question sounded stupid. Clara didn't look okay. The woman's nose was twisted at an odd angle, and blood covered her face. She'd obviously broken her nose.

Clara's eyelids fluttered open then squeezed shut, and she started to mumble. "No, it can't. It can't."

"You might want to tell Buchanan to send an ambulance," Nonie said to Fezzo. "It looks like Clara broke her nose when she fell."

"Now you've gone and done it," Guy said. "The police are going to get involved and who's going to be in the thick of it? You, that's who."

Nonie wanted to yell at Guy to shut up, or even better to kiss her ass, but she was stuck, unable to say a word with Clara in her lap.

When Fezzo finished his call to Buchanan, he hung up the phone and brought it over to Nonie. He looked down at Clara who was moaning and moving her head from side to side.

"No . . . it's . . . no . . . it's . . ." Clara mumbled.

"Mon petite," Fezzo said to Nonie. "What made you want to come into the backyard like dat? Did you see something?"

Nonie looked up at her uncle reluctantly and nodded. Hoping that Clara wouldn't hear her much less understand what she was saying, she whispered to Fezzo, "Guy told me. He told me that Anna Mae was dead. He said she was the one slamming the cabinet doors, probably to get someone's attention."

"And you didn't see her in de house?"

"No. Not even a glimpse."

"Hmm."

About that time Nonie heard sirens in the distance. They grew louder quickly and within minutes she heard the crunch of gravel in the front driveway.

Fezzo went to the side gate of the privacy fence, opened it, and signaled for whoever had showed up to come this way. He stepped back and Nonie saw Sheriff Buchanan hurry into the backyard. Right behind him was Nate Lopez.

"What's going on here?" Buchanan asked.

"Looks like we got us a dead body," Fezzo said, and pointed to the mound with two feet sticking up from it. "And I think Clara here's got a broke nose."

"The ambulance is on its way," Nate said.

"Now y'all start from the beginning and tell me what happened," Buchanan said.

Nonie nodded at Fezzo, signaling for him to take the lead.

Fezzo filled Buchanan in on the reason they were at Clara's, about Anna Mae having gone missing, and Clara wanting them to help search for clues. To his credit, Fezzo left out the part about the slamming cabinet doors and didn't let on that Guy had been the one who'd told Nonie that Anna Mae was dead. He mentioned that just as they were getting ready to leave, they realized that the one place they hadn't checked was the backyard. They decided to investigate it and discovered the concrete mound, which Clara claimed she knew nothing about, and she'd welcomed their help getting rid of it.

"Check in the shed for a trowel," Buchanan told Nate, then he went over to the mound, took a handkerchief out of his back pocket, and used it to move the feet from side to side.

"Got one," Nate said, hurrying back to Buchanan with a trowel in hand.

Buchanan took several pictures of the mound and feet with his camera phone. "Let's work the rest of the concrete and dirt off the body," Buchanan said, then asked Fezzo to step back.

Everyone stood quietly by as more of the legs attached to the feet were revealed. As they watched, a voice suddenly boomed in Nonie's left ear.

"Now they gonna catch that bastard!"

Nonie jumped and jerked her head in the direction of the voice. Looming behind her, bigger than life was Tiana Lewis. She stood with her hands on her hips and a look of fury on her face.

"That woman died, and the man who killed her, he's not going to get away with it. Not like they did with me, my boy and my man. No siree, not this time. I'm going to make sure of that!"

Unable to talk to Tiana and find out how she'd gotten here or what she was doing here made Nonie feel like her brain would explode. She had Guy, Helen, and now Tiana all in the backyard along with the sheriff, Nate, Clara and Uncle Fezzo. It felt like some macabre nightmare she couldn't wake from.

When they had the bottom half of Anna Mae uncovered, Nonie heard the ambulance sirens coming down a nearby highway.

"Ambulance is here," Nate said, lifting his head. "Mr. Broussard, would you mind going out front and leading the paramedics back here?"

"Not a problem," Fezzo said, then went off to the side gate once more.

Clara was still moaning and moving her head from side to side when Fezzo reappeared in the backyard with two paramedics carrying a collapsible gurney following close behind. They looked from Clara to the bent legs now exposed.

Buchanan, who was on his knees, trowel in hand, looked up at the paramedics and motioned toward Clara with his chin. "Take her to the hospital and have her checked out."

The paramedics went over to Clara, removed her from Nonie's left, and one took her blood pressure while the other one checked the responsiveness of her pupils. Clara moaned louder. After checking her over thoroughly, they soon lifted her onto the gurney and wheeled her out of the backyard.

Before they made it out of the gate, Buchanan called after them. "Send backup, another unit and send for the coroner."

"Yes, sir," one of the paramedics said, then both wheeled Clara through the gate and out of sight.

A gust of wind kicked up suddenly, sending bits of dirt and small chips of concrete tumbling across the lawn. Nonie got to her feet and went over to Fezzo. Now that Clara was gone, she could speak a bit more freely.

"Do you think that's really Anna Mae?" she whispered to Fezzo.

"Dat's a question I should ask you," he whispered back. "You don't see her anywhere?"

"No. I haven't seen her since we got here."

"Then how did you know she was back here?"

"I told you. Guy's the one who told me."

Fezzo shook his head and looked back over to where the sheriff and Nate were still carefully moving dirt away from the body.

The concrete had covered the top of a hole, which they were about a foot into at the moment. It looked as if someone had dug the hole, dropped Anna Mae into it headfirst, then realized too late that the hole wasn't deep enough. Instead of pulling her back out and digging deeper, they evidently considered it a better idea to cover what was exposed with leftover dirt and concrete.

After what seemed like an eternity, Buchanan finally tossed the trowel to one side and Nate the shovel. They both leaned over the hole and took hold of the body and started to lift it up. Inch by inch more of the body came into view, and after one huge heave and pull, Anna Mae Turner's face suddenly appeared. Buchanan and Nate laid her gently on the ground.

Anna Mae's face and hair were covered with dirt, and the pants suit she wore, which Nonie recognized as the same one she'd worn to Dover's funeral, had turned a putrid brown color. How anyone could just dump a body in a hole that way was beyond Nonie's comprehension. It felt worse than wrong. It felt evil.

Seeing a dead person wasn't something new to Nonie but seeing one that had been treated with such disrespect made her stomach roil with nausea. She turned away and put her head against her uncle's shoulder.

Fezzo smoothed Nonie's hair with a hand. "It'll be okay, mon petite. It'll be okay."

"She won't be okay, Uncle Fezzo. I can't believe somebody killed her."

"Dere's all kinds of people in dis world. Some good, some bad. Dat's why you always got to be careful. That's why nonc worries about you whenever you go somewhere. You just never know what people gonna do dese days."

With Anna Mae lying prone on the ground, except for her legs, which Buchanan seemed unable to straighten, Nate took off his deputy's jacket and laid it over her face.

About that time, the smoky gray sky gave way to drizzle. Nonie couldn't bear to look at the woman. Dead, dirty, now being rained on. She heard sirens in the distance and let out a sigh of relief. The second ambulance was on its way to pick up Anna Mae.

"Uncle Fezzo, if you don't mind, I'm going to go into Clara's and help myself to a glass of water," Nonie said.

"You bes' ask de sheriff if dat's okay first," Fezzo said.

"Sheriff Buchanan," Nonie called out. "Is it all right if I go into Ms. Clara's for a drink of water?"

The sheriff shook his head. "Sorry, Nonie, no can do. All of this is a crime scene now, and we can't afford to have anything disturbed. We'll have to cordon off the yard, as well. "

Suddenly, Tiana Lewis appeared right beside Buchanan. "Oh, no you not. This here ain't no crime scene. Look in the hole stupid. Look in the hole."

Buchanan frowned and looked from left to right. "Did y'all hear anything?"

Fezzo shook his head.

"Uh, no," Nonie lied.

"Probably a neighbor's dog." Buchanan said. "Whatever."

Fezzo patted Nonie's shoulder. "Take the car and head back to you house. There's no reason you gotta stay and watch all dis. I'll get a ride back wit' de Sheriff." He dug into the front pocket of his slacks.

"We came in my car," Nonie said, figuring he was hunting for car keys.

"Dat's right. Okay, den. Be careful, huh?"

"I will."

"Hold up a minute, Nonie," Buchanan said. "I need you to stick around for a bit longer. I have some more questions to ask you."

"Okay."

"Tell him to look in the hole," Tiana insisted, this time right in Nonie's left ear. "The hole. They got to go back and look in the hole. They can't let that bastard get away with it." She stormed over to the mounds of dirt and pointed adamantly at one spot. "Here."

Nonie was about to ask the sheriff for permission to look in the hole when she noticed he was talking on the radio that was attached to his shoulder pad.

She turned to Nate. "Do you mind if I take a look in the hole?"

He shook his head. "Sorry, crime scene. Don't want it disturbed anymore than it already has been."

Nonie thought fast while Tiana continued to bust her chops about somebody looking in the hole where Anna Mae had been dumped. "Would you mind looking in the hole or around it for me? When I started moving away some of the concrete I had a bracelet on. Now it's gone. I'm afraid it might be in that pile of dirt you have over there or in the hole."

Fezzo looked at Nonie like she'd just farted loudly in church, but he didn't say a word.

"I hate to bother you about it," Nonie continued. "But that bracelet was pretty important to me. Would you mind taking a peek? It might have fallen inside the hole while you were digging."

Nate shook his head. "I don't know. Sheriff isn't going to like that."

"Please," Nonie said.

"Just go look in the damn hole yourself," Tiana barked in her ear. "What's the matter with you, girl. It's right there in your face. All you've got to do is walk over there and get it. Better to say you sorry than ask that white boy for permission."

Nonie sighed. "Please?" she said again.

The drizzle soon turned into fat droplets, and Buchanan covered his radio with a hand and said to

Nate, "Go to the car and get a blanket so we can cover the body."

Nate nodded, and when Buchanan turned back to his radio and walked off a couple of feet, Nate mouthed to Nonie, "Sorry."

When Nate left to get the blanket as ordered and with Buchanan busy on his radio, Nonie felt Tiana give her a little shove on her back.

"Go now," Tiana said. "You blind, girl? Nobody's lookin'. So go already."

Nonie sighed, then held a finger up against her lips, motioning to Fezzo to stay quiet. Holding her breath, she inched her way closer to the hole. Concrete and dirt lay in piles along the perimeter of the hole, she glanced over the pile and looked into the hole. She didn't see anything but dirt.

Just then she heard Buchanan say, "You need to step back, Nonie. We can't have you disturbing the crime scene."

Nonie held up a hand. "Oh, I'm sorry. Sorry, I didn't mean to—" In that moment, Nonie caught a glimpse of something shiny stuck in a pile of dirt near the top of the hole, right where Tiana had indicated. "Sheriff, you might want to come check this out. I see something in the dirt over here." Nonie pointed to the shiny object and waited for Buchanan to make his way to it.

When Buchanan reached the area she pointed to, he frowned, leaned over and plucked a pen out of his shirt pocket and used it to pull something out of the dirt. It was a ring. An LSU class ring.

"What the hell?" Buchanan said.

About that time Nate had returned with a blanket. He removed his jacket from Anna Mae's face, then recovered her face and body with the blanket.

"Nate, grab me an evidence bag, will you?" Buchanan called out to him.

Nate hurried back out of the yard again and returned a moment later with what looked like a clear, plastic sandwich bag. He held it open, and Buchanan tilted his pencil towards the opening, and the ring plopped into the bag.

"Do you mind if I take a look at that?" Nonie asked. She'd seen a ring like that before, only she couldn't remember where. The sight of it haunted her even more than Guy, Helen and Tiana put together.

"Woot, they got it," Tiana yelled. "They gonna get that bastard now! In your eye, you lowlife. They's gonna be comin' for you for sure!"

CHAPTER TWENTY-FOUR

As Sheriff Buchanan and Nate poked around in the dirt for more evidence, Nonie said to Buchanan, "Sheriff, I've got to run out to my car and grab a couple of things if that's all right." It was the only excuse she could think of to get away so she could talk to Guy, Helen and Tiana to find out what they knew.

Buchanan looked up from his digging. "Sure. Just don't go anywhere until I have a chance to talk with you again."

"No problem. I'll be right back."

With that, Nonie signaled to Fezzo. "I won't be long," she assured him.

He gave her a questioning look, but remained silent.

Grabbing her keys from the front pocket of her slacks, Nonie hurried out of the side gate and walked around the house, unlocked the Acura and slipped into the driver's seat. As expected, Guy, Helen and Tiana followed her inside. Guy suddenly appeared sitting shotgun and Helen and Tiana had taken over the backseat.

Tiana clapped her hands and gave a loud whoop. "Now they gonna get it. The man that killed that woman is gonna get his what for. I may not have been able to get to those sumabitches who took me, my man and my boy, but this one's not going to get away. My job is done!"

Nonie turned to look at Tiana. "What are you talking about?"

"The ring they found? The one that wore that ring is the man who killed that woman. All they have to do is find the man. They'll see then. They'll see."

"Do you know who did it?" Nonie asked. "Did you see him kill her? How did you find us? How did you get here?"

"You gots a lot of questions. I didn't have to find you because I followed him when you left my house." She pointed to Guy. "I figured if you could see me and him then maybe you could help me find who killed me and my family."

"But Tiana, that was so long ago, those people are more than likely all dead by now," Nonie said.

"Yeah, I know that now. But I liked getting out of my house. You house is nicer than mine."

Nonie frowned. "I never saw you in my apartment."

Tiana chuckled. "I know. I was hiding the whole time. Made myself go *poof*. That way nobody can sees me, but I can sees them."

Nonie looked over at Guy and Helen. "Did either of you see her?"

Both shook their head.

"Can you teach me that trick?" Helen asked. "To go poof so nobody, not even Nonie can see me?"

"What I look like?" Tiana asked with a scowl. "A secret teller? That's all my business."

"What about the other stuff?" Nonie asked, still confused as to how she never knew Tiana had been at her house. The killer? The ring? Do you know who did it? Did you see him kill her?"

"No, but I just know. I knows it was the man who wore that ring. I seen it in the hole. And something inside of me said it's a match. The man who wore that ring is the man who did the murder. So now my job here is done."

"What do you mean?" Nonie asked.

"I found me a murderer, so my jobs done here. It wasn't the ones who killed me and my man and boy, but it's a murderer just the same."

"What are you going to do now, Tiana?" Guy asked.

"Me? It's been a long time on this earth by myself, waiting to get me some revenge. Like your woman said, the men that killed me and my family might all be dead by now because it was so long ago. They probably getting their due paid somewhere else. But at least I was able to settle somebody else's business." She looked at Nonie. "Thank you for giving me that chance. Thank you for finding me. Now I can go find that light and go home to my boy and my man."

"But what about the plantation?" Nonie asked. "Are you going to leave there now?"

"Oh, I'll hang around a little bit longer. I owe you one. Your man here tells me that there's some people with some machines like y'all had when you came to the plantation the first time, and they need to get pictures and stuff. I'll give them a good scare just for you, so it'll look good on your name. So that your word would be good. That way when you tell them a place has a ghost they gonna believe you. But once I'm done with that, I'm gonna find me that light and go home. Thank you Nonie Broussard for helping Tiana Lewis. I owe you, and for that I'll stick around. I was the only one in there, so if they go and I'm not there, they not gonna get nothing on their machines."

"Talking about being the only one in there," Nonie said. "Were you the one who pushed me down the stairs?"

Tiana gave her a sheepish look. "Yeah, that was me. If I don't knows somebody and they snooping around my house, I get mad. I didn't want to hurt you, no. Just give you a little scare so you would leave." Tiana yawned. "I'm gonna go back to my house now and wait for them people with the machines. Then I'm gonna go home. See my man and my boy."

Nonie was about to tell Tiana that there was no need for her to stick around. That if she knew it was time for her to seek the light, she should go now in order to be with her family. Before she could say anything, however, Tiana blipped out of sight.

"Now isn't that something?" Helen said from the backseat. "Look at what you did. Your gift gave somebody resolution and hope. Not only Tiana, but Anna Mae, too."

"What do you mean?" Nonie asked.

"We saw her," Guy said. "Remember, I told you Anna Mae was the one banging the cabinet doors."

"That's right," Helen said. "Now because of you, they found Anna Mae's body, and she was able to have peace enough to go to the light."

Guy nodded. "We saw her go to it. Remember that gust of wind in the backyard earlier before it started to rain? That was her crossing over. And that was all because of you. You're the hero of the day."

Nonie sat dumbstruck. "Oh, I'm no hero. You and Helen told me Anna Mae was dead and told me not to get involved."

"Yes, dear, we did, but fortunately, you didn't listen to us," Helen said. "And look at all the good that came out of it."

"Yeah, but now the police want to talk to me again," Nonie said. "Maybe they think I had something to do with Anna Mae's death. How else would I have known to go into the backyard and find that lump of concrete? I can't exactly tell them y'all told me."

"No," Guy said. "But you already gave them a plausible explanation. It'll hold water. No worries, Nonie my little bologna."

"Why do you think she was buried like that?" Helen asked. "You know, upside down?"

"I have no idea," Nonie said. "I can only guess that whoever meant to bury her didn't want to bother digging a six-foot-long hole. So they tried making it round and deep, hoping that would work. From the looks of it, they dropped her in the hole, discovered it wasn't deep enough, then folded up her legs and feet and covered them over with concrete. They or he probably thought no one would notice."

"What a dumb ass," Guy said.

"What's got me is the ring they found," Nonie said. "I know I've seen it somewhere, I just can't remember where."

"Sure you can remember," Guy said. "I've seen that ring, too. Think back. The mayor's funeral. Who was wearing a ring like that? I don't know their names, but there were two guys wearing rings identical to the one found in the dirt where they buried Anna Mae."

Nonie gasped. "Clarence and Stefren Fontenot! The mayor's sons. You're right. They were both wearing L.S.U. class rings."

Guy nodded. "You got it."

"Oh, my God," Nonie said. "You think one of them killed Anna Mae?"

"It sort of makes sense, don't you think? Their mom was made to look like a laughingstock at her own husband's funeral. They could have done it for family honor. Sure, I can see them doing it. Getting rid of the woman who'd soon be prancing all around town like she owned the world. Their mother wouldn't have been able to deal with that, and they were mama's boys that's for sure."

"We've got to let the sheriff know," Nonie said. "At least it'll help him know where to start searching for Anna Mae's killer."

"Just know that the more you get involved, dear, the more difficult things will be for you," Helen said. "They're going to want to know how you know. Seems a little convenient. You find the ring and just happen to remember that the Fontenot boys wore the same type of ring."

"It might be convenient," Nonie said, "but it's the truth. I saw those boys and their rings at the funeral. That's not going to implicate me in any kind of way."

"I would stay out of it if I were you," Guy said. "Let them do their investigation, and things will unfold on their own. You've done enough. With

Tiana's help you found the ring. You should leave it at that."

"Not only that," Helen said, scooting to the edge of the backseat so she was closer to Nonie. "If word gets out that you were the one who pointed them out to the police, one brother might go down for the murder, but the other one might come after you."

"Oh, I seriously doubt that," Nonie said. "Anyway, for all we know, both of them could be involved in the murder."

"We won't know for sure until the police check it out," Guy said.

"Yeah, but they might not know to check the Fontenot boys out first unless somebody says something. There are a lot of people in Louisiana who wear L.S.U. class rings. How'll they know where to start looking unless I give them a clue?"

"But how many people from Clay Point have that kind of ring?" Helen said. "It shouldn't take them long to figure it out."

"There were a lot of people at the funeral," Nonie said. "Most of Clay Point and quite a few from out of town."

"The sheriff's not stupid," Guy said. "I'm sure he'll figure it out soon enough."

Nonie swiped a hand over her face. "No, I've got to tell them what I know. For Anna Mae's sake as well as Tiana's. She's been hanging around for so long, waiting for some kind of restitution to be paid for her loved ones."

"Yeah, but this one doesn't belong to her," Guy said. "It might help make things right enough for her to want to go to the light, but it's not worth you getting into trouble over."

Nonie shook her head. "It just wouldn't be right. Tiana owned that clue. She's the one who saw it and made me go look for it. I owe it to her."

Guy leaned over to Nonie until he was nearly nose to nose with her. "I'm telling you to stay out of it. You've done enough already."

Nonie tsked. "You know it would be the right thing for me to do, Guy Philip." She suddenly picked up an odd vibration from Guy that made her chuckle. "You just don't want me to be around Nate Lopez anymore than I have to. That's it, isn't it?"

Guy chuffed. "Like I've got a problem with that dude."

"You've always had a problem with Nate because he asks me out on dates. You don't like him."

"Here we go again," Helen said to Guy. "You're sticking your nose in that girl's business, telling her who she can and can't date? What's wrong with you, son?"

Guy sat back, then shrugged. "Go ahead and tell them," he said to Nonie. "You're going to do what you want to anyway. Don't listen to me. I'm just a guy that's been hanging around you since high school. What do I know? Just don't come crying to me if things turn upside down on you, Nonie Marie."

CHAPTER TWENTY-FIVE

When Nonie went back into the backyard, thankful that the rain had stopped, she was surprised to see the coroner doing a quick exam of Anna Mae's body. She'd been so busy talking with Guy and Helen that she hadn't even seen him arrive. He gave a proclamation of death, then the paramedics loaded her onto a stretcher, keeping the blanket Nate had covered her with draped over her body.

Nonie walked over to Fezzo, leaned close to him and whispered, "I think I know who that ring belongs to. You know, the ring they found earlier in the dirt."

Fezzo looked at her in surprise. "You gonna tell 'em?"

"I have to."

"But—"

"Nonie? Mr. Broussard?" Sheriff Buchanan interrupted. He walked over to them with Nate in tow. "I hate to inconvenience the two of you, but would you mind coming down to the station and giving a statement on what you found and saw here?"

"No problem," Fezzo said. "We'll be there."

"Sure," Nonie said when Buchanan looked over at her. "Uh . . . Nate, do you mind if I speak with you for a moment?" If she was going to let the cat out of the back about the ring, she wanted to test it out on someone more approachable than the sheriff.

"Sure," Nate said, and followed her as she walked away from the sheriff and Fezzo.

When they reached the privacy fence, Nate asked, "What's up?"

"That ring that the sheriff found in the dirt. I saw two of them just like it at the funeral home the other day. Clarence and Stefren Fontenot, the mayor's sons, were wearing identical rings. I have a feeling if you talk to both of them, you'll find that one of them has a missing ring."

Nate arched a brow. "Are you sure the rings were exactly the same?"

"Positive."

Nate studied her for a moment, then said, "Thanks for the tip. Gives us something to work with right away. Narrows the playing field. I appreciate it."

"No problem."

After a long, awkward pause, Nate finally said, "By the way, you know Festival International is a couple of weekends from now in Lafayette. Different music from musicians around the world will be playing there."

"Yeah, I've heard it advertised on TV. Sounds like it'll be a cool event."

"Would you like to go with me?" Nate said, a hopeful look in his eyes.

Guy suddenly appeared right beside Nonie, causing her to start.

"Are you okay?" Nate asked.

"Uh . . . yeah, "Nonie said. "Thought I saw a bee buzzing around, that's all."

"Oh." Nate looked about. "If there was one, it's gone now."

"Good," Nonie said, playing along. "I'm allergic to bees." She didn't know why she added that last caveat because it had been a bold-faced lie.

"Anyway," Nate said. "Would you like to go?"

Nonie turned to Nate, purposely taking Guy out of her line of sight. "I'd love to."

Nate's grin spread from ear to ear. "Great. I'll give you a call as the date gets closer, and we can talk in more detail. You know, what time I'll pick you up. Stuff like that."

"Sounds great."

They stood in awkward silence again, and Nonie could feel Guy seething behind her.

"Well," she said, "I guess Fezzo and I will go on down to the station and give our statements."

"Sure thing," Nate said. "Good to get that out of the way." He gave her a little nod, then walked back to Buchanan and Fezzo.

Nonie turned toward the fence so no one could see her and faced Guy, who was sulking now. He suddenly blipped out of sight, and Nonie felt a twinge of guilt. She could have been less blatant about accepting Nate's date offer in front of Guy.

As she mulled over her predicament with her dead boyfriend, Sheriff Buchanan walked up to her and said. "Nate tells me y'all are coming to the station now. I'll head that way myself. I've got a couple of detectives from Lafayette on their way over to Clay Point now. They'll be taking your statements."

Nonie swallowed hard. Detectives? No one had mentioned giving statements to any detectives. She'd figured they would be talking to Nate or Buchanan. Now she'd have to start from the beginning and retell her story to two strangers. The news thrilled her about as much as a dentist telling her she needed a root canal.

"If y'all will follow me out, I'd appreciate it," Buchanan continued. "I'm going to have Nate wrap the house and yard with police tape to keep everyone out for now."

Nonie and Fezzo followed Buchanan out of the side gate and left Nate to his duties. When Fezzo and Nonie were locked away in the Acura, Nonie noticed that Helen and Guy had decided to hitch a ride, as well. They both sat in the backseat. Helen smiling. Guy frowning with his arms crossed over his chest.

"How did you know about dat ring?" Fezzo asked Nonie as she backed out of the driveway.

"Someone told me."

"Dat someone was Guy?"

"No. Someone else." Nonie said. She filled Fezzo in on the story about discovering Tiana at the plantation and that Tiana was the one who had chased the men out of the house with a skillet. She also told him that Tiana had led her to the ring.

Fezzo chuckled. "You bes' be glad it was just dem men she chased out dat house. Most of de time I suspect dem ghosts take to you because you can see them, but if you not careful, you can wind up being chased out just like dem men in you crew."

"I'm careful, Uncle Fezzo."

"Why her you think? How come dis Tiana ghost was the one who told you? Guy didn't see it?"

"I don't think he did. But Tiana had a reason to keep a close eye on things." Nonie told Fezzo about how Tiana and her family had been murdered over a hundred years ago and that all Tiana ever wanted was revenge for their deaths. To her, snitching out the murderer for Anna Mae was just as good as snitching out her own.

After hearing her story, Fezzo nodded. "I can understand dat. If dat was me, I'd be looking to tear up some hide if somebody hurt my family. Tiana's problem, poor thing, is dat probably all dem men dat hurt her and her family are dead by now."

"That's what I told her. But at least she feels a part of having justice served with Anna Mae, and that was good enough for her."

Fezzo nodded, then glanced over at Nonie. "You a good girl, you know dat? Helping even dead people like dat. You like you grandma. You got a big heart. " He smiled. "Just protect that big heart. Protect my Nonie because you family loves you very much, and I don't want nothing to happen to you."

"I love you, too, Uncle Fezzo."

Just then Nonie's phone rang. She dug it out of her back pocket and answered it. It was Jack Nagan.

"How goes it?" Nonie asked him. "I'm driving so we've got to make this fast."

"Can we all meet at your house later?" Jack asked. "Like around six or so. If you can get hold of Buggy and let her know I'd appreciate it. I'll give Tatman and Shaundelle a call. I've got the evidence ready from the two locations we investigated."

"Anything good?" Nonie asked.

"Really good. I've already met with the producers so I'll be showing up with checks in hand."

Nonie grinned. "Six will be great. I'm sure it won't be a problem with Buggy either."

"Great. See you later."

Nonie hung up the phone and slipped it back into her pocket.

"Must be good news de way you smiling like dat," Fezzo said.

"Really good," Nonie said. "Looks like we got a hit on the two houses we did. That was one of the investigators who was with us that night. He went over all the equipment we used and found some good evidence."

"Mah, I'm glad you got a hit," Fezzo said. "Just make sure, mon petite, if you keep doing dat ghost hunting that you don't wind up getting hit by dem ghosts."

CHAPTER TWENTY-SIX

That night, before Jack and the rest of the Boo Krewe showed up at her apartment, Nonie had made sure to stop off at Roy's Grocery and load up on beer and snacks. She was putting potato chips in a serving platter along with dip when she heard someone whisper loudly, "Boo!"

Nonie whirled about, chips flying across the floor. Guy was standing across from her with a mischievous grin on his face.

"How many times have I told you not to do that, Guy Philip!" Nonie said, bending down to pick up the scattered chips from the floor. "I've got people coming over. What are you doing here? Why don't you go play with Helen?"

"We have been playing," Guy whined. "I wanted to spend some time with you before Jack Sprat and the gang showed up."

"His name's not Jack Sprat and you know it," Nonie said. "And what's got you so cheerful all of a sudden. The last time I saw you, you were pouting in the backseat of my Acura."

"Yeah, well I got over that," Guy said with a twinkle in his eye.

Nonie tossed some chips into the trash and dusted her hands together. "Why isn't that comforting to me?"

"Paranoid?"

"Yep. With good reason."

"Why are you being so pissy?"

"I told you. I'm expecting the crew, and I don't want you all up in my face when they get here."

Nonie heard a clinking sound behind her, and she turned on her heels and saw Helen placing drinking glasses side by side on the kitchen counter. She still wore her pink housedress and slippers.

"What are you doing here, Ms. Helen?"

"Oh, this is the big meeting, isn't it? Don't you find out tonight whether we're going to be on television or not?"

"Yes, supposedly so."

"Well, there you have it. No way was I going to miss hearing the news."

"I can't have the two of you hanging out here while the meeting is going on," Nonie said. "It's too distracting for me. It's hard for me to pay attention to the living while the dead are blabbering in my ear."

"Oh, my dear, I promise I won't say a word," Helen assured her. She clasped her hands together. "You won't hear a peep out of me. All I want to do is find out if I'll be on television. Well, my house anyway. I'm really hoping it happens. That might convince my son to leave the house as it is."

"I understand your predicament, Helen, but I can't help what your son does. Yes, we should find out tonight whether your home will be on television or not, but you have to remember if it's going to be on TV you'll need to be over there so the film crew can pick up more evidence. It won't do any good if you're following Guy around and the crew isn't able to collect anything paranormal from your house."

"Oh, I'll be there, not to worry. And, Guy, maybe you can come to my house, too. Since you can move things around, we can give them a really good show," Helen said, her eyes bright.

"No, no, none of that," Nonie said. "We don't need anything over the top. Just you, Helen, and Captain will do perfectly fine. Guy will wind up causing more trouble than anyone's prepared for."

"That's not fair," Guy said. "I wouldn't cause any trouble."

"Right, and the tooth fairy collects dust bunnies," Nonie said.

"Huh? The tooth fairy doesn't collect dust."

"My point exactly," Nonie said. "She doesn't collect dust and you can't not cause trouble."

"But I want to help her," Guy insisted. "Helen helped us at Clara's, and she taught me to blip. I need to return the favor."

"What do you mean she taught you to blip? What the heck is that?"

"You know, blip. In one place one minute, somewhere else in the next. I don't have to worry about walking or hitching a ride anywhere. Now all I have to do is blip myself to wherever I want to go."

"Great," Nonie said, shaking her head. "That's so comforting. But no on going to Helen's and making things move. I can't afford the chance that things will get screwed up."

"I won't screw anything up!" Guy insisted.

Nonie batted a hand at him. "Whatever. I don't even know why I'm wasting my breath with you. You're going to do whatever you want to anyway. Just don't cause such a big hoorah that you'll cause one of the investigators to stroke out."

"Well, if they're investigating for ghosts they should be ready for anything, right?" Guy asked. "Why should I have to tone anything down? If I move a piece of furniture around or toss a picture off the wall, they should love it. It's more evidence."

Just then, Nonie heard the front door open. She'd forgotten to lock it. Someone called out, "Anybody home?" It was Buggy.

"Where you at, girl?" Nonie recognized the voice as Shaundelle's.

"In here," Nonie called back. "Be there in a sec." Then she said to Helen and Guy, "I need y'all to keep it down in here. Stay put and keep quiet."

"But why?" Helen asked. "It's not like they can hear us."

"Because Nonie can hear us," Guy said. "And it makes her all pissy when they're talking to her and we're talking to her at the same time."

"Oh," Helen said. "Okay, I get it."

Nonie grabbed a dishtowel, wiped her hands, then tossed the dishtowel into the sink and headed for the living room.

Shaundelle, Tatman, and Buggy surrounded her as soon as she entered the room.

"Girl, I heard what happened over at Clara's earlier today," Buggy said. "You were there when all that went down?"

"Oh, don't tell me you got all the scoop," Shaundelle said. "Tell us everything. The entire 4-1-1."

In that moment, Tatman walked into the house followed by Jack who was wearing black jeans, a black pullover shirt and black boots. To Nonie, he looked utterly lickable. A black computer bag hung from his left shoulder.

Walking through the house like he owned it, Tatman bypassed Nonie and headed for her kitchen. "Got anything to munch on, Nonie? I didn't get to eat supper yet."

"There's chips, crackers and dip on the counter," Nonie said. "Beer's in the fridge."

"Beautiful," Tatman said, rubbing his stomach.

"Where can I set this up?" Jack said, sliding the computer bag off his shoulder.

"What is it?" Buggy asked.

"The evidence I showed the producers. I wanted all of you to get a chance to see it."

"Oh, hell, yeah," Shaundelle said. "Put it on the coffee table so we can all sit around it and see."

"There's the kitchen table," Nonie offered.

"Yeah, but it'll be crowded over there. We can all see it better from here," Shaundelle said. "We bring your kitchen chairs in here then we've got the couch and your big chair. We can all sit and watch theater style." She smiled a big toothy grin and headed for the kitchen after Tatman. "Where's the beer at?"

"We definitely want to see the evidence," Buggy said to Jack, "but just tell us. Are they going to shoot those two locations we investigated or not?"

Jack smiled, showing beautiful white, straight teeth. "Both locations are a go."

"Woohoo!" Buggy shouted.

"That's what I'm talking about!" Shaundelle said, and did a little bump and grind in the kitchen. "We in the money now, honey."

"That's awesome," Tatman said. "You go, dude!"

"It's not just me," Jack said. "We were all in this together. All of you did a great job collecting evidence, especially since none of you have done this before. And by the way, I found out why the Richardson house was in front of that plantation. Seems like the folks who owned the plantation were distant relatives of Helen's. They gave her a piece of land near the road as a wedding present so she and her husband could build their own house there."

"That was awful nice of them," Nonie said. She cleared off a couple of magazines she had sitting on the coffee table and motioned for Jack to set his computer bag on the table.

"Shaundelle's right," Nonie said. "We'll all get to see much better from here."

"What I want to see is them checks," Shaundelle said. "Did you bring 'em with you, Mr. Jack the Money Man?"

"I sure did," Jack said. He reached into a side pouch of his bag and pulled out four envelopes. He handed one to Nonie, another to Buggy, then one each to Shaundelle and Tatman as they hurried into the living room. "A grand a piece. As promised."

Shaundelle hugged the envelope against her large breasts then gave it a huge wet kiss. "You comin' home with mama!" She folded the envelope and slid it down into the orange, V-neck spandex shirt she was wearing then tucked it in her bra.

"Yes, ma'am, yes, ma'am," Tatman said, folding his envelope and shoving it into his back jeans' pocket. "I can get used to this."

Buggy slipped her envelope in her back pocket, as well, then said, "Okay, before we get started with evidence, I wanna know what happened at Clara's."

"Who's Clara?" Jack asked.

"Didn't you hear?" Buggy said. "They found Anna Mae Turner—"

"Wait, who's Anna Mae Turner?"

"Aw, dude, you've got a lot of catching up to do," Buggy said. She told him about the mayor's funeral and the fight between Anna Mae and Hazel.

"Oh, man," Jack said. "Got it. Now what about Anna Mae and Clara?"

"They found Anna Mae buried in a hole in Clara's backyard," Buggy announced.

"Yeah," Shaundelle chimed in. "They'd buried her ass up, head down."

"What?" Jack said.

"For real, dude," Tatman said. "They stuck her in this hole that was too small then poured concrete over her legs and shit so nobody would see it."

"Are you kidding me?" Jack said.

"No, man. I'm as serious as a quadruple bypass. Tell him Nonie," Tatman said.

"Not much left to tell," Nonie said, not wanting to get into the details of how she'd found Anna Mae. "Y'all know about as much as I do."

"Yeah, but the way I hears it, you was there," Shaundelle said. "You've got to have more skinny on the deal than the rest of us. And what was you doing there anyway?"

"Helping Clara with something in her house," Nonie said, dancing around the issue as best she could.

"And?" Buggy said.

"And there's not much more to tell," Nonie said, giving Buggy a look that told her not to push the issue in front of everyone.

"You got no more than that?" Shaundelle said. "Girl, you holdin' back. I can sees you holdin' back. Now fork up the goods."

"The only other thing I know is they found a ring near the grave," Nonie said. "A class ring from L.S.U.. So far I think that's the only lead they have on the case. Uncle Fezzo and I had to go down to the police station and give our statements to a couple of detectives."

"And did y'all see the whole thing?" Tatman asked.

"We didn't see her murdered and put in the hole," Nonie said. "We just saw her in the hole."

"Who found her there?" Buggy asked.

"That's a longer story," Nonie said. "And it's not why we're here. Let's take a look at the evidence. I'd like to see what we came up with that got us each a grand, wouldn't you? Maybe we can do it again?"

"Hell, yeah, "Shaundelle said. "We keep going at this rate, and I'll be able to get my own Tips and Tint shop. To hell with workin' for the man. No offense, Jack."

"None taken," Jack said.

"Girl, you're not going to get away with that," Buggy said. "We'll look at the evidence, but I want the full deal scoop about Clara and Anna Mae later on, you hear?"

"Yeah, me, too," Shaundelle said. "All I got was what's been floatin' around the Tips and Tint, and you know how them women be. They be spreadin' rumors sideways, longways, downways, every which way they can make it up. By tomorrow they'll be sayin' that Anna Mae was cut up in little pieces and buried in holes all around Clara's house. I want to know what really happened so I can set all them hussies straight."

"Yeah, yeah," Nonie said, and tossed Buggy a scowl. Couldn't she take a hint for heaven's sake?

Jack took his computer out of his bag, set it on the coffee table and turned it on. While they waited for it to boot up, he pulled a thumb drive out of the bag and held it up. "It's all on here." When the computer sing-songed that it was booted up and ready to go, he put the drive into a USB port. "Ready?"

"Hang on a sec, I'm coming," Tatman said. "Want a beer, brother?"

"No, I'm good."

After draining the first Budweiser he'd taken when he arrived, Tatman went into the fridge, grabbed another can, popped the top on it, and hurried back over to the group. "Ready," he said, then guzzled down more beer.

"Okay, the first thing you'll see are some still shots we took at the Richardson house." He ran a finger over the touch pad on his computer and clicked on a photo. "This was taken in the attic."

Everyone leaned in for a better look.

"What's all those white, blue and green squiggly lines that run across the picture?" Tatman asked.

"It's called ectoplasm," Jack said. "Sometimes an entity—"

"What you mean an entity?" Shaundelle asked. "You talkin' about a ghost?"

"In a way, yes."

"In a way?" Buggy asked. "What's that mean? What else could it be if not a ghost."

"A ghost, is typically a human who's lived before, and is either residual or intelligent," Jack explained. "Residual is like an echo, it's not a real ghost, but more like the reflection of a person who keeps reliving an event that happened in their life over and over. An intelligent spirit is one who's earthbound for whatever reason. Many of them will try to interact with you in some way. We call both entities, but there is another type. An entity that was never human. That can either be a shadow person or . . .well, a demon. There are other things, like djinn, but we'll stick to spirits for now."

"Oh, huh-uh," Shaundelle said. "Nobody said anything about no demon when we got started with this gig. I don't want no part of no demon. No, siree, you can all have the demons."

"I wouldn't allow us to stay and investigate a location if I thought it had a demonic influence," Jack said. "I wouldn't even want the film crew there. That's something left to people with much more experience, like demonologists, which we're not."

"So go on about the ectoplasm," Tatman said, pointing to the picture on the computer screen.

"Sometimes an entity . . . or ghost, doesn't have enough energy to present itself as a full apparition, so it leaves a trail of energy, like this." He touched his computer and another picture appeared on the screen. It had a bright white ball of light over one of the cots that sat in the Richardson's attic.

"What the heck is that?" Buggy asked.

"An orb," Jack explained. "Same principal as the ectoplasm. I don't usually put a lot of stock in orbs because many of them wind up being bugs or light reflections from a window or mirror in a room. But this one is different. It's bright white, huge, and perfectly round. And get this." He clicked a couple of keys, and the ball of light took flight. It circled around the cot three or four times, then shot out of view like a comet. "We caught that on video."

"Wow," Buggy said. "I didn't see any lights like that in the attic."

"More times than not you can't see them with the naked eye,' Jack said. "They typically show up on film. Now keep your eye on this cot." He pointed to the cot in the middle of the room. Nothing happened for a long moment, then suddenly the mattress on the cot depressed, as if someone had settled onto it. In that same moment, the gray blanket that lay across the foot of the cot moved upward slightly.

"Holy shit and crackers!" Shaundelle said. "It moved by itself."

"Man, bro, that's some heavy-duty crap," Tatman said. "No wonder the producers jumped on this."

Jack grinned and nodded. "Who wouldn't. This is some great stuff, and we're just getting started. He pulled up another file. This one looked like a bar graph with hundreds of white lines running horizontally through it. "This is an audio file. It shows what's been picked up by the digital recorders we were carrying around to do EVPs." He clicked a button and a vertical bar ran slowly through the horizontal white lines. He turned the volume up on the computer. "The voice you'll hear first is Nonie's. What you're listening for is what comes after she speaks."

"I don't know if anyone would be able to see you," they heard Nonie say.

What followed was an audible murmur, "Why . . . you?"

The faintest white noise followed, then they heard Nonie ask, "Do you want me to give that message to your son?"

Another murmur, ". . . for sure." Then two seconds later, " . . . television."

Nonie spoke again. "Okay, Helen. Thank you again for your help."

" . . . welcome."

"Whoa!" Tatman said, looking at Nonie. "Who were you talking to?"

"I was talking to Buggy," Nonie said, her eyes flitting to her friend.

"Uh- yeah," Buggy said. "She was talking to me."

Shaundelle harrumphed. "Who you kiddin'? You was talking to a ghost, wasn't you? You even said her name. Helen. We all heard it."

"I guessed," Nonie said, knowing the excuse sounded lame as it came out of her mouth.

"Bullshit," Shaundelle said. "You was talking to a ghost. Plain as day."

"Would you have stuck around up there if you'd have seen a ghost?" Nonie asked Shaundelle.

"Oh, hell to the no!" I'd have been out of that house faster than a cop after my cousin Tyree."

"Same here," Nonie said.

Nonie wanted to slap herself upside the head. She hadn't thought things through during the investigation. If she had, she would have kept her questions simple, like Jack had taught them. She'd been so wrapped up in seeing and talking to Helen that she'd forgotten that both parts of the conversation would be picked up on audio. What a dope.

Jack continued to click through pictures and video, bringing up the floating skillet in the plantation and the Rem Pod on the kitchen table that had squawked and blinked multicolored lights the entire time it had been set in place. Once again, he switched over to an audio file. "These are the EVPs we got from the plantation."

Jack's voice came through loud and clear over the speakers of his computer. "Are you a man or a woman?"

The response was immediate. " . . . woman, fool."

"Wow," Shaundelle, Tatman and Buggy said collectively.

More faint white noise then, " . . . name be Tiana."

Thankfully, Nonie had company during the confrontation with Tiana so she hadn't asked any direct questions. The film clip that followed, though, showed the iron skillet swinging in midair of its own volition and caught Nonie giving someone they couldn't see a shrug.

"See, there you go again," Shaundelle said. "You actin' like somebody's standing right in front of you. What gives, Nonie?"

Nonie held her palms up. "I figured somebody had to be holding that skillet, so I motioned to them like I could see them. Only made sense."

"How come that skillet didn't chase after you and Buggy?" Tatman asked. "Why just me and Jack?"

"Who knows," Nonie said. "Maybe she has a problem with men."

"She?" Shaundelle said, narrowing her eyes. "How you know it was a she unless you seen her?"

Nonie bit her bottom lip for a second, then bounced back with what sounded like a plausible answer. "You heard the EVPs. Didn't it sound like a woman to you?"

"Yeah, it did," Tatman said.

"That's all fine and good," Shaundelle said, "but you wasn't listening to no EVPs when you was there, so how'd you know it was a she?"

"I said it was a she after I just heard the EVP, like you did a second ago," Nonie said.

Nonie felt sweat form on her forehead. Thankfully, Jack jumped in and changed the subject.

"Well, he or she, I can tell you the producers were pretty impressed." He closed his laptop.

"You were a huge help," Nonie said to him. "If it hadn't been for you, we wouldn't have known what to do with all that equipment."

Jack grinned. "I'll take that beer now, if you don't mind."

"You got it, brother," Tatman said, already heading for the kitchen.

"When's our next hunt going to be?" Buggy asked Jack.

"Next Saturday night. It's an old hospital in north Louisiana. Used to be an insane asylum, too."

"Oh, huh-uh," Shaundelle said. "You mean a place where they kept crazy people?"

"The asylum was back in the forties and fifties," Jack said. "It became a V.A. hospital after that but the state closed it down in the late nineties."

"Aw, hell, there's gonna be all kinds of dead people up in there," Shaundelle said, tapping the arm of the couch where she sat.

"Yeah, but you can't be running off like you did at the plantation," Tatman said. "If we see anything moving around, you've got to hang with us. All for one, one for all, I say. Jack said that if he thought some place was dangerous he'd have us leave. We just have to trust him to make that call."

"Yeah, but if there's gonna be crazy people running around in there, don't you think that's gonna be dangerous? There's no telling what they can do. They could get all up in our heads and make us crazy, too."

"That's ridiculous," Buggy said.

"How you know?" Shaundelle asked. "You ever been in one of them crazy places?"

"No, but—"

"Shaundelle if you're not up for this, we'll understand," Jack said. "We can find somebody to replace you on the team if you're too scared."

She pursed her lips and frowned. After a long pause she finally said, "Hell to the no. Ain't nobody gonna be getting my check but me. I took off from the plantation because it was my first time, so y'all need to cut me some slack. That boogity swinging that skillet scared the piss out of me, so I took off. But now I know what could happen so I'll buck up and deal. Y'all will see. I'll get all kinds of evidence of them crazy people in that aslum."

"Asylum," Jack corrected.

"Yeah, there, too," Shaundelle said, then harrumphed. "But if I start yellin', one of y'all best be paying attention."

"You can stick with me," Tatman said.

"Oh, I'll stick to you like butt glue," Shaundelle assured him. She turned to Jack. "Why an aslum? Couldn't you find a department store or something like that? You got to get us into an old hospital and crazy place?"

"Word around is that it has great potential," Jack said. "Look at it this way. We can either waste our time hunting places that are maybes or stick to the ones that have a reputation for being haunted. I mean, have you ever heard of a haunted Walmart anywhere around the state?"

"No," Shaundelle said.

"What about a haunted CVS?"

"No, but that don't mean there ain't one. We just ain't found it yet."

"Well, I haven't heard of either. The bottom line is that the maybes won't get you paid."

Shaundelle sighed, her right foot tapping nervously on the floor. "Yeah, I guess you right about that."

"Who's picking out these locations anyway?" Nonie asked Jack. "You?"

"I did a lot of investigations with a few groups around the state and get word from them as to what locations have potential."

"Well you sure got the last two right on the money," Tatman said.

Nonie watched the group as they talked amongst each other, most of them blabbering about what they were going to do with their new checks. She and Jack were the only ones who remained silent, and she could see him watching her out of the corner of her eye. It made her nervous. What made her even more nervous was the thought of going to an old hospital and insane asylum. The money was nice, no doubt, but for once she hoped the reports were wrong, and the place was empty. With Helen having followed her home and Tiana showing up at Clara's, she feared what might follow her back from that hospital. The last thing she needed was some insane ghost taking up residence in her house. Guy would have a hissy fit, and it would wind up being an all-out ghost war.

She blew out a quiet breath. Between Helen, Tiana, Anna Mae's poltergeist activity and now the possibility of someone new from the insane asylum, it made her wonder. Maybe working at the funeral home wasn't such a bad idea after all.

CHAPTER TWENTY-SEVEN

It was nearing nine-thirty when Jack grabbed his computer bag and hoisted it over one shoulder. Everyone else was preparing to leave Nonie's. He took his time, wanting to be the last to leave. Fortunately, he'd come alone. Buggy had hitched a ride to Nonie's with Shaundelle and Tatman, so they'd be leaving together.

Everyone had been as excited as he'd hoped they'd be over the checks they'd earned and witnessing the evidence they'd collected. He wasn't surprised when they'd questioned Nonie about who she'd been talking to. He'd done the same thing when they were on location.

Although a bit apprehensive, they seemed excited about the new hunt in north Louisiana on Saturday, which was only three days away.

"See you tomorrow, girl," Buggy called out to Nonie as she headed out the door with Shaundelle.

Nonie smiled and waved. "Tomorrow."

"Thanks for the grub and beer," Tatman told Nonie as he followed Shaundelle to the door.

"Anytime," Nonie said, then walked over to the doorway and gave them one final wave goodbye. She looked over her shoulder at Jack. "You heading out now?"

"In a couple," he said, then got up from the couch and carried his empty beer can into the kitchen and tossed it into the trash.

Nonie stood at her front door, which was half-closed. She felt stuck. Should she leave it open and encourage Jack to leave or close it and be left alone with him?

When he walked back into the living room, Jack said, "You did a really good job. Not only with the investigation but from what I heard from the group, you did a pretty good job helping out at Clara's. I don't know how you did either but I think you're a special person."

Nonie lowered her head slightly, feeling her cheeks grow hot.

Jack stepped closer to her, and she held her breath. Before she realized what he was doing, Jack leaned over, tucked a finger under her chin, lifting her head so she had to see him. Then he kissed her. She froze under his touch, but only for a second, then her lips seemed to melt onto his.

Their kiss quickly turned passionate, hungry, and just as Jack pulled her closer to him so their bodies were touching, he suddenly slapped a hand to the side of his neck, which broke their kiss.

"Damn," he said, then looked at his hand.

"What's wrong?" Nonie asked.

"Felt like a bee sting on the back of my neck," Jack said. He turned his head to one side. "Do you see anything?"

Nonie stepped to his side, moved his hair aside and examined his neck. "You've got a small red spot here, but it doesn't look like a bite."

"That's odd," Jack said. "It pinched like all get out."

Nonie quickly dropped her hand from his neck and stepped back.

"What's wrong?" he asked.

Nonie looked at him, then past him and saw Guy

standing a few feet behind Jack. "Uh .

nothing . . .nothing. I thought I heard something,

that's all.

Jack took her by the hand as if to recapture her

attention. "About that dinner you agreed to . . . How

about we make it this Friday night? Will that work

for you?"

Nonie glanced over his shoulder before looking

back at him. "I'd love to. Friday's perfect."

"Great. I'll be here to pick you up about around

seven. We'll go to Randall's in Lafayette. They

have great seafood and steaks there."

"Sounds wonderful. I'll look forward to it."

In that moment, Jack slapped a hand against the

back of his neck again. "I don't know if it's fleas or

some invisible bee, but something just stung me

again." He grimaced, rubbing the back of his neck.
"Anyway, I'd better get going."

Nonie gave him a hesitant smile and walked him
to the door. Jack leaned over and gave her a small
kiss goodnight.

"See you on Friday," he said.

She nodded. "Seven."

Jack stepped onto the porch and waited for
Nonie to close the door, then headed for his van.
When he reached it, he climbed inside, turned on
the interior lights and angled the rearview mirror so
he could check the side of his neck. He spotted a red
welt forming but no pustule. He saw half-moon-
shaped divots around the welt, like someone had
pinched him with their fingernails. He scrubbed the

back of his neck, straightened the rearview mirror, then backed out of Nonie's driveway.

Now he was on countdown until Friday, and he knew she would be the only thing on his mind until then. The one passionate kiss they shared tasted like spring water to a man dying of thirst. Refreshing, breathless. He thought about how her slender body felt pressed against his, so firm, so perfectly proportioned. Her hair smelled of lavender shampoo and the scent of her skin, a mixture of cinnamon and freshly baked cookies that had drilled its way to his manhood like none other.

He glanced at the rearview mirror again, wishing he'd see Nonie's reflection in it. Friday couldn't come soon enough.

CHAPTER TWENTY-EIGHT

"What do you think you were doing kissing that guy? That Jack goddamn Sprat?" Guy demanded as soon as Nonie closed the door. He stood in the middle of the living room with his hands balled into fists at his sides. He'd been standing behind Jack as soon as Tatman, Buggy, and Shaundelle had left her apartment and had witnessed the date confirmation and the kiss. He knocked over a beer can that someone had left on the coffee table.

"Don't get your drawers all stuck up in your butt," Helen said, suddenly appearing beside Guy. "Just how hard is that head of yours? We've already had the discussion about you letting Nonie live her own life. What's wrong with you?"

"That's got nothing to do with kissing," Guy said to Helen.

"What business did you have kissing that guy on the lips?" Guy demanded of Nonie. "You haven't kissed a man since I died."

"Not that you saw anyway," Nonie shot back.

Guy gasped. "You mean you have kissed someone else?"

"I have been on other dates before," Nonie said. "You know, like the times you'd go MIA and I could have a real date, which are rare. What did you think? That I suddenly went into a nunnery for nine years? I've got needs you know."

"Oh, my God, are you saying you've had sex with other men?" Guy asked breathlessly.

"I'd be lying if I told you no," Nonie said.

"Good for you, dear," Helen said.

"Look, I'm getting pretty tired of your possessiveness," Nonie said. "You don't own me, Guy."

"Oh, dear," Helen said and backed away from Guy.

"And don't even think about trashing my apartment again," Nonie warned. "If you do, I'll kick you out of here and not allow you back in. I'm tired of picking up your messes. If you've got a hissy fit to pitch, you can do it somewhere else."

"He'll calm down," Helen said. "Won't you, my boy?"

"I'm not your boy," Guy said.

"Don't you be ugly to Helen," Nonie said. "She's the only voice of reason you've got."

Helen patted the sides of her hair as if to straighten her hairdo. "He just got a bit miffed when he saw you kissing that man, that's all."

"He had no business being here in the first place," Nonie said. "I asked both of you to leave, but here you are, and he saw what he saw."

"Yeah," Guy said. "I saw it with both eyes. That man kissing you, and you kissing him back."

"So you pinched him," Nonie said. "That's so damn childish, Guy."

"Well, I could've punched him. Which would you've preferred I do?"

"Neither doggone it," Nonie said. "You can act like a grown-up human being even though you're dead. Not like a spoiled five-year-old."

"You've got to admit, my pinching him got his attention. It got him out of here, didn't it?"

"Who said I wanted him out of here?" Nonie fumed.

"I wanted him out, and that's all there is to it," Guy said with a quick nod.

"Is that why you did it? Just to get him out of my apartment?"

"Duh."

"Look, I'm going to dinner with him on Friday whether you like it or not," Nonie said. "And you're definitely off-limits on that date. On the date, in the van, in the restaurant."

"Well, I don't like it, and I plan on being right there with you."

"Oh, no, you're not, mister," Helen said suddenly. "You need to let her go on this date and decide for herself what she wants. The living or the dead."

"Ms. Helen I appreciate everything you've taught me," Guy said, "but when it comes to Nonie, she's my girl. And I don't want another man's mouth on hers. I don't want another man touching her. She's my woman."

Helen shook her head. "I just can't get it into his thick head," she said to Nonie. "He won't listen. I keep telling him that he's dead and you're not, but all he wants to hear is that you're his and that you belong to him."

Nonie sighed. "Guy Philip Skinard, if you do anything to mess up my date on Friday, I'll never speak to you again. Every time you show up in my apartment, I'll kick you out. You need to think about that. If you want to spend any more time with me, then you need to let me try to live a normal life. At least go on dates."

"So what you're saying is you're blowing me off," Guy said. "That you don't love me anymore."

"Don't pull the guilt trip thing with me, okay? Helen is right. You're dead, in case you forgot. I'll always love you, but how much of a future do I have with a dead man? I need a warm, male body in my life. I'm almost thirty-years-old. What am I supposed to do as long as you're here? Dry rot until it's time for me to pass on? Or go to a convent and become a nun?"

"But you've got to allow me to protect you from some of these guys," Guy said. "The ones that want nothing more from you than a little poontang before they move onto someone else."

"What do you know about men who only want poontang and then move on? Do you plan on interviewing everyone I want to date?"

"You're planning to date?" Guy asked
incredulously.

"You know what I mean. Answer the question."

"Oh, I have my way of knowing. I'm a man
myself, remember?"

"What you are is a ghost, remember?"

"Yeah, but I was a living breathing man not so
long ago. I know how men operate. And I
think Jack Sprat wants a little more from you than
dinner and a conversation. I think he wants a bit of
poontang."

"That's a stupid word, you know that? Poontang.
Makes you sound like some kind of hick
cowboy. Regardless, if there's any poontanging
going on, it'll be my business and not yours. And if
it does happen, I'd suggest you step out of the room.
Out of the house. Out of Clay Point. Go on out to

the bayou and have yourself a war dance or something. Get over it. Look, if you plan on sticking around, we're going to have to come to some kind of terms. I can't keep living like a monk the rest of my life. I love you, but if you love me the way you say you do then you owe me some kind of freedom."

Helen nodded in agreement. "There's no reason why she can't love you and love someone who's alive, Guy. You're the one who chose to leave the light. Nonie didn't make you stay here. There are a lot of women who lose their husbands and carry a love for them that will never die. But they remarry and move on with life. You've got to accept that same thing."

"Whose side are you on anyway?" Guy asked, gawking at Helen. "I thought you were my friend.

"I am your friend. But I'm on the side of what's right."

"But I'm right here," Guy said. "Right here. She can see me and feel me . . . sometimes. There's no need for her to be taking on with someone else." He turned to Nonie. "Why can't you just love me? Why can't it just be me? Nonie, my one and only. You always were and always will be. I could never be with another woman. Living or dead. You were always my entire life and still are. I wouldn't know what to do without you. I know that puts a lot of pressure on you, and I'm sorry, but it's how I feel. If you want me to go, I'll go and won't come back. If you feel that strongly about moving on with your life and not having me interfere, I can just disappear. You'd never have to see me again. Is that what you really want? You wouldn't miss me even a little bit?"

Nonie's heart ached from his words. "Guy, you know I love you, and, yes, I'd miss you terribly. But we've got to establish some kind of boundaries. I'm not telling you to leave permanently. I want you to find peace, too. I want you to find that welcoming light that you turned away from. That's your destiny. That's where you're supposed to be right now. That's the only way you can move on with your journey. There's a lot more for you out there than there is for you here. All you experience here is frustration, especially where I'm concerned. I'm getting older and you stay at the same age. I don't want to grow old and feeble alone."

"You wouldn't be alone, Nonie. I'd be there with you."

"You know what I mean. Don't make this any harder than it already is. I . . .I'd like to find a good man. One just like you, only one that can breathe and doesn't blip out every now and again."

Guy's face clouded with hurt and anger. Without another word, he blipped out of sight. And for all the words Nonie had spoken, she felt anguish squeeze her heart. This time she feared Guy would never come back.

Guy found himself sitting atop a cypress tree in the bayou, right near the place where he'd had the boat accident that had killed him. He hadn't meant to blip himself back here, but he supposed it was where he belonged. For without Nonie he'd die all over again. He didn't know how to deal with what she was asking for. How could he just let her date other men? Kiss other men? Sleep with other men? She always was and still was his whole life. He didn't want to leave her. He wanted to protect her.

If he could only make her understand that there were so many men out there just waiting to use her. If she wanted to be with another man, then fine. That was something he'd have to learn how to deal with. But at least he could help her find the right one. She'd probably say it was none of his business, but it was. Nonie was always his business, ever since the day he'd proposed to her in high school. They'd promised to marry and have a brood of kids together. How could she just forget that?

Guy had never forgotten those promises. The ability to keep them was taken away, which was something he could do nothing about. He wanted to make her happy. That was the most important thing to him. He'd just have to find a way to make it work so she wouldn't stay so frustrated with him all the time. She'd always be his Nonie. His one and only. But maybe part of his growth in this journey of death was learning how to share. Learn how to let go. It was the hardest lesson, the most difficult test he'd been given so far.

CHAPTER TWENTY-NINE

The next morning, Nonie arrived at the funeral home around 10 a.m. According to her dad, whom she'd spoken to before leaving home, there were no arrangements or viewings scheduled for today. That meant it would be a spit-and-polish day. The funeral home would get a thorough cleaning in preparation for its next event. Not that it really needed it. As far as Nonie was concerned, the funeral home was always in immaculate condition, when compared to her apartment anyway. But spit-and-polish days had been something they always did when things were slow, and doing something simply because that's the way it had always been done was what her dad was about.

In preparation, Nonie had dressed in jeans and a pink T-shirt with a white anchor embossed on the front along with the saying "Never Sink," written below it. The only good thing about cleaning days was it was the only time she could dress down and not have her mom ride her butt about it.

She parked her car in the visitor's parking lot and made her way around the funeral home to the garage. There she found Fezzo, washing and waxing the hearse. Margaret stood not far away blatantly puffing on a cigarette.

"Mornin' mon petite," Fezzo said when he spotted her. "You had a good night?"

"It was okay," Nonie said, offering him a smile. She threw Margaret a glance. "I thought you gave up that nasty habit."

Margaret gave a dismissive wave of her hand that held the cigarette. "Oh, for Pete's sake, it's only one."

"Yeah," Fezzo said. "One after de other. Dat's the third one you had since you been out here Margaret Ann."

"Snitch," Margaret said, and briskly walked out of the garage to the adjoining lawn and tamped out her cigarette in the grass. "Now, y'all happy? I swear some people need to mind their own beeswax."

Nonie pasted her lips in a hard line, trying to keep a smile in check. "What's on my agenda today?" she asked Margaret.

"Floors," Margaret said, standing upright and brushing a hand over the front of her navy blue dress. As usual, she had a wide white belt cinching the dress at the waist. Her blue pumps tapped against the concrete as she made her way back into the garage.

Nonie groaned. Floors meant manhandling a utility buffer throughout the funeral home. The machine was so old and bulky she felt like she was driving a monster truck without a steering wheel every time she used it. She following Margaret to the garage.

"Isn't there another job you can give me?" Nonie asked. "I hate doing the floors."

"Well, you certainly can't expect me to do them dressed like this," Margaret said motioning to her dress and pumps.

So much for dressing down, Nonie thought. "What about Butchy?"

"He's in de embalming room," Fezzo said. "Your daddy's got him scrubbing down all de machines and tools."

"Where is Dad anyway?"

"In his office messing with paperwork," Margaret said. "I'm going to be clearing out the reception area and do a bit of dusting."

"What about Mom?"

Fezzo cleared his throat and put a bit more elbow grease into his scrubbing.

"She's home with a headache," Margaret said. "Said she'd be in later when she was feeling better."

"You mean once the work's all done," Nonie mumbled.

Fezzo glanced at her with a little frown. Nonie knew he didn't like her talking about her mother like that, but the truth didn't always look like roses and gardenias.

"What was that, hon?" Margaret asked.

"Nothing," Nonie said.

Fezzo winked at her.

"So where's the monster truck?" Nonie asked.

"What monster truck?" Margaret said, glancing over her shoulder to North Street, which ran east of the funeral home.

"The buffer," Nonie said.

"Oh . . ." Margaret said, looking a bit confused. "Why do you call it a monster truck?"

"Because it handles like one," Nonie said with a sigh. "It's as old as dirt, and it never goes in the right direction. I want to go straight, it hooks a left. I want to go left, it decides to go right. We need a new one."

Margaret tsked. "No need spending money that doesn't need to be spent now, missy. That old buffer works just fine. You've just got to get the hang of it."

"Have *you* ever tried to get the hang of it?" Nonie asked.

Plopping a hand on her hip, Margaret shook her head. "Don't be silly, young lady. Now go on and get about your business. The buffer's where it always is. In the supply closet."

Still grumbling, Nonie was making her way out of the garage and into the funeral home when Guy and Helen appeared, flanking her on either side.

"So when am I going to be on television?" Helen asked, clasping her hands together.

Nonie let out a sigh of frustration and held up a finger, indicating that she should wait. She went into the funeral home through the back door, which led into her father's office. He was sitting at his desk, licking a finger and flicking through reams of paperwork.

"Hey, Dad," Nonie said.

He glanced up at her, his reading glasses perched on the end of his nose. "Hey punkin', what's new?"

There was so much going on that was new that it would take a week for her to fill her father in on all the news. The problem was that it would be news he wouldn't want to hear. Nonie too readily recalled the time she had told her mom and dad about seeing her grandfather at the foot of her bed and how upset they'd gotten. Not because they believed her but because they figured their beloved daughter was flying one branch shy of a cuckoo's nest.

"Same ol'," she lied as she headed out of his office and into the hallway. "Going to do the floors today."

"Good, girl," he called after her, then went back to his paperwork.

"Can we talk now?" Helen asked.

"Let's go in the coffee room," Guy said. "Nobody should hear you talking in there. They're too busy doing their own thing."

Nonie nodded and took a quick detour into the lounge then peeked back out into the hallway to make sure her father's office door, which had a hydraulic arm, had closed after her.

"Margaret's probably going to be coming down the hall any minute so let's make this fast," Nonie said, turning back to Guy and Helen.

"So tell me, tell me," Helen said. "Is it real? Are they really going to use my house on TV?"

Nonie grinned. There was so much excitement and anticipation on Helen's face it was contagious.

"It's definitely a go, Helen," Nonie said, and waited for a squeal of delight. Instead a look of confusion crossed Helen's face.

"What's that mean exactly . . . a go?"

"It means the producers want to use your house in one of their episodes."

Helen gasped, clapped her hands and did a little jig, her cap of white curls bouncing with her. "Oh, my word, I can't believe it! Thank you, thank you!"

Nonie chuckled. "I didn't have anything to do with it. It was all you and Captain."

"Did they catch them on video?" Guy asked.

"Captain showed up as a shadow in the shape of a man lying on the cot upstairs. Ms. Helen showed up as white and colored ectoplasm, and she generated some impressive EVPs."

"I showed up as ectogasm?" Helen asked, suddenly coming to a halt. "Should I be embarrassed?"

"No, no," Nonie assured her. "It's called ectoplasm. It's a stream of lights that show up in wavering lines either on video or on a still camera shot. It just means that some entity, that being you, pushed out enough energy to be caught on film that way."

"Whew," Helen said dramatically. "And what else is it you said I did that was impressive?"

"EVPs. That stands for electronic voice phenomena. They didn't get everything you said upstairs, only a few words here and there, but the words were clear. They were very impressed."

Helen clapped again. "Okay, okay, so what do we do now?"

"Well, my job with them is over now. I'm not sure when they plan to send a film crew out to your house, so I'd suggest that you go home and stay put. You wouldn't want to miss them, right?"

"Oh, absolutely not!" Helen said. "I'll go there right now, just to make sure." She turned to Guy. "Are you coming with me?"

"I'll catch up with you a bit later," Guy said. "I'd like to talk to Nonie for a while."

Helen cocked her head and gave him a wary look. "Just remember what we talked about."

Guy gave her a forced smile, then Helen clapped her hands once more and blipped out of the room.

"That blipping thing takes some getting used to," Nonie said. "I'm used to you doing a fade out."

"It took a few tries when Helen was teaching me to get it down right. She told me to concentrate hard on where I wanted to be, and the first time I did, I wound up in the bayou, not far from the boat accident. The second time I found myself in the dairy aisle at Roy's grocery."

Nonie laughed.

"It's not funny," Guy said with a pout. "Both times I was trying to get to you."

"Oh, stop taking yourself so seriously," Nonie said. "Unless I'm missing something, you've got like what . . . eternity to get it down pat."

"Yeah, well—"

"Nonie?" Margaret suddenly appeared in the coffee room, her face flushed. "There you are. I've been looking everywhere for you." She glanced around the room. "Who were you talking to just now?"

"Uh . . .nobody."

"Well, it had to be somebody because I heard you talking plain as the nose on my face."

Nonie shrugged. "Must have been talking to myself. You know, making a mind list of what I needed to do while I'm here."

"Have you even started on the floors yet?"

"Uh, no. I just got in here about five or ten minutes ago."

"Those floors aren't going to polish themselves."

"I know, I know," Nonie said, heading toward Margaret.

Margaret held out a hand. "Might as well stay put for now because Nate Lopez is here to see you."

Nonie felt her a right eye give a nervous twitch. "Did he say what he wanted?"

"Do I look like your secretary?" Margaret asked. "He asked to see you is all I know.

Probably has something to do with Anna Mae and Clara is my best guess. Anyway, instead of having him traipse all over the funeral home, I told him to stay put, and I'd come find you. He's out by the reception desk."

With that, Margaret marched out of the room, glancing back once or twice, evidently expecting Nonie to follow her lead.

Nonie did, hesitantly.

True to her word, Nonie found Nate near the front of the funeral home. He had a hand propped on the receptionist's desk, leaning with one foot crossed over the other. When he spotted Margaret and Nonie, he immediately stood at attention. Nonie couldn't help but appreciate how good he looked in his deputy's uniform. His black, tousled hair, his gray-green eyes seemed to sparkle every time he looked her way.

"How're you doing, Nonie?" he asked, hooking his thumbs in his front pockets.

"Okay. You?"

"Making it. Just wanted to come by and talk with you about a few things," Nate said, then glanced over at Margaret, giving her a look that said, "If you'll excuse us for a minute . . ."

Margaret ignored him and sat behind the receptionist's desk, busying herself with pencils, paperclips, and pens.

"Is there somewhere we can talk in private?" Nate asked.

"Sure," Nonie said. "Follow me." She didn't know why she hadn't told Margaret to invite Nate back into the coffee room because that's where she was taking him back to now. It was the only private place she could think of.

Nate followed Nonie dutifully. When they entered the lounge, Nonie pulled out a chair and offered it to him.

"Would you care for something to drink?" Nonie asked.

"No, I'm good," Nate said.

"Well, have a seat at least."

"I can't stay for long. Still on duty. I just wanted to come by, ask you a couple of questions and give you an update on the Turner case."

"Turner?"

"Yeah, you know, Anna Mae."

"Oh, yeah, sorry."

Nonie pulled out a second chair and sat at the table closest to him. "How can I help you?"

"Well," Nate scuffed the toe of his boot against the floor as if embarrassed. "I was wondering . . ."

"Yes?"

"How did you know that Anna Mae was under that partially dried cement?"

Taken aback by the question, Nonie chewed her bottom lip for a moment. Her brain scuttled around at a hundred miles an hour searching for a plausible answer. If she told him the truth, they'd send the loony wagon for her. After a long moment, she said, "Well, Clara had asked us to come to her house to look around. See if we might spot anything that looked out of the ordinary that would give her a clue to Anna

Mae's whereabouts. We were about to leave the house when I thought of the backyard. Clara told me that she hadn't been back there in some time so I figured it wouldn't be a bad idea for us to take a look. That's when we noticed the concrete. Clara didn't know anything about it, so I went over to it and checked it out. Noticed that it was only partially dry. Clara seemed a little upset over it being there. Claimed it made her yard look terrible, which, she thought, reflected badly on her. So, Uncle Fezzo and I offered to clear it away for her. That's when we found Anna Mae. Only we didn't know it was Anna Mae right away."

"Did you notice anything out of place or out of sorts in her house?"

"No, not a thing."

"So nobody told you to go into the backyard to look for any particular reason?"

"No," Nonie said. "It happened just like I said. Besides, it was only Clara, Uncle Fezzo and me. Who else would have told me to look in the backyard?"

"I don't know," Nate said. "Just asking."

There was a glint in Nate's eyes that Nonie couldn't quite identify. "Anyway," she said. "The rest is history. We called Sheriff Buchanan right away."

"So you finding the ring in that pile of dirt was purely coincidental?"

"Of course," Nonie said. "You know that. You were there at the time. I caught a glimpse of something shiny and brought it to the sheriff's attention. You guys made the find. Why are you asking all these questions? Am I like a suspect or something?"

"No, nothing like that at all. In fact you helped us sew this case up quickly. If you hadn't spotted that ring we might still be looking for Anna Mae's killer."

"You mean you found the person who killed her?"

Nate nodded. "When you identified the ring as looking like the same ones you saw on Stefren and Clarence Fontenot, we went over there to have a little chat with them. To make a long story short, it seems like Stefren didn't take to kindly to anyone upsetting his mother so much. So he decided to take care of the woman who caused his mother so much grief. He waited until Clarence left the house, then went in search of

Anna Mae. Found her at Roy's Grocery. Waited for her to come out and followed her home. From the way he tells it, he warned Anna Mae to get out of town and she told him where she lived was none of his business, so he hit her over the head with a blunt object, right across her left temple. Not sure what he used yet. He won't say. Doesn't matter, though, with a bit of pressure, we got a full confession out of him. He claims he didn't mean to kill her, just give her what for. You know, drive the message home about her leaving town. When he figured out what he'd done, he dragged Anna Mae into the backyard, got a shovel out of her shed and started digging a hole. Found out it wasn't deep enough when he dumped her in it headfirst. He wasn't strong enough to pull her back out, so he covered what was still showing with concrete. It was probably around that time his ring slipped off. Anyway, we found an empty sack of concrete in the same shed. He must have used the water hose next to the house to wet it down."

"I can't believe he spilled his guts that easily," Nonie said.

"His mama was in on the interrogation, and she read him the riot act about telling the truth or else. I don't think she was expecting him to confess. Not her precious boy. But the guy was so scared he started blubbering out of both sides of his mouth.

"How awful," Nonie said. She shook her head, trying to shake the image of Anna Mae's dirt-covered face.

"Yeah. Just like there's some people who can't hold their liquor, I guess there's some people who can't hold onto their tempers."

Nonie couldn't help but think of Guy trashing her apartment the last time he'd gotten upset with her. "I suppose you're right."

"So, we got the guy who did it, thanks to you. I just thought it was a bit coincidental that you went into the backyard, then caught a glimpse of that ring. I had to ask. Hope you didn't take offense."

"Not at all," Nonie lied. It wasn't that she'd taken offense. It was the fact that she'd had to lie about why she'd gone into the backyard in the first place.

Nate pushed the chair she had pulled out for him back under the table. "You know, Nonie, I feel sort of obligated to let you know . . . There's word going on around town about you."

Nonie felt her pulse quicken. "What word?" She got to her feet. "That I had something to do with Anna Mae's death?"

"No. What's being said is that you can see dead people. That you see and hear them."

Nonie forced a chuckle. "Why on earth would anybody say something like that?"

"I don't know. You know how people in a small town love to gossip."

"Who told you that?"

"Old man Guidry over at the hardware store. Claims one of the guys who works for him is doing a project with you and swears he saw you talking to the dead."

"That's ridiculous," Nonie said. She thought of Tatman and was glad he wasn't around at the moment or Clay Point would have had two murders on its hands.

"Anyway, just thought, I'd give you a heads-up about that," Nate said.

"I appreciate it . . . I think."

Nate laughed. "Yeah, it's not exactly like telling you you've won the lottery. But if you go walking around town and see people looking at you funny, at least you'll know why."

Great, Nonie thought. *Just what I need.*

"We're still on for weekend after next, right?" Nate asked.

For a moment, his question didn't register with Nonie.

"The festival."

"Oh, yes, right. Definitely still on," Nonie said and smiled.

Nate reached over and moved a strand of hair from her cheek. "Good. I'm looking forward to it."

"M-me too, Nonie said, finding she had a hard time getting the words out. When Nate had touched her cheek, she felt heat flow over her body like a hot shower. It came so unexpectedly that it stole any further words from her mouth. His hands were large, soft to the touch, and his caress gentle.

Snapping to attention, Nonie tried giving the room an inconspicuous sweep, looking for Guy. Nowhere in sight. Even if he was around, he'd have only heard her accepting the date. He couldn't read her mind, couldn't feel the change her body experienced at Nate's touch. If he could

have, he'd really have something to bitch about.

CHAPTER THIRTY

That night, after shoveling down a bowl of Spaghettios, Nonie went into the bathroom, took a shower and brushed her teeth.

Feeling exhausted, she went into her bedroom, got into bed and rolled over on her stomach, pulling her pillow in close. Her body still vibrated from the buffing machine that had bucked her around the funeral home most of the afternoon. She was tired physically and mentally. Tired of dead people. People who'd died by natural causes, by murder, the ones who were dead but refused to move on. She just wanted to be left in peace and get a good night's sleep.

No sooner did that thought cross her mind than Nonie heard someone whisper, "Psst," in her left ear. She groaned and rolled over on her back. Guy was standing over her.

"You know you're going to kill me, right?" Guy said.

Nonie rubbed an eye with the back of her hand. "What the heck are you talking about? You're already dead."

"My heart, Nonie. You're going to kill my heart."

"I can't kill it. It's already dead."

"How can it be dead if I feel so much love for you?"

"Can we have this conversation again tomorrow? I'm really burned out."

"I heard you talking to that deputy and you agreeing to go to the festival with him. You're going to dinner with that Jack Sprat guy, too."

"Quit calling him that. It makes you sound like a kindergartener."

"I've got the right to call him whatever I want."

"Stop," Nonie whined. "I just want to get some sleep. Go play with Helen or something."

"It almost feels like you're two-timing me," Guy said. "How would you feel if I was going out with two different women, all the while claiming I loved you?"

"You want to go out with two different women, have at it. I don't know what else to tell you."

"You barely give me the time of day anymore."

"In case you haven't noticed, I've been a little busy lately. Puuulease can we talk about this tomorrow?"

Guy sighed. "You haven't even let me give you the present I told you about the other day."

Nonie opened one eye and looked at him. "You told me your present was showing me that you could move stuff around. So I've already gotten it."

"That wasn't the real present. This is." He leaned over, and Nonie felt a whisper of a touch against her lips as he pressed his to hers. His lips were surprisingly warm, like when he was alive. So soft, so passionate. It brought tears to Nonie's eyes. His kiss made her hungry for more of him. She needed more.

When Guy broke the kiss, Nonie groaned.

"There'll be more," Guy said. "The better I get at manipulating things in this world, I'll get better at physically loving you. You'll feel my lips better. You'll feel me better. I have to practice, and I have been really hard. See, that's why I don't want you with other men. You're mine. Eventually, maybe not right now, but eventually, I'll be able to give you all you need."

"Oh, Guy," she said, feeling so confused. How was it possible for a dead man's lips to feel so warm, so deliciously passionate?

Evidently taking her words as a sign of acceptance, Guy moved the covers up closer to her chin and kissed her lightly on the forehead.

"I'll be quiet and let you get some sleep," Guy said. "Helen needs some help from me tonight anyway, so I'll see you tomorrow."

With that Guy blipped out of sight, leaving behind a slight chill in the air.

Nonie turned on her side, then onto her stomach, then back on her side. Restless now. What was she supposed to do? She struggled with guilt, with desire. Life was becoming a struggle. Especially now that word was going around town that she saw dead people. It had to be Tatman who started the rumor after he heard the audio of her speaking to Helen. Now that she'd discovered Anna Mae's body, word would spread even faster. A gossip fire gone amok.

Nonie blew out a frustrated breath and slammed a fist into her pillow, mauling it into a more comfortable shape. She wondered if she'd made a mistake getting involved in the paranormal investigations, then thought about the thousand-dollar check sitting in her kitchen drawer. The money was great, she had to admit it. But what was it going to cost her in the long run? Was she going to be dragging more ghosts home? And what about Tatman and Shaundelle now that they suspected she saw spirits. Would that change their team dynamics?

Closing her eyes, Nonie told herself she'd simply have to be more careful during the investigations. Not talk to what others perceived as thin air. She'd have to force herself to unsee whatever ghosts she saw. Otherwise she'd slip again and get busted. The problem had been that she'd spoken to Helen and Tiana. If she had acted like they weren't there or used some kind of signal with Buggy like they originally planned to let her know spirits were around, the rumors wouldn't have started. It was all her fault. Not Tatman's or Shaundelle. If the shoe had been on the other foot, she'd have probably told Buggy that Tatman talked to ghosts. Problem was that word had already gotten out. No matter how careful she was on other investigations, she might already be too late to squelch the rumor mill.

That's all she needed. Two men wanting to date her, a dead man sworn to love her forever, and the town of Clay Point thinking she was the next Edgar Cayce.

What a life. Sewing labels on men's underwear had sure been a lot easier than this. The only thing she'd had to worry about back then was making sure the labels were straight. Now the only thing that seemed to be straight in her life was a road to ruin. The next investigation

was at an insane asylum. Heaven only knew

what would follow her home from there.

THE END

Made in the USA
Middletown, DE
03 July 2021

43575946R00392

JUL 2 0 2021